Dark Gold

Samuel J Riddles

First published in Great Britain by Samuel J Riddles 2010

Copyright© Samuel J Riddles 2010
All Rights Reserved

The moral right of the authors has been asserted

This is a work of fiction. Names, characters, places and incidents either are the product of the author's imagination or are used fictitiously, and any resemblance to actual persons, living or dead, businesses, companies, events or locales is entirely coincidental.

I Thank God for this gift I have been given.
For my wife and son who have supported me throughout.
Also for all who believed in me, I thank you…

PROLOGUE

Arundel, West Sussex
August 22nd 1852

The news of his friend's death struck Howard Bruce like a fist to the stomach. His palms were starting to sweat and he could feel himself shaking. He could hardly believe the fact that he would never see his life long friend again. It was unimaginable.

It all started when Charles Davis and Michael Woodward knocked at his door. They had been out since the early hours picking berries for making pies and preserves when they had come across an old abandoned mine hidden in the overgrowth. Swiftly they rushed back to get Bruce so they could all share the adventure together. He swiftly threw on a pair of shorts and an old T-shirt and followed them to the destination.

Charles was a bright young man, the leader of the pack. Standing at six foot and weighing well in excess of two hundred fifty pounds he was also the largest of the three. His dark brown eyes were camouflaged by his well tanned skin. Thick dark brown hair sat above his forehead like a poor quality wig. Charles' father had high hopes for his only son, planning for him to break into politics and one day possibly become Prime Minister.

Woodward and Bruce wore similar features; both had dark blonde, almost bordering mousey brown hair, and were blessed with bright green eyes which stunned all who looked deep in to them. Anyone whom had never known them would have sworn blind they were brothers.

One feature that Bruce didn't share with Woodward was the small scar on his forehead, which he got while playing on one of the local chalk pits.

The three young men wandered along the hillside pathway, taking in the beauty of the South Downs. At that time of year, all that had to be offered by nature was on full show. They ate the blackberries that grew along the side of the pathway as they made their way towards the mine.

"It's just through the trees on your right, not far now" explained Davis

They fought through the overgrown brambles and weeds before they came to the entrance of the mine that stood at around twelve feet tall, but stretched to over twenty feet wide. Visibility inside the mine was barely at ten feet.
"How deep do you think it is?" asked Davis

Bruce shook his head, standing in utter amazement at the discovery "I have no idea. But I've heard they could go to a depth of around one thousand feet"
"Well. I guess there's only one way of finding out" Davis stated as he stepped towards the entrance.

Bruce turned and stared at Davis, hoping he would reconsider, the thought of that filthy place was playing havoc on his mind, but he knew that the chance of that happening was less than inviting.

The thing that stood out about Bruce was the fact that he hated dirt and grime. If he came into contact with overly filthy places or objects, He would scrub himself until his skin was raw. He hated that he was like that, but he couldn't help it, it was something he had to live with.

After searching for a while, Davis found a large stick that he wrapped with a piece of old rag he had taken from his mothers sewing desk; he then doused it in paraffin ready to use as a torch. He repeated the process twice more, making a torch for each of them. Now comes the hardest part- he thought. He picked up two good sizes pieces of flint and started smashing them together over one of the torches. Finally, after about five minutes the rag caught light. Bruce and Woodward gave a huge sigh of relief, as they were both thinking they would be there all day. They each picked up a torch and lit off Davis'.

Before entering the mine, Bruce took the time to put on the gloves that were always kept in his pocket, just in case anything like this ever came up. Now though, he had added a small mask that covered his mouth and nose, the thought of breathing in the dirt scared him more than touching it.

"Must you insist on wearing that silly outfit? It doesn't exactly do much for you." Said Woodward; shaking his head in disapproval.

"Have you seen how dirty it is in there" Replied Bruce. "Even with this on, I'll need to take two baths at the end of the day"

Davis turned to Bruce and Woodward. He gave a wry smile and asked "Do you think we'll find anything of value?"

"I wouldn't have thought so" Answered Bruce. "If we're lucky, we might find some old tools. There's probably nothing but chalk and rocks down there."

Each of them took a deep breath of fresh air, filling their lungs before they made their journey in to the stale atmosphere of the damp, cold mine. They each agreed to stay as quiet as possible, in case of any unwanted visitors such as bats or anything else that gruesome that lives underground.

Davis and Woodward didn't hold back one bit, they were to excited to see what was at the end. Bruce felt very apprehensive about the trip though, as he knew that the mine had been shut down in 1786 due to a virus epidemic, killing over a hundred miners. But Bruce felt something deeper than that, a feeling that just would not go away. He couldn't put his finger on what it was, no matter how hard he tried, all he knew was that going in was a bad idea and not just because it was filthy.

After around half hour they stared in horror at the gruesome discovery they had just made. Each became uneasy as they stared at the remains of what they could only have imagined to be one of the miners that had died and been left to rot where he lay. The bones seemed darker in colour than they imagined, even though in the poor light, they couldn't really see them perfectly. One thing that struck Woodward, was that they looked as if they had been placed in a perfect pile, as if the mine had been visited before.

"What do you think happened to that poor fellow?" Asked Davis

"Who knows, to be quite honest, I'd rather not know." Woodward answered

Bruce looked at his two friends, wondering why they didn't know about the mine prior to finding it. He thought it best not to tell them, driving fear into them would just make them run and he was now thinking to much about making the discovery of the century. "Best we move on" He advised "We can't do much for him."

Davis and Woodward both looked at each other and

nodded in agreement. They kept walking, taking each step with more caution, their minds clearly focused on the human remains. None of them had any idea of how far they had walked. Bruce could only guess that their short steps had only taken them about four hundred feet in the hour and a half they had been down there. They took short breaks every forty five minutes to take in the surroundings and take a sip of the water canister strapped to Woodward's shorts.

"Why would anyone mine in this spot" Asked Woodward "There's nothing here but rock and chalk"

No one answered for a few seconds. Davis took a swift look around and studied the area. "No idea." Perhaps it's because us British are greedy. If there is any way we can grab a quick profit, we do it. Even if it is just by selling crappy chalk" Bruce and Woodward shrugged their shoulders and started their trek once more.

The atmosphere grew damper and heavier as they travelled a further two hundred feet, each of them were finding it increasingly hard to breathe. Woodward had the idea of turning back and going home, the combination of the damp, musty air, his difficulty in breathing and the thought of coming across another corpse was more than he could bear. The idea soon passed out of his mind when all three noticed a slight glimmer of light about fifty feet ahead. As they came closer and closer, the light became brighter and they came to realise that it was the reflection of a chamber. Many thoughts came into their minds as to the contents of the chamber, but only one stuck; Gold.

As they entered the chamber, their jaws dropped in utter amazement. They stood and stared in awe at what had gone from dark, damp rocks, to brightly shining shades that reminded them of the colours of the sun. The light from each of the torches, reflected off the golden walls

"My God, it's an Egyptian treasure cave" Stated Bruce, trying his best to keep his jaw closed.

"I've never seen anything like it" muttered Woodward, almost too silent for the others to hear.

Davis stood in silence, the only thing on his mind, was how much it was all worth. He walked at snails pace up to the wall, slowly stretching out his arm. As his palm touched the picturesque wall, the gold crumbled like powder to the floor. "What the hell is this stuff?" he asked

"God only knows my friend, but I think you've just established that it's not gold." Bruce replied

Davis and Woodward began tearing chunks out of the wall, each chunk just crumbling like before into their hands. Davis thought of trying to find any large pieces that he could take home, so he asked Bruce to help, but Bruce simply shook his head and said "I can't even begin to imagine how many germs are in that stuff"

The heat as they dug became unbearable, even though they had only been digging for a few minutes. Davis and Woodward continuously wiped their brows, each fighting the heat and digging as if their lives depended on gathering as much as possible. Bruce stood and watched as his friends worked for a further ten minutes. As the water ran out, the feeling of thirst soon became too much to bare. Fatigue was now set in. They had no other choice but to agree to stop.

"I say we come back tomorrow with something to carry it back with." Davis suggested

"Good idea" replied Bruce "it's probably going to get dark soon anyhow, we should think about heading back."

Woodward took a quick glance around, his green eyes filled with excitement. "I can't believe no one has ever found this" He said. "Don't you think it's odd that none of the miners told people about this?"

"Perhaps they didn't want anyone else to get their hands on it." Davis Replied

Bruce shook his head "No" he said, matter-of -factly. "If that was the case, they would have been back to get it, just another one of those unsolved mysteries." Bruce gave the others a blank look. He still held back his knowledge of the mines history. He remembered reading that the survivors of the mine plague were all executed; no reason was given for the executions. He just figured that the town's people thought they were contaminated.

"Just think chaps" said Woodward. "This time tomorrow, we could be the richest men in the world."

"I wouldn't go that far." Bruce answered his tone a lot less enthusiastic than his friends.

The walk back to the entrance seemed a lot shorter than the trek down. No stops were taken apart from the quick glance at the skeleton they had passed on the way down. All in all, considering it took nearly three hours to reach the chamber, it took only half that on the return journey. Bruce's expression was still blank when they reached day light, his mind clearly on getting home to wash. Davis and Woodward had never met anyone who was so concerned about personal hygiene. They always thought he was just a bit of an attention seeker.

They fought their way back through the overgrown weeds and brambles and walked back down the same path they had used to locate the mine. Their home town of Arundel was only a twenty minute walk through the fields, but after trekking down to the end of the mine and back, it felt a lot longer.

"Let's keep this quiet for a while." Davis ordered "If we go public straight away, we'll never get a look in."

"Charles is right" Answered Bruce. "This is too big for anyone to let us take the glory."

As they reached the high street, they all said their farewells and went off in different directions to their homes. Bruce's thought were split between the discovery and the fact hat he was only five minutes away from a nice hot bath, although now, the thought of the gold was greater than ever. He could possibly give his family the life they all deserved with the riches he could gain from the gold. The thought made him smile but he quickly shrugged the thought off as he looked at the state of his clothes when he reached his home, he rushed straight to the bathroom, without any acknowledgment to his parents.

When he felt he was as clean as he could get, he went and sat down at the dinner table, ready to eat the Fish and Potato's that his mother had prepared for the family. His Mother, a kind, affectionate woman with the brightest blonde hair he had ever seen, sat opposite him at the table. She looked upon him in a confused manner.

"Where exactly have you been all day Howard?" She asked

Bruce didn't answer right away, he sat silent, trying to think of a good story to tell. In the end he could only think of one thing. "Just out and about really."

Davis was a boy who liked to plan his days and nights. After leaving the mine, he had planned his evening to the dot, Dinner then bed. He couldn't wait to get back down the mine and collect his findings. He sat down to dinner with his Mum and Dad, swiftly finishing his beef stew, then headed straight for his bed. The excitement played on his mind continuously, as much as he tried to sleep, the effort was just too great. He sat up in his bed and stared out of the window, each minute seeming like an hour.

He sat for about thirty minutes, staring at the same spot on the wall. He started to feel an aching pain in his stomach, which grew with every second. As the ache grew to an unbearable pain, he tried to think of what he could have eaten in the day, coming to the conclusion that it must have been the beef stew. Mother didn't cook the beef properly again- he thought. He dared not cry out in pain, his father was a man who believed that children should be seen and not heard, even though he was sixteen years old and no longer considered himself to be a child. He tried to vomit, hoping the pain would diminish if he did. He leaned over, holding his stomach, still trying his best not to scream. After another ten minutes or so the pain seemed to subside. He had no idea what had happened, but he knew he never wanted that feeling again.

The bright early morning sun rose over Sussex, into another cloudless sky. Bruce was woken by a loud knock at the door. He left it for a few seconds before the knock came again, this time louder. His parents were heavy sleepers, and waking them would surely mean punishment so he opened the door.

He was greeted by a tall man with a full beard and beady eyes. His police uniform was freshly pressed and his shoes freshly polished. His face showed nothing but sadness.

Police chief White hated passing on bad news, especially to people he had grown fond of. Bruce was the first person Davies had asked him to tell and he respected him to much to ignore the request.

"How did he die?" Bruce asked, gaining control of his emotions long enough to ask the question.

"My guess would be poisoning." White replied with a sense of remorse in his voice.

"Who could have done such a thing?"

"I don't think he was murdered, I think it was accidental, which brings me to the other reason I am here. I believe that you were out with him yesterday, do you have any idea of what might have caused such a tragedy?"

"No I'm sorry" Bruce replied softly "I cant believe that he is gone"

"My apologies again Master Bruce. I hate to be the one to bring good folk bad news. I will need to speak to you again, to disclose what you did yesterday."

Bruce began to think of Davis digging the gold in the mine. He pictured his friend wiping the sweat off his face and licking his lips. That had to be it, there was no other explanation.

As soon as he realised the gold was the most likely reason, he pictured Woodward doing the same. He rushed out of his front door and down the street towards Woodward's house. He had neglected to put anything on his feet and the sharp road was cutting into his feet but he paid no notice to the pain. His main concern was getting to Woodward in time.

When he approached Woodward's door, he slammed on the door as hard as he could. After the third slam Woodward's dad answered. "Howard." He said in a slightly angered manner, he was still dressed in his night clothes. "What can I do for you at…"

He didn't have time to finish, Bruce barged passed him and ran through the house and up the stairs. He opened the door to the bedroom, almost ripping it off the wall. Woodward was still lying in bed, he seemed motionless. Bruce froze in the doorway for a second before he stepped slowly towards the bed; his heart was racing faster than it ever had before. He felt a sickening feeling in his stomach and could feel himself shaking.

Ho stood for a second next to the head of the bed; the covered were pulled over Woodward's head. He took a deep breath and pulled the covers back to reveal his friend, he was still. The colour in his face had changed from a slight tan to a cold blue. Bruce could see he was not breathing. He placed his fingers against Woodward's neck to check for a pulse, it wasn't there.

Bruce sat frozen in Woodward's living room twenty minutes after discovering the body. Chief White had already questioned him but it was a wasted effort. The thought that he had now lost both of his closest friends was too much to cope with. His mind wandered to the mine. He couldn't understand why he had been spared, then he realised the illness that had haunted him all his life had saved him. If he hadn't have been so afraid of the dirt, he would more than likely, he knew, have shared the same fate as the other two.

What ever was in that mine was the killer and Bruce knew he had to take it upon himself to make sure that no one ever finds it again.

1

**Worthing, West Sussex
Present Day**

The night sky was clear; no clouds blocked the sight of the stars. The moon cast rays over the still seas and the light flickered off the gentle ripples like tiny diamonds. People drove along the seafront enjoying the crisp, clean, warm air flowing through their open windows and lowered convertible roofs. Couples took romantic walks along the promenade, hand in hand after enjoying cold beverages at some of the local pubs, who were now calling time. The smells of the many kebab and pizza shops dotted around the town were tempting those who needed a little sobering before heading home.

A black Mercedes Benz pulled in to the bus stop outside the Pavilion Theatre. Two men sat inside. The passenger, a small man with balding hair and three day old stubble on his face, stared out of the window. He watched the pedestrians walking to and fro. He thought back to the days he and his wife did the same. They would walk for miles along the beach when the tide was out talking for hours about nothing that held any importance. It seemed to him though, that the only talking they would do recently was in raised voices. Things had been tough for them for a great number of years, it wasn't they he they no longer loved each other, he loved her more than anything but the passion had just diminished. Every now and again, they would get the incredible urge to be with one another and the spark they longed for shone once again, but it didn't last long. He guessed the relationship he once had with her was now a distant memory.

The driver spoke. His voice was deep and stern. "Are you ready?" He passed over a small black box.

The passenger looked at him. His eyes told all. He was scared. Not just about what he was about to do. In fact he was more scared of the driver than anything. "Yes Sir." He replied.

"You're sure you can go ahead with this?"

"Do I have any choice?" The passenger waited for an answer. One never came. He took a deep breath and opened the car door. He stopped in his tracks as he started to exit and turned back to the driver. "Make sure you do as I asked. It's important to me." The only response he got was a slight nod.

He walked towards the entrance of the theatre. His stride was short and slow kept his face pointing to the ground hiding his nervousness so not to attract any unneeded attention. The sweat poured from his forehead like a waterfall. His mouth felt dry and the palms of his hands were moist. He looked behind him every few seconds, checking no one was watching. His whole body shook under the stress; it was like nothing he had ever experienced before.

He walked towards a tall, lanky man dressed all in black. The man had an eerie look about him. His stare was cold; there was no sense of emotion in his eyes. The hard expression that seemed permanently painted on his face proved that this man was nothing less than evil. The passenger stopped next to him and took a quick look around, checking once again that no one was watching. He handed the man a small phone shaped device and carried on walking. No words were spoken, there was no need. They both had their own missions. Both had their own agendas. Nothing else was on their minds.

The young people of Worthing made their way towards Horizon, the number one clubbing hotspot in town. The club sat in perfect illumination on the end of the pier. It could be seen from miles across the English Channel and was a big focal point of the town.

The guard booth stood at the front end of the nine-hundred and seven foot long, thirty six foot wide pier. Two guards would search everybody that came through, while a staff member, a slim young woman with long copper hair, sat in the booth taking the fees. With weapon crime increasing by the year, every resource was needed to make sure that no one was hurt while trying to have a good time. Violence was a common occurrence during the course of most nights; drunken fights would break out if clubbers simply bumped in to each other, the result of the young people not knowing their limits when it came to drink. With plenty of door staff on hand to reduce this however, the number of fights that broke out was slowly but surely decreasing

The clubbers made their way along the wooden planked walkway that sat above the calm seas. The man dressed in all black followed closely behind them. The man, well in his forties, seemed out of place among the young people, who looked to be in their late teens and early twenties. As he passed through the guard's booth, he paid the entrance fee and turned to one of the large guards who were standing on the left side of the gate. As he was searched he discreetly placed a small envelope in the guards pocket then walked on through the gate.

He walked through the main club entrance and found himself in a small hallway with a cloakroom on the left and toilets on the right. Ahead was another set of doors. He walked through and glanced around the main room of the club. The illuminations were even more intense than those on the outside. The strobe lighting dazed him as he entered. The music seemed to be turned up as high as the DJ system would allow, and to those who were not used to the excessive volume, it would have verged on deafening. The circular dance floor in front of him was surrounded by a water fall of reds, greens and blues.

Barmen rushed around pouring drinks and tossing mixers in the air showing off their talents hoping to impress the punters enough to leave a generous tip. People lined the bar gripping their cash, yearning for their next shot of whatever was available. The smell of alcohol lingered in the air adding to the masterful Saturday night feeling that everyone inside had. All was perfect. For the ones who had worked hard all week, this was their reward, to unwind and let their hair down. For others it was just an excuse to escape the rat race. Either way, they were all there to have a great night.

The man walked around the gangway that led to a second bar situated at the back of the club. This bar had no dance floor. Instead, the smaller area had seating around the wall with tables in front for those who needed to take a break from hours of dancing. As he walked a little further around, he came to a cigarette machine. Taking a few coins from his pocket, he inserted them into the machine and pressed the button for the brand he wanted. The temptation to light up was unbearable, though he knew he couldn't. With the smoking ban that had been bought into action some two years before, he would have drawn the attention of the staff and his mission would be a failure.

Next to the machine was a small alcove that had a neon fire exit sign above. He moved unnoticed into the alcove and picked up the small black package which had been left by the guard. The package was hidden inside a small air vent and out of view. He pulled the box from the vent and opened it. He took a small mobile phone from his pocket and placed it inside the box on top of the contents. After a few seconds of fiddling with phone he shut the box and slid it back into the vent. He turned and scanned the room, making sure no one had seen him, and then he made his way back to the entrance and left the club.

A few minutes later, he sat on a bench just down the beach from the pier. He watched the public make their way into the club. This was a moment he had waited for, for a long time. The feeling excited him. He felt an adrenaline rush flow through his body like a heard of wild horses. The feeling of power gave him a great sense of victory, a sense of well being, a sense that he was in charge.

He took the device that he had been given by his comrade from his inside breast pocket and flipped the lid down. The face had the numbers one to nine at the bottom and a large green button at the top. He dialled the number he had been given earlier in the day. A moment of hesitation came over him and he stared at the club before he pushed the green button. That final look at his victim made it all the more beautiful.

The dark night sky was suddenly lit up in a bright

orange glow. The club went form a thriving party to a giant fire ball in a fraction of a second. Glass and shrapnel flew through the air and crashed into the sea below. The structures of the pier buckled under the force of the explosion and crashed down into the water. Bodies lay still across the wooden floors. Pedestrians stood in shock on the promenade as they witnessed the travesty unfold. Many scrambled in their pockets and bags searching for their buried phones to call the emergency services. Thick black smoke lifted in to the night and gently blew out to sea. Charred smells filled the air immediately. After a few seconds, the roar of fire died down.

    The Man in black sat and watched the whole show. He felt proud of the work he had accomplished. Once the display had finished he simply stood and walked away.

2

Alex York stood on the balcony of his penthouse apartment overlooking the crisp, calm sea. He slowly nurtured a bottle of Jack Daniels Whiskey. After a hard days work, this was the only way he had ever been able to unwind. Especially on days like today.

He had spent over nine hours in the court rooms putting to bed the cases that he had spent the last few months working on. It was long, gruelling work, the only thing that kept him going was the two coffees every hour and the occasional shot from his hidden hip flask. It was worth every minute though. He loved working for the National Anti-Terrorism Service. It gave him a great sense of well being. He felt he was really helping make a difference.

York stood at six feet tall. Hours spent in the gym resulted in a well toned body, mixed with his facial stubble that gave him a rough look, and his smooth, charming way around the opposite sex, made them cling to him like a moth to a light bulb. He stared through musty oak eyes that acted as a window in to the depth of his mind and soul.

He stood watching the local drunks stumbling about for over an hour. He found them amusing. The thought that people would go out for one simple reason, to get leathered and struggle to even take a few steps, seemed like a complete waste of time to him. Looking down at the half empty bottle in front of him, he couldn't help but smile. Yeah, he liked a drink but he knew his limit. Or at least he thought he did. Drinking seemed to be the only way he could unwind these days. As soon as he walked through the door from work, the first thing he would do was open a bottle of whatever alcohol he had in the cupboard. It was only a couple of glasses, just enough to settle him in for the night.

He placed the lid back on the bottle and put it back down on the patio table next to him, then continued to enjoy the beautiful seascape and the illuminations of the club opposite. The vast, calm and open landscape of the ocean helped him to forget the parts of his life that were less than perfect.

After a few minutes he turned back towards the door to his living room. He barely took a step inside when the explosion happened. The force of the blast knocked him to the floor. He felt the building shake briefly around him and he had to take a couple of seconds to shake off the shock of the blast before he got up. As he stared out at the giant fire ball and the thick cloud of smoke that was climbing in to the dark skies above, his heart felt as though it had stopped. A sick pain grew in his stomach.

He stood for a few moments, taking in what had just happened. He had never seen anything like it. In his four years with the Anti-Terrorism Service, he had only ever seen the aftermath. He was used to that. It was like a nightmare, something you wouldn't wish on your worst enemy. Straight away, York knew the death toll would be high.

He seemed to be in a daze as he stared at the remains of the club. It was as if the whole world had come to a complete stop. He snapped out of the trance and ran for the door.

The small amount of traffic on the road had come to standstill, the drivers staring in shock at what they saw. People were rushing out of their homes and hotels to see what was happening. Most stood in shock at the sight; others had the same reaction as York. Men ran towards the wreckage to try their best to lend a helping hand to anyone whom may have survived the blast.

York ran on to the pier at full speed. Bodies lay everywhere. Those who had been standing outside smoking when the blast happened were thrown through the air like leaves being blown from a tree; some were thrown well over sixty feet.

The smell of burning flesh was almost unbearable, he began to feel queasy. Most that had come to help were forced to turn back; the sight was just too unbearable for them to take. Even York was bewildered at the sight. The whole of the end of the structure where the club once sat was now in pieces at the bottom of the ocean.

He ran past the amusement arcade that sat directly in the centre of the long pier and up to young girl laying at the edge of the wooden walkway. She was face down and her arm was hanging over the edge of the railing. Her skin had been stained with blood and soot, one of her legs had been bent forwards from the impact. He rolled her over and checked for a pulse. It was faint, she wasn't breathing. He began CPR, every piece of energy he had went in to giving this girl the chance to see out the rest of her life. He checked her pulse again after a couple of minutes, it was getting weaker.

A Stocky Security guard who worked in the booth at the front of the pier ran up to help. He placed his hands under the girl's neck and raised her head. York continued to try to revive her. It was no good. The slight pulse had gone; he looked straight in to her frozen eyes. He felt guilt. Had he done everything he could? She was pretty and had her whole life in front of her; there was no way she deserved to die. He pulled himself away from her body and checked others. The stocky man stayed with him. "What's your name sir?" York asked.

"The names Mike." The guard replied, out of breath. "You look like you know what you're doing. Point the way and I'll follow." He stared at York expectantly. Although York had been to First aid courses, the knowledge seemed to have left him in the time that he needed it the most. He shook his head to wake from the slight daze he was in and answered "Walk down the right hand side of the pier, check the bodies for a pulse. Do you know how to do that?"

"Remind me"

"Place two fingers on the side of the neck, hold it for a couple of seconds, if you feel nothing I'm afraid they're dead."

Mike nodded his head in agreement. He took a gulp and turned to walk away. Sweat was now pouring down from his shaven head. There was a slight cut on his head from being struck by a piece of shrapnel. He stopped and turned back "What should I do if I feel something?" He asked.

"Call me. I'll come over and try to give first aid."

York took the left side. He counted at least ten bodies between him and the end of the path. He hoped that he could save at least one. He checked them one by one. None were breathing, none had pulses. He looked in to the fixed and frozen eyes of a young man who, in York's mind, couldn't have been any older than twenty. Death had come quick and painlessly. York closed the young mans eyes as he heard Mike calling from across the way.

As he got to the other side he saw Mike standing over the body of another young man. He ran over to him, praying he had found at least one survivor. He hadn't, the young lad was lying in a motionless heap. "What's up?" York asked

"This boy." There was a sense of deep sorrow in Mike's voice. "He's sixteen years old. He used a fake ID to get in." He passed the ID card to York.

"You weren't to know." York knew exactly what Mike was feeling, the mistake that cost a child his life was one that he had experienced on more than one occasion in his life. "He looks well over eighteen. I would have made the same mistake. It's not your fault." The words were useless.

York moved swiftly towards the side bars and looked over the edge. People were struggling against the current; most of them were giving up and slipping under the surface of the water. Some doing all they could even though they had lost limbs. "Mike, you a good swimmer?" He shouted.

"I'm no Olympian." Mike said as he moved next to York, he looked over and knew what he was thinking "You don't have to ask me twice." Without second thought he launched his bulky structure off the side, he hit the water with the force of a ten ton truck. He floated on the top for a few seconds to catch his breath then dived beneath the surface in search of the helpless.

York was amazed at the bravery of the giant man. He had to compose himself before he could even think of jumping. When he did, it was only half the force of his accomplice. The water was nowhere near as cold as he imagined. He prepared himself for freezing temperatures, so when he landed in the dark abyss, he was almost pleasantly surprised. Bodies were floating on the surface around him. The sight sent shivers down his spine.

York swam to the aid of a young man fighting against the current with his one remaining arm. The shore was only about twenty metres away but it seemed like a mile, but he put all his effort into pulling the young him to safety. York hoped the man still had full use of his legs, he did. Although wobbly at first, he balanced himself as walked to dry land.

As York swam back towards the wreckage, he watched Mike dive under the water again. The groan of twisted metal filled the air. He looked up in time to see a steel pillar that had survived the blast crumble to the sea. It fell in the same place that Mike had gone down. Time seemed to slow down for the split second that the pillar took to crash into the water.

He swam as fast as he could then dived under the surface of the water. He could see next to nothing. The fire that still burned from the pieces of wood sitting above the surface lit the water underneath to give only slight vision. After a few seconds he found Mike. The pillar had crushed his legs. York looked at him, he was struggling to get his legs free, but York could see the chance of him getting loose were slimmer than winning the lottery. He barely had a chance to make a first effort to get him free. Mike jolted as his lungs suddenly filled with water. York could see the life drain from the man's eyes. He squirmed in pain, and then fell still.

3

York spent the next twenty minutes trying to free Mike from the trap. He had to come to the surface for air every couple of minutes. When he did, the pillar just fell back into the same place. He managed to gather the strength for one last attempt. The pillar moved enough for him to pull the body free and drag it back to the shore. He laid Mike's body down on the shingle then sat next to him. He looked down at him, the thought that there were still people in the world that would risk their lives for others comforted him some what. Every person he knew was adamant that the world was selfish and if a man were dying in the middle of a crowded street, no one would stop. This man was proof that they were wrong.

He stared out over the disaster area. The fire was still burning and thick black smoke still poured into the air. There were at least two hundred bodies floating on the surface of the water. The wreckage was like nothing York had seen in a long time. Not since the bombing that changed the course of his life forever.

He was nine when his parents had been killed in a terrorist bombing. Their plane had been hijacked while waiting to take off. The terrorists kept the plane grounded for hours. After much negotiation they agreed to let the children off the plane. As they were helped towards the terminal by police, the plane exploded. York and the other children watched in horror as the plane carrying their parents was turned to nothing but rubble. The memory still lived vividly in his mind, and the nightmare would haunt him for the rest of his life.

The sound of sirens filled the air. The town was now illuminated in a sea of blue lights. York walked back to the promenade. He looked around at the busy emergency service men and women working hard to control the situation. Police officers cordoned off the area and evacuated the local residents. Paramedics saw to the pedestrians hit by debris. Fire fighters unreeled the hoses and ran up the on to the pier. Not one of them seemed to be even slightly taken back by the sheer devastation in front of them. They all simply got on with what they did best.

Paramedics tended to the gash on his leg that he had received from a sharp piece of metal in the water, and then he escorted them to the place where Mike's body lay. He watched as they placed the body carefully in a bag and lifted it up on to a stretcher, and then they carried him away. He felt sorry for the big man. He was brave, a real hero. His life; like so many there that night, was cut short at the hands of terrorists. Now; he knew it was time to do what he did best.

York sat on the back step of the ambulance. He took a look around at the emergency crew all still hard at work. As he sat watching, a Jaguar XF pulled up on to the pathway and two men got out. The driver was an older man. A strong, neat freshly combed moustache sat above his lips. His hair was neatly combed over to hide the slight receding line. He wore a freshly pressed dark suit; he didn't bother with a tie. Captain Tom Henshaw's dress sense was impeccable. Having never married and having no intention of marrying, he always made an effort to look good while he was at work. Some would say he was married to his job, and they would be right.

The passenger was the man he wanted to see. Agent Andy Myers had always been there for York in every bad time since they were five years old. They had a friendship that was for life. After going through school life together, York enrolled in the army, while Myers went to college to gain a Law Degree. Myers then went on to join the police force until he and York joined the ARTS team when it was launched some three years ago. He stood at six foot two with spiked jet black hair and a thin structure. He was a lot simpler in his choice of clothing than his boss. He looked as if he had just picked up the nearest and easiest piece of clothing available but he made the polo neck and black jeans work. It wasn't his facial features or general appearance that made him attractive to women; It was more his personality. He could walk in to any bar and take a pick of a number of females to take home with him. Although he always confessed he longed for someone to settle down with, York always knew he loved the promiscuous lifestyle.

Myers walked up to York looking him up and down. He was unshaven, his clothes were soaking and his t-shirt was torn. "You look like crap" he said with a sarcastic smile on his face.

York smiled back "You should see the other guy!" He replied. "You got a cig? The sea ate mine." Myers pulled out a cigarette and handed it to York, and then he offered out a light. York turned to Henshaw and nodded towards the Jaguar. "Nice car boss."

"Ain't she a beauty" whoever met him for the fist time, were always surprised by the way he spoke. His dress sense made him look posh and well to do, but in reality he was a common as the every day man. "Got her yesterday morning.

So what are we looking at?" Henshaw inquired nodding towards the crime scene.

They all walked towards the entrance to the pier stared out over the site where the club once stood. "What ever it was sir, the blast was big. I was at home over five hundred yards away and I was thrown back by the blast."

"You think it was a bomb?" Myers inquired.

"If I had to guess, I'd say it was PE4, and a lot of it. Whoever did this, wanted to make a serious statement. From what I could tell and judging by the structural damage, I'd also say that charges were placed on the steel pillars to maximise the damage"

They walked along the wood planks towards the end. Myers and Henshaw looked at the bodies that lay motionless in front of them. Henshaw was seldom knocked back by bombings and death, but this was different. This sent a sharp pain through his heart like a strike from an arrow. He hadn't seen anything like this since serving a tour in the Middle East where he witnessed several suicide bombings; even most of those weren't as bad as what he was seeing in front of him. Henshaw turned to York. "Any survivors?" He asked in a hopeless tone.

"I tried to resuscitate one girl that I found with a faint pulse. But I was too late. I also pulled one guy from the water, but that was it. The guard who helped me pulled a couple of girls in to." The thought of losing Mike in the rescue upset him for a moment. He rarely liked anyone when he first met them, but Mike had a likeability factor that was hard to ignore.

"Where is he now?" Henshaw asked.

York paused "A pillar that was still standing after the

blast fell on him whilst he was under water; I was too late to rescue him. His name was Mike; he was a security door man here for the club." He paused again for thought. "I want to know where he lives and if he has any family. If he does I want to be the one to tell them face to face. I owe him that much"

Henshaw looked at York for a few seconds. Although York tried to hide his emotions, he knew what was really going on. As did Myers. "Ok." Henshaw replied.

They turned and began to walk back. "Police are questioning the witness. As for you Alex, I think you should go home and take a break. Leave this one to us."

York stopped. "With all due respect sir, I want to help with this one. I want nothing more than to bring down the son of a bitch that did this."

Henshaw turned and looked at him. "I knew you were going to say that." He gave a wry smile and started to walk again. "Ok Alex, but for now there is not much we can do. I say we let the emergency services do their jobs then we can start our investigation."

As they made their way back to the promenade, they spotted Detective Will Carter running towards them. The overweight Scot had an urgent look painted across his chubby face. His overgrown stomach wobbled about like a bowl of jelly as he ran. On his shirt collar, he had a bright red stain that suggested he had been working a case of jam donuts when he was called away.

"Captain Henshaw." He called as he neared them. He stopped directly in front of them then took a few seconds to catch his breath. He had only run a few feet, but from the sound of his breathing, anyone would have thought he had just completed a marathon. As he managed to bring himself back from his half dead state, he gave the news over to Henshaw.

"It seems we have a bigger problem at hand sir."

"Which is?" Henshaw replied.

"I have just been talking to a witness who thinks she saw a man going into the Theatre a few hours ago with a gun and he hasn't come out yet."

4

Prime Minister James Whitburn hadn't had a full nights sleep since moving in to 10 Downing street two and a half years ago. Something would always have him working well in to the night. If by chance he managed to get to sleep at a reasonable hour, something would happen to have him up before the sun had a chance to rise. The bags that had formed under his eyes seemed to be a permanent feature now. Lines around his face made him look in his fifties, though he was only forty eight.

The news of the club bombing reached his office only a few minutes after it happened. The news struck him hard. It was the worst terrorist attack since 7/7 and the first since he had been elected.

After a quick shower and slipping in to any suit that he could pull from his wardrobe, he didn't bother to shave; he just made his way towards the meeting room.

There to greet him when he arrived was the Defence secretary Gavin Connors and Sheldon Murphy, the Director General of MI5. Whitburn's slightly greying hair was unkempt and his suit looked as though it had seen better days. Neither of the men bothered to notice, it was a sight they had both gotten used to.

The atmosphere in the room was bleak. None of them could quite take in the events that had unfolded a little over half an hour before. Coffee and pastries had been laid out on a table in the back right corner of the room, but no one could bring themselves to eat, each of them just poured a cup of coffee and sat down.

Whitburn took a sip of his coffee and began to speak.

"Thank you for coming in at such short notice gentlemen. You all know why we are here, so lets cut to the chase."

Murphy spoke first. He was of similar age to Whitburn but looked far less weathered. His hair still held its natural light brown colour and unknown to everyone else; his complexion was kept youthful by regular moisturising. "I have to say Mr Prime Minister; this is completely out of the blue. We have been monitoring all terrorist activity in the country for the past year and there has been nothing to suggest that an attack was about to happen."

"So we may have new cells working within the country?" Whitburn inquired.

Connors came in to the conversation "There is no real way of proving that. We don't even know that any known terrorist organisations are responsible for this. With security in the airports and docks so tight since the London bombings, it's not likely that we could let anyone who poses a threat in easily."

"True." Murphy responded "But there could be hundreds of cells working all over the world that we don't know about. We can only work on what intelligence we have and I am afraid gentlemen, in this case, the intelligence is limited."

The room fell silent for a few seconds. They all received terror threats from various groups all over the world on a regular basis, but something like this happening under their noses, without them getting wind of at least a little information was almost embarrassing for all of them, especially

Murphy.

Whitburn finally broke the silence "Ok, the worst has happened. Now let's look to the future. I want all airports, docks and train services going in and out of the country to put full and thorough bag searches in to action. No one leaves or enters the country without being eliminated from our suspect list."

"I don't mean to sound rude sir." Said Connors after taking a sip of coffee "But it sounds to me like you want to treat every member of our society as a suspect. With respect, I have to seriously advise you to reconsider. An action like that could seriously damage your reputation."

Whitburn let out a sigh and bowed his head. "When the people of our nation hear of the tragedy this morning, they are going to be looking in my direction for answers and they are going to demand action. At this point in time we have no idea who is responsible and I can't see that changing in the next few hours unless someone steps forward. I can honestly say I am willing to put my whole career on the line to find those responsible."

No one had a chance to answer. The phone in front of Whitburn rang; he pressed the answer button and put the phone on speaker. "Whitburn."

"I have Captain Henshaw holding on the line for you sir." His receptionist advised him.

"Thank you Cathy, put him through."

The phone went dead for a few seconds then Henshaw's voice came through. "Mr Prime Minister, Tom Henshaw."

"Tom, good to speak to you again."

"Thank you sir, I just wish it was under different circumstances." The pair had been friends for many years. After flying together in the Royal Air Force, they went on to become regular golf buddies. Although the regular weekly game had now dwindled down to just one game when they have some spare time, which wasn't very often.

"That's regrettable. So what is going on down there Tom?" The PM asked

"It seems the situation is far more severe than we first anticipated. I have just received word that a number of people are being held hostage in the theatre here."

"Do we know the number of fatalities in the bombing?" Connors inquired

"We have no way of telling at this point in time, however we believe the number to be in the region of around two to three hundred."

Whitburn fell silent. He felt a sense of sorrow grow inside of him, for the victims and their families. He wasn't one to take death well, even if he wasn't acquainted with the deceased, he still felt for them.

"What's being done about the hostages?" He asked

"I am going to lead the recovery operation and I have my two best agents Alex York and Andy Myers working on resolving the situation in the theatre."

"Would you like MI5 to offer assistance?" Murphy offered.

"We have the support of the local police, but thank you anyway Sheldon; I will keep your offer in mind."

Whitburn rose and walked around the table towards the coffee table and picked up a bagel, as he spread some butter on the only meal he would more than likely get all day, he continued the call "Tom. I want you to tell your guys to use any means necessary to resolve the situation in the theatre quickly and without innocent casualties."

"Will do sir." Henshaw answered, and then the phone cut off.

Whitburn walked to the door and opened it. He turned back to the two men in the room. "Let's get to work gentlemen."

5

York took a dark blue polo neck from the boot of Henshaw's Jag and replaced his wet t-shirt. Even though the Jag was only a couple of days old, it had already been converted and readied for action. The boot had been completely kitted out with combat gear. Separate compartments were made for different things. The box at the back had drawers for weapons; firearms, knives etc. The side boxes had uniform and bullet proof vests and an under carpet box had been made for explosives and grenades. What was a luxury car before was now a combat machine.

York pulled a vest from the side box and pulled it on over his polo neck. Then he strapped a holster belt to his waist and placed a communication radio in the breast pocket of the vest. He opened the firearms box and pulled out a Heckler and Koch G36K assault Rifle. He placed the strap over his shoulder and pushed the gun to the back. He then pulled out an H&K MK23 handgun and placed it in the holster.

He looked up at the building in front of him. The Pavilion Theatre was one of the focal points of Worthing. Built in 1926 it became a hit straight away. People from across the county as well as the locals would come to enjoy the shows. After being destroyed by fire in 1933, it was rebuilt with some of the great architectural features of the original. The building was big, with a dome shaped roof on the main building, the ticket office that sat in the front centre had great detailing around the front and sides; it was a great site to behold. The restaurant stuck out to the side of the main building and attracted extra trade to the site.

York looked at his watch, which read 03:36am. It had been a little over two hours since the explosion. Since they had turned up, he spent most of his time talking to police officers and giving statements. He wasn't much help though. After all he only saw the explosion and even that was after a few drinks, but he wasn't about to share that part.

He peered over at Henshaw who was talking to Carter. Then he caught sight of Myers walking towards him. He walked up to the car and began kitting himself out in the same gear as York.

"Police and local lifeguards are working together to retrieve the bodies from the water. Henshaw is going out with them in a few minutes" Myers informed his friend.

"Has the area been closed off to the public?" York asked

"Yeah, but local residents who refused to leave their homes are still enjoying the show. How you doing?"

Although the words were sincere, York still hated that Myers asked. Every time they were called to bomb site it was the same old questions. Myers knew that York had been hitting the bottle hard in the past few months and when he turned up on scene tonight, the smell of alcohol was still fresh in his breath.

York couldn't help but let out a slight chuckle "The answer is no, I am not drunk but I damn well wish I was about now." Using humour to get out of conversations or situations he didn't like was a usual trait for him, and Myers knew it. He could read his pal like a book.

"You did all you could you know." Myers said comfortingly. The words were a long shot and he knew they would have no effect, but they seemed to flow out anyway. "And as for the doorman who helped you, there was no way you could have predicted that pillar was going to fall."

York managed a smile, Myers was right. Although he felt sorrow for those innocent people who had lost their lives, his life long pal always had the knack to make him feel slightly better about the situation, whatever it was. "I say we take down the idiot inside, save the hostages and make it to the café for a full English 'coz I'm starving."

Myers finished kitting out then they made their way to the surveillance truck across the road. The truck looked like any normal white Luton on the outside. On the inside though, it was a completely different story. CCTV monitors sat along the left wall with hundreds of buttons and dials underneath them. The right hand side was kitted out with high tech sound equipment and to the rear was a small table with a kettle and a microwave for those long stakeouts.

The man at the helm of all the equipment was the stereotypical geek. He wore thick rimmed glasses and never seemed to make an effort to comb his thin, greying, light brown hair. He was a short, thin man. Although he was nearing 30, the only thing that made him look even close to his age was the unsuccessful goatee, which was greying early to match his hair. Kirk Stevens had worked for the Anti Terrorist Service since they formed three years earlier and always played a leading roll. His love of space and astrology was well known in the service and was the reason he had picked up the nickname Captain Kirk.

York and Myers entered the truck. "Kirky boy, how's it hanging?" York asked sarcastically while patting Kirk's back.

"Ask the hot girl I was with last night." Kirk came back.

York and Myers said nothing; they just looked at the skinny technician with raised eyebrows "So what have you got for us?" Myers inquired.

Kirk moved his wheelie chair over to the monitors the pressed a few button. "I managed to pick up the wireless signal that the theatre had installed a few months back." He explained. "It took a bit of hacking to get through the password but most of these amateur tech guys are all the same, and they use the same passwords."

"Don't suppose your gonna tell us what that might be?" York interrupted.

"What and reveal my trade secret. I don't think so." Kirk flipped a switch and the monitors came to life. There were seven in total and they all made up one picture. "I pulled up the image from the camera above the left entrance." He continued. "It's positioned to overlook the left side of the auditorium. As you can see the, place is empty."

York stared at the image on the screen. The seats were deserted. Everything seemed normal. Kirk pressed a few more buttons and the image on the screen changed. "This however, shows a different story."

The image was now on the right hand side of the auditorium. The scene had changed dramatically. York figured there to be about ninety people huddled together at the back right next to the stage. One man was sitting on a seat in front of them. "Can you get a close up of him from another angle?" Myers asked.

Kirk shook his head. "These are the only two cameras

in there." Kirk replied. "But thanks to my being a genius and all, I guessed you would ask that so." He stopped talking and brought another image up on the screen. "I looked back over the recording of the night and found this."

Neither York or Myers bothered to ask how he managed to get the recordings, frankly they didn't care. They were now looking at an image of the man face on. He wore denim jeans, a dark blue turtle neck and a sleeveless jacket. York stared at the picture; the man on the screen certainly didn't seem the type to be holding people to ransom. Something just didn't add up in his mind. He was dressed like a thug but his eyes told a different story, they seemed to tell York he was harmless.

"Kirky my boy, you are a genius." York stated with an excited tone. "If I could just ask one last thing of you."

"If it will keep me busy." Kirk responded.

"Get me all the info on this guy as you can and I'll pay for an all expenses trip to the Kennedy space station for you."

"Come on Alex." Kirk said in a cocky tone "I thought you could have at least challenged me."

A mile down the road, the man in black reached his apartment. He walked up the stairs and fetched the keys from his pocket. The events from the last few hours stuck in his head. He felt no remorse for the lives he had taken, it was all in a days work for him. He placed the key in the lock. As he was about to turn it, he heard a car pull up behind him. He turned and saw the Black Mercedes that dropped off his comrade. He immediately knew something was wrong. They had only agreed to meet again if there was a problem or if one of them had been caught,

He walked back down the steps and up to the car. He crouched down beside the driver's side window and waited for him to wind it down. As the window opened slightly, the man found himself staring at the silenced barrel of a pistol. Before he could make a move, the driver pulled the trigger. The man fell in to a lump on the floor. Blood trickled from the wound in his head and stained the pavement. The black Mercedes pulled away and disappeared down the road.

6

While York waited for the computer to bring up the info he wanted, he stepped out of the truck and scanned the area. He spotted Henshaw down on the shingle beach co-ordinating the divers for the recovery of the bodies in the water. "SIR." He shouted to get Henshaw's attention as he ran over to where his boss was standing.

"How's it going?" Henshaw asked.

"We have managed to get a full facial picture of the hostage taker." York informed. "Kirk is searching through the database now to get his ID and background. Once we do, I'm going to talk to him."

"Good work, but go easy on him; we don't know what sort of state of mind this man is in and I know some of your negotiation techniques. We don't want him to do anything stupid."

York smiled. "Trust me Captain." He paused for a few seconds before asking, "Captain, any idea why there are only about ninety people in there? There was a show planned for last night and by my calculation there should be ten times that."

"Apparently." Henshaw said, turning back to York after shouting some commands at the divers. "The show was cancelled due to three cast illnesses." The scepticism showed in Henshaw's voice.

York knew exactly what his boss was thinking; he was thinking the same thing. If one had gone sick, there would have been no reason to think it was suspect. The fact that three had gone was a completely different matter. "Have the local police paid them a visit yet?"

"They've got a car on route now." Henshaw glanced over to the divers again. York knew he didn't have his full attention.

A yell came from across the street. "ALEX." Myers called.

"Listen captain." York said in a sympathetic manner. "I know you feel somewhat responsible when people die in these situations. Just remember that there was nothing you or any of us could have done to avoid this. All we can do is ensure justice is served."

Henshaw turned and walked away without answering. York didn't need to hear a reply; he knew his words had been taken onboard.

A yell came from across the street. "ALEX." Myers called.

York ran over to the truck and jumped in. He looked down at the computer screen. The picture was a match to the still shot taken of the terrorist. Before York could begin to read the information on the screen, Kirk started to read it aloud. "The man's definitely not what I expected," he informed his colleagues with a smug voice after completing a potential two and a half hour job in twenty minutes. "And all I can say about him is that he has a cleaner record than you Alex."

York gave Kirk a hard glare. "My record is as clean as they get. Everyone knows I'm a good boy."

Kirk didn't bother to answer, he just continued on. "He finished school at 16. From there he went on to work for a construction company, mainly working in and around the London area, he worked for them for around twenty years. He

46

was signed off permanently six years ago after falling two floors from a scaffolding tower and damaging his back. The only thing wrong with him is the amount of money he owes various loan and mortgage companies" He looked up at York. "And no, I don't think he really fits the bill of a terrorist either."

York patted Kirk on the back. "Nice one Kirky, You did good." York glanced at the name and the address under the picture and wrote them on a small note pad, and then he and Myers left the truck.

York searched for his boss, who was now aboard the lifeboat heading out to the disaster site. His attention was pulled to the Toyota Land Cruiser pulling up next to Henshaw's Jaguar. Inside, the six ATS assault team members looked ready for a fight. Each of them were dressed in black combat gear and wore black baseball caps with ATS written on the front. Each of them had a look of sheer concentration on their faces.

York headed over to the car as each of them collected their equipment from the boot and loaded up with weapons. York called for Detective Carter to join them, who was busy talking to the few passers by who had witnessed the tragedy.

They all gathered around the front of the four-by-four vehicle. Agent Jack Simmons, the leader of the assault team, placed a large copy of the theatre's architectural drawings on the bonnet.

"Ok gentlemen." York began "We have one terrorist inside with about ninety hostages." He pointed to a spot on the drawing "They are currently being held here just by the stage on the right hand side."

Simmons jumped in "I have pinpointed the best point of entry to be the kitchen. There is a door from the main dining room to the auditorium. If we're quick and take him by surprise, then we may be able to keep the civilian casualties to zero."

York nodded in agreement "Agent Myers will lead your team in if you have no problem with that Jack."

Simmons nodded "That's cool with me, Mr Myers and I have worked together on numerous occasions, and it will be a pleasure."

York looked at Myers "You mean you have worked cases without me. I'm hurt."

Myers pulled a sad face then continued ON with the briefing. "Alex and I both feel that there is something amiss about this man we are dealing with. He has never put a foot wrong in his life. He has no criminal record and to be perfectly honest, I would say from experience, he is no terrorist."

"What do you plan to do?" Detective Carter inquired, making his first addition to the briefing.

"I want to try and get inside to talk to him and gain some level of trust. If he doesn't budge, I can check the area inside to ensure we can get in safely. Also I want to make sure that all of the hostages are ok and none are hurt."

"Do you really think he is going to let you in?" Carter asked sceptically.

York shrugged his shoulders "I hope so, it may take a little convincing but if I can assure him that I will be going in unarmed, and then I believe he will comply."

They all went over the entry plan once more. York told carter to have his armed officers to be ready on standby. He knew that they wouldn't be needed, but he felt compelled to make the detective feel that he was involved. The ATS team were more than capable of entering a building filled with twenty highly trained terrorists and still get the job done with zero civilian casualties and be out for an early breakfast.

As Carter rushed off to brief his officers on the plan, the ATS team members took their positions. York pulled Simmons to the side.

"Jack," York said "I read that this guy has a family. If I am right thinking he has been coerced into doing this, then I can bet my year's salary that they will want to make sure there is no way to trace this shit back to them."

"You think they will go after the family?" Simmons responded "There is a strong possibility that they have no idea what he is doing."

York nodded and continued "That's true and I may well be barking up the wrong tree with this but if they are pro's, then they will leave nothing to chance. Also, I want the wife brought here. She may be able to help us settle this peacefully"

Simmons thought for a few seconds then gave the thumbs up "Ok, I'll send two of my guys to their house, do you have the address."

York handed him the piece of paper he had written the address on earlier and Simmons walked over to pull his two men up and give them their new assignment. They jumped into the Toyota and pulled away.

With the team in position and Myers taking the lead, it was time for him to do his part. He rushed back to the surveillance truck and sat at the desk in the back. He ordered

Kirk to dial the number for the ticket office. He placed a headset that was connected to the computer over his ears, and then sat back in the chair, keeping his eye on the live CCTV feed on the screen on front of him. The phone rang but there was no answer. He tried again and then a third time, but it was to no avail, the man inside was not playing ball.

The hostages huddled together under the stage. They tried their hardest not to let their fear show, to stay calm and in control of themselves, but it was a hard task. Most sat silent and still, some whimpered under their breath and quickly wiped away any tears that rolled down their cheeks. No one dared talk; they all just sat and contemplated what their futures would hold in store. Even after the explosion, they simply sat and waited for their captor's next move.

They stared at the man sitting in front of them on the seat. He didn't seem like the type to be holding people hostage. He was short with balding hair and a chubby, soft face. Surprisingly he seemed almost as scared as they were. His stomach stuck out and hung over his belt line and when he sat down it laid comfortably on his lap. The only thing that was alarming about the man was the machine gun sitting on his knees.

He spent most of the seven hours he had kept them there staring at his mobile phone in an apprehensive manner. No one could quite understand why. The only time he got up from his seat, was to do a quick check of the area, searching for any intruders.

The ringing phone startled him. He began to rise from his chair when the thought hit him. What if this was a ploy to get him out in the open. If he answered the phone in the ticket office; he would be in full view of anyone outside ready to put a bullet in his head. It was a risk he was unwilling to take. He sat back in his chair and stared at the hostages again.

After another twenty minutes in silence, one man, a short, thin man in his early thirties with thick rimmed glasses spoke up. He had been the stage director of the theatre for many years and for many productions, so he was a naturally assertive man. This was a different circumstance though; he was used to talking to unhappy audience members or unruly cast members, not armed terrorists. It took him a few moments to build the confidence to speak. "How long are you planning on keeping us here?" He asked hoping the answer wouldn't come from the barrel of the gun.

The terrorist smiled. "I wondered how long it would be before one of you said something." He replied. "I was beginning to think that you had all taken a vow of silence." He tried his best to lighten the atmosphere with a bit of humour, but it was a wasted effort. His voice surprised the group, when he came in and took them all hostage; his tone was hard and loud. Now, it had calmed and he sounded almost as gentle as he looked. "I promise I will not keep you here any longer than is necessary."

"Are you…..going to kill us?" A woman asked in a low, stammered voice.

Before he could answer, a loud voice came from outside. "Mr Miles Bennett. This is the National Anti-Terrorist Service." He stood up from his seat and walked quickly over to the window. He pulled back the curtain slightly and peered out. Standing only thirty feet from the entrance was a tall, well built man holding a megaphone. He wore stone jeans and a dark polo neck with a bullet proof vest covering his upper body. He knew that the trouble was just beginning.

7

York waited for a response but none came. He noticed the curtain move to the right of the ticket office. The man was listening, now he just had to convince him he was in no danger.

"Mr Bennett my name is Alex York. I am an Agent with the Anti-Terrorism Service. I am not here to hurt you I just want to talk."

Again he waited for a response. All of the emergency service personnel had fallen silent. Apart from the paramedics on the pier and the sound of the lifeboats engine that echoed around in the early morning air, you could have heard a pin drop. York saw the window where he noticed the curtain move open slightly. He was making progress, it was slow but sure.

"What do you want?" Bennett shouted back.

"Like I said." York came back "I want to talk to you. But not like this. I would like you to answer the phone."

There was silence again for a few seconds. Bennett was considering the request. Gaining someone's trust in this situation was something York had always been good at. He had a quality about him that could have people catering to his every need. That wasn't just useful on the job; quite often he made use of it in other areas of his life too.

"What about your guys with the weapons. I want them to fall back; you can at least give me that." Bennett finally replied.

York turned to Myers who was standing a few yards behind him. He motioned for him to move the assault team out of direct vision of the ticket office. They moved slowly back towards the truck on the other side of the road. York turned back to the window.

"Ok, there you have it. I have moved them back and the armed police are lowering their weapons too." He spoke in a suggestive tone and turned to Carter as he did. Carter nodded and gave the order for his team to holster their weapons.

This time York didn't have to wait long for the response. "Ok." Bennett's voice came from behind the window. This was York's chance to end the siege. If he could just convince Bennett throw down his weapon and come out, then he could finally get home for some sleep.

He didn't bother to go back to the truck; he had dialled the number into his mobile before he came out. He paused for a few moments to give Bennett the chance to get into the office where the phone was situated. He peered through the glass doors into the office. There was no movement. He figured that the man inside was playing safe, keeping low and out of line of sight of any hotshot shooters.

York pressed the send key on his phone and waited for the reply. The phone rang only twice before being answered.

"Go ahead. Talk." Bennett's vice was stern but shaky. The fear that the man was feeling could be felt even down the phone.

"Thank you Miles, I appreciate the..." York didn't get to finish his sentence.

"Just cut to the chase." Bennett interrupted.

York thought for a second, he began questioning his original judgement of the man on the other end. The hard tone made him think perhaps he wasn't the angel his file made him out to be.

"Ok." York eventually replied. "I want you to tell me Miles. Do you have any injured hostages in there? Anyone who may need some medical attention?"

"No. Everyone is ok." His tone began to soften again.

York was now beginning to get a new idea of the man they were dealing with. His mood seemed to change every minute. He knew he had to get inside to gain a better picture.

"Listen, Miles." York said calmly as he began to pace up and down. "I want to try this another way. The last thing I want is for my team to burst inside and start firing bullets all over the place. So this is what I am proposing. Why don't you let me come in? We can talk properly then."

"How do I know your men won't just come in any way? For all I know you could just be a distraction."

York smiled and looked over to Myers "Believe me. My boss would never let any harm come to me from a stray bullet." Myers nodded his head and mouthed the words 'Yes he would'

All York could hear down the line was breathing. Again, he had made Bennett consider his request. He moved left slightly to try and gain a line of sight in to the booth where he assumed Bennett was hiding. Still he could see nothing.

"Ok, but you must do something for me, like before. I want you to pick up my wife and daughters. I want to make sure they are safe."

"I requested they be picked up about half an hour ago. If I am correct, they should be on their way to the police station as we speak."

Little was York to know that this was not the case. As

the two team members pulled into the road where Bennett's house was situated half way down, they spotted a black Ford Transit van parked outside. The back doors were open and there were two men armed with automatic weapons pulling masks over their faces.

    They pulled the Toyota to the side of the road a hundred yards back and killed the engine. They hadn't been noticed by the hostiles, as they arrived, the driver had turned the head lights off as soon as they noticed the rifles. They watched the two assassins shut the door and move slowly and quietly towards the house on the opposite side of the road. The driver, Agent Coombs ran through an adjacent ally way towards the rear entrance to the house.

    The passenger, Agent Timms moved towards the front of the house and ducked below a hedge two doors down. He crouched low and watched the pair as they made a mess of picking the lock on the door. He took a glance over to the van and noticed a driver sitting behind the wheel. Under the cover of the night, he moved over and kept low as he came to the rear of the van. He took a quick glance over to the pair in the door way, who had now gained entry to the house. One went in but the other stood guard. Timms moved down the side of the truck and opened the passenger side door. Before the driver knew what had happened, the silenced G36K rifle popped a round off. The bullet hit him directly in the temple and killed him instantly. Timms then directed the barrel to the man standing by the door and fired again. The bullet struck the man in the heart and he fell to the floor. He made a slight movement then fell still.

    "Front of the house clear, one x-ray inside." Timms

said in to his throat communication radio.

Coombs moved through the ally and through the gate with stealth. The only thing he needed to do now was get in the house and take down the assassin before he could complete his mission. He pulled the handle down on the rear door and to his surprise, it was open. Luck was definitely on his side. On the odd occasion Bennett would go to a friend's house for a late night poker game. When he did, his wife would leave the back door open instead of trusting a drunk with a set of house keys. Tonight, she had assumed he was at a game.

Coombs slowly and silently opened the door. He moved in through the kitchen and into the hallway. He could see the shadow cast by the slight moon light of a man standing by the door. Before he reached the stairs, the guard had been taken down and was now lying face down on the porch in a pool of blood.

He moved up the stairs, careful not to disturb any loose floor boards. As he reached the landing, he peered into the master bedroom directly opposite. The assassin was standing over Mrs Bennett's bed with his rifle pointed at her head. The fact that he had taken the time to look at the lady who was lying naked and half covered by the duvet, gave Coombs the time to strike. His bullet struck the assassin in the side of the neck. Blood poured onto the carpet. The thud of the body hitting the floor woke Mrs Bennett with a start. When she saw the man standing in her doorway holding a gun and the dead man lying on her floor, she screamed at the top of her voice. Coombs placed his hand over her mouth and showed her his ID badge in his left breast pocket. Then while he waited for her to dress, he gathered the two girls together and took the family to the car.

8

York waited for the word that the family were safe and then called Bennett to let him know. Although York had been in situations like this before, he felt slightly nervous. The man inside was still a mystery to him. By this time in past operations, he knew exactly who he was dealing with, and exactly how to take them down. The confusion made him uneasy.

He pulled his rifle from over his shoulder and gave it to Myers. Then he handed over his pistol. He looked up at Myers, who had a concerned look about him.

"Don't worry mate, I've done this before you know." York said in a sarcastic manner.

"It's not that, I am just worried that you haven't put me down for the apartment in your will." The humour between the two seemed to calm York's nerves a little. He knew that was exactly Myers' plan, and he appreciated it. After handing Myers his communication radio he started towards the theatre. After taking a few steps he turned back to his friend.

"By the way, I don't suppose you could let the boss know what is going on could you?" He asked.

Myers looked at him irritably "Why do you always leave me with the best jobs."

York turned and started walking away. He listened to Myers talking to Henshaw over the comm. radio as he walked. He heard the raised, angered voice reply, Henshaw was obviously less than satisfied with the plan. York knew his actions were completely against what his training had taught him. Henshaw was strict on many things when it came to the safety of his staff and when one of his agents put themselves in unnecessary danger, he kicked off big time. York was seldom one to stick to the rules and play by the book and Henshaw knew this. York spent many hours in Henshaw's office taking and grilling over rule breaking and here he was about to do it once again.

He walked up to the entrance to the ticket office. He could feel a bead of sweat trickling down his face and his palm felt moist. Although he had been watching the CCTV footage, he still felt unsure of what he was walking in to, that made him nervous. He stopped momentarily to take a deep breath then he opened the door and walked inside.

The room was unlit, the only light coming from the headlights of the cars outside. He walked around the enclosed counter slowly. Bennett materialised as if from no where. It wasn't the sudden appearance that made York jump however; it was the AK-47 pointing towards his chest.

He held his hands up and spun around slowly "As you can see, I am unarmed, so there is no need for the weapon."

Bennett nodded his head towards the bottom of York's trousers. "And what about the gun attached to your ankle."

York let out a slight laugh then shook his head "I'm afraid it seems you have seen one to many bond films. We real Agents don't have such luxuries."

Bennett didn't lower his weapon; he kept it aimed at York's heart. He had never even fired a gun before until three days ago. He had been taken to a remote field and used cans for target practice. At first he didn't hit a thing. But after a few attempts he soon began to master the task. He found holding so much power at his fingertips almost exciting. It was completely out of character, but he liked it.

"So what do you want?" Bennett asked; his tone had become firm once again.

"I want to see the hostages." York said lowering his arms. "I need to make sure they are unharmed."

Bennett tried to read York's body language. He couldn't tell if the man in front of him was playing a trick or was genuine. "Why should I let you?"

"Because." York replied taking a step forward towards Bennett. "If you have harmed any of them, then I will be unable to help you. My trigger happy friends outside are just itching to get in and blow you into the next world. But I would much rather have no one else die tonight."

"Ok, but if I so much as smell one of your guys heading in this direction, we all die. Do you understand?"

The words were like an arrow to the heart. The stakes had just been raised in one sentence. York was now starting to understand what Bennett had been asked to do. He had to come up with an idea quick or they would, he figured, end up pulling more bodies out of another disaster scene.

York walked through the double glass doors to the auditorium first, closely followed by Bennett who still had the rifle aimed at him. On the other side of the doors, directly in front of them was a small door that led to the sound and lighting room. To the right and left were openings that led to the seating area. York took the opening to the right. He walked down the two steps from the rear gangway to the seating aisle. As the hostages, who were still huddled together near the stage, came into view Bennett moved past him and stopped him in his tracks.

"That's as far as you go." Bennett said "You can see they are unharmed."

York stared at the captives. They all looked scared. Some of the women had a constant stream of tears running down their faces, yet they remained quiet. The men held the women close, doing everything in their power to comfort them. It seemed like a failed effort.

He pulled his attention away from the hostages to scan the huge oval shaped room. Large posters hung behind Perspex frames advertising up and coming shows were dotted around the walls. Thick red velvet drapes were hung over the windows. The seating had been upholstered in a similar colour to match in with the curtains. On the right hand side of the room, York noticed a large double door that led through the restaurant. They had been wedged shut by a metal framed chair. The entry point that Simmons had pointed out was now compromised. It would take more than a kick to budge the doors and York cursed the fact that the only entry point now seemed to be the front entrance.

"You'll never find it you know." Bennett stated.

York stared at him quizzically "Find what?"

"You know what I mean."

He did know, but he wanted to hear it out loud "Why don't you tell me what you think I am looking for and I'll tell you if you are right."

Bennett leaned in closer "The bomb." He whispered.

The fact that Bennett had whispered the answer helped York understand Bennett a little more. The hostages were obviously unaware of the explosive and he wanted to keep it that way. He was showing signs of compassion, which meant here was room for negotiation. He also knew that the man in front of him, as he suspected, was no terrorist. With most of the hostage situations he had found himself in, the hostage takers had been ruthless. Some showed levels of consideration when it came to the captives, especially the injured ones. But they were still willing to kill for their cause. York couldn't see a killer in Bennett. When he looked in to his eyes, he saw plain and simple fear.

"You haven't told them about the bomb yet have you?" York asked motioning to the hostages.

Bennett shook his head; the expression on his face confirmed it. He seemed almost ashamed at what he was doing. "I didn't want to make them anymore scared than they are already." He said softly.

"Then why the hell are you doing this?" The question was a long shot and York had no expectation of getting a reply.

"Do you have a family Mr York?"

York shook his head.

"Then you could not possibly understand the strain of trying to provide for the people that mean more to you in the world than anything. The constant battle to give them everything that they need is harder than anything you could ever imagine."

York was surprised to get an answer. A tear began to roll down Bennett's cheek as he stood silent for a moment, thinking of his wife and children. After a few seconds, he shook the emotional state and raised the rifle in the direction of York again after lowering it for a split second. "I think it's time you left Agent York. I have a mission to complete."

York almost felt sorry for the man before him. He had

never had anyone to provide for and realised that Bennett was right, he had no idea how hard it was. "Ok, I'm going. But please, think about what you doing. You will not help your family in any way by bringing harm to these people."

He didn't get a reply; Bennett just motioned towards the door with the end of the rifle.

9

York left Theatre and made his way over to the truck where Myers, Simmons and now Henshaw, who had returned to shore after learning that York had entered the building, were standing. As he approached the truck, he waved Carter over to join in the briefing.

Henshaw had a look on his face that was all too familiar to York, the disapproving look that he gave every time one of his agents acted without permission.

"Alex, are you completely insane?" Henshaw barked. "I swear if you ever…"

"Calm down captain." York interrupted "You'll give yourself a heart attack."

The comment only enraged Henshaw further and York knew it. He didn't bother to respond. All too many times they had been in disagreement about certain things and York would just treat it as a joke.

York grabbed his weapons back from Myers and waited for Carter to make his way over to them.

"Ok gentlemen" York started. "Here's the low down. We have a worse situation than we originally projected. It seems our friend also has an explosive device. To add insult to serious injury, the entry point that we suggested earlier has been blocked. The bottom line is we are completely screwed."

"Did you see the device?" Carter asked.

York shook his head "I didn't get the chance, he had me out of there as soon as he could."

They all stood dumfounded. The news was the worst that they could have expected. With no entry point and the knowledge of a bomb inside, the situation was looking less than promising.

"Did you manage to get a reason for the attacks from him?" Henshaw inquired.

"No, but I believe he's doing this for financial reasons."

"How can you be so sure?" Carter came in.

York ran through everything that was said inside. "I would say who ever is paying him, is paying him well. There is no way that he would martyr himself if he wasn't certain that his family would be safe."

Simmons let out a snigger then told York what had happened at the family's home. "I'll tell you one thing. These guys are well funded. The men who attacked his home were nothing short of professional."

Myers raised his hand to join in on the conversation "Are we not forgetting that he is more than likely the one who detonated the bomb in the club."

Carter shook his head "I have just spoken to a witness who claims she saw a man acting suspiciously down the beach to the west from here, he apparently was yielding some sort of phone like device." He pulled his note pad from his inside jacket pocket and continued. "She said he took the device from his pocket shortly before the explosion, then he placed it back after and calmly walked away. I would bet a years salary on him being your guy."

"What makes you so certain?" York asked.

Carter looked down at his notebook "Because a man matching his description was found dead outside his home. Gun shot wound point blank to the head."

There were a few questions beating around in York's brain. Why had Bennett not detonated earlier? What was he waiting for? And York knew that there had to be an agenda. Or was Bennett just to terrified to press the trigger? It was obvious to York that the other bomber had to be more experienced than Bennett. But why hire two attackers?

"So do you still think he is the innocent man you said he was?" Simmons asked.

York shook his head and sat down on the foot plate at the rear of the truck "Honestly, I don't know. The man standing inside is definitely not what his profile makes him out to be. When we were talking, he seemed to blow hot and cold. One minute we were talking normally, the next he is pushing me out of the door. To be honest, if you are asking, 'do think that he will blow the place into the next millennium'? Then I would have to say no."

"What if you're wrong?" Henshaw interjected.

York sat silent for a second and let out a sigh "Then god help those hostages."

The group were disturbed by the sound of a vehicle pulling up close by. York looked around the truck to see Coombs and Timms in the 4x4 with Bennett's wife in the back. She had a strange sense of calm about her as she stepped from the car. Her dark permed hair flickered in the slight breeze that now blew in off the sea. York judged her to be around five foot four and for a mother of two, she had kept herself in good shape.

He walked over to her and extended his arm towards her, "Mrs Bennett. My name is Alex York I w…"

The introduction went unfinished. As soon as he began

to speak, Claire Bennett interrupted. "What the hell is going on?" She demanded in a strong, harsh manner. "One minute I am asleep, the next I am woken by a man pointing a gun at my head."

York motioned her over to the truck. He explained everything, from the bombing at the club, to the hostage taking in the theatre. She sat silent in the back of the truck for a few seconds, and then she looked at York and said "Why is he doing this?" Her tone had changed now. She spoke softer; York could sense the fear in her voice.

"Mrs Bennett." He crouched down in front of her and looked in to her eyes "I know this is a lot to take in, but we are running out of time. We have one chance to end things peacefully, for that I need your help. Will you help us?"

She bowed her head as a tear rolled down her face. The past hour had become almost a blur. The thought that the man she loved was holding innocent people hostage was almost too much to cope with, but she held herself together. Wiping the tear away she looked back at York "Ok, what do you want me to do?"

York leaned over and picked up the telephone. "I need you to talk to him. If there is one person that he will listen to, it's you."

She hesitated before taking the phone. The urge to break down was greater than ever now. Her hands were shaking and sweating, and she could feel her eyes filling up every second.

York slowly dialled the number; the conversation was played over the loud speaker.

"What now?" Bennett answered.

His wife didn't respond she sat silent and shaking. York answered for her "Mr Bennett. We have someone here who wants to talk to you. He nodded at Claire.

"Miles." She said softly.

"Claire, what the hell are you doing here?"

"I was brought here by the police. They stopped some men from killing us in our home. Miles, what is going on?"

Bennett didn't answer straight away; when he did he said "I'm sorry Claire. I'm doing this for our family, for you."

"Miles didn't you hear me, some men tried to kill us."

"Please don't think any less of me. I am in too deep now; I have a job to do. I love you."

The line fell silent. Claire broke down in uncontrollable panic. York lifted her to her feet and passed her over to a paramedic who was working close by. The thought that this had been their last hope of a peaceful ending played on his mind. He knew also that the chances of getting in undetected were slim at best. In his mind, the whole thing was a nightmare.

Silence encircled the ATS Team as they thought about what to do next. They all knew if they were going to storm the building, they would have to do it soon. Defeat was a foreign concept to them. Since their launch four years earlier, the team had built a solid reputation amongst the law enforcement agencies of Britain. They had tackled many hostage situations with a one hundred percent success rate and they didn't plan on changing things today. The idea that they had no way into the building without Bennett detecting them and triggering the explosive just made them more determined.

Simmons stepped into the back of the truck. Materialising a few seconds later with the copy of the theatre blueprint, he placed the drawing down on the floor of the truck next to York and secured it down with his torch and pistol.

They all stared intently at the drawing in front of them, all looking for something they may have missed the first time round. A few suggestions were put forwards and then quickly cast aside. After a few minutes, York noticed something that hadn't come into his mind before. He rose to his feet and stepped to the side of the truck. Looking up at the roof of the old building, he stared at the windows that ascended vertically from the roof. They encircled the top of the dome like the final tier of a cake. Although big enough for a man of York's stature to fit through, he felt the bars inside the windows that formed an X would hinder his access.

He stepped back to the rear of the truck and cursed that yet another idea had materialised to nothing. As he started to sit back on the footstep, it struck him. The solution had been staring him straight in the face the whole time. He peered back around the truck and down the beach. In the distance he noticed a news helicopter hovering around the police cordon. A devilish smile spread across York's face that was all too familiar to his colleagues.

Henshaw looked at him expectantly "Well?"

York said nothing, looked at his boss and smiled.

Whitburn sat at his desk and nurtured his seventh cup of coffee. He thoughtfully glared at the piled of paperwork on his solid oak desk. The piles of paper were growing by the day.

With the current recession now finally beginning to diminish, the workload hadn't. Many financial institutions had fallen over the past eighteen months. Government funded organisations were abolished and thousands of the British public were being left workless and in the most severe circumstances, homeless.

At the beginning of 2009, Whitburn and a small group of other leaders had come together with some of the world's wealthy and top business men to try desperately to control the situation. In a shock tactic to save his country from financial meltdown, Whitburn gave the people of Britain a lifeline. Immigration had to be controlled, financial institutions would be temporarily taken over by the government to oversee unnecessary spending and to aid the general public, and tax rates were frozen and in some circumstances cut. The shocking and potentially dangerous move could have cost Whitburn his place as PM, but it was well worth it. Despite the few businesses that were lashing out at him, mainly loan and credit card companies, the people of his nation were finally beginning to fall back on their feet.

He continually went over in his mind the events of the past few hours. In a couple of hours, he would have to address the nation with the devastating news. He desperately wanted to tell them that the people responsible would pay, but he knew it would be a lie. The fact was they had no idea who was responsible. No one had owned up and there was no evidence pointing in any direction. It was almost amusing to him that even with the sophisticated intelligence agencies at his fingertips; he still could not have stopped this attack.

His deep thoughts were disturbed by the phone that sat centrally on his desk.

"Sir, I have Captain Henshaw on line one for you." His secretary informed him. He noticed slight fatigue showing in her voice after another early wakeup call. No matter what time of day or night, she would drop everything to be at his aid. For that he was grateful.

"Put him through." He replied "And take a half hour break to grab a coffee and some breakfast. You've earned it."

"Yes sir, thank you."

After a momentary silence, Henshaw's voice came through. "Mr Prime Minister, Tom Henshaw."

"Hello Tom. How are things looking down there?" He asked with slight apprehension in his voice.

"I'm afraid things have taken a turn for the worse sir." The words struck Whitburn like a bullet to the head. "We have now come to learn that the hostage taker has an explosive device."

Whitburn let out a long sigh and rubbed his temple. The hope of a peaceful ending, he knew, was now out of the question. "Is he the man who was responsible for the club bombing?"

"Detective Carter believes that we may have a different suspect for that. A witness said she saw a man acting suspiciously just before the explosion."

A brief silence came over Whitburn as he digested the news. The lifeline he had hoped for slowly fading away. If the hostage taker had been the bomber, things would be a lot simpler. "Ok Tom. We have tightened security on all transport, if you could send a description to MI5; they can begin searching for him."

"Ok sir." Henshaw replied "Agent York is planning a

stealth assault on the theatre, we may have found a way to get in unnoticed, we shall keep you up to date sir."

"Thank you Tom, be sure that you do. I want you to do everything in your power to make sure he comes out alive. If he has information, we need it."

"Yes sir."

As the line fell silent, Whitburn leaned back in his chair. The situation was becoming more complex by the hour. What he wasn't to know, was that things were going to get a whole lot worse.

10

The pilot of the Bell 206 long ranger pushed the controls forward and brought the helicopter out of its hovering position. The Rolls Royce turbine engine revved up and the Bell moved along at a slow speed. When the call had come through, the pilot hadn't bothered to argue. The fact was he would be praised for being able to get in close for the reporter, sitting in the rear, to get a few close snap shots of the bomb site and the theatre.

He flew the Bell in low towards the building. As he approached, he pulled back slightly on the control and hovered around and over the top, giving the reporter great views from all angles. Once all the shots had been taken, the pilot banked right and flew towards the wreckage, which was free of the water now the tide was fully out. After a few more shots were taken, he manoeuvred the helicopter back to the theatre and began the process again, as he was ordered to do.

Once he had completed three passes, he aimed the Bell towards a multi storey car park to the west of the theatre a few hundred yards down the road. As the top level came in to view, he noticed two men standing beside a silver Jaguar, both had automatic weapons hanging over their shoulders.

The first man seemed almost out of place. The thick moustache, well presented hair and freshly pressed suite gave him the look of someone who should be sitting in an up town bar drinking expensive brandy while enjoying imported Cuban cigars.

The second man was a lot younger than the first, the pilot judged him to be in his mid to late twenties. His biceps almost bulged out of the sleeves of his polo shirt, the result of much spare time spent in the gym.

Moving the Bell in to position, the pilot landed forty feet from the two men. The younger of the two ran up and opened the sliding door then jumped in. He pulled a head set over his ears and after a wink and a smile at the pretty, young blonde haired reporter, the pilot spoke to him through the on board communications. "Alex York?"

York nodded and replied "Yeah. Here's the plan. Make one more fly by over the top of the theatre, be sure to go in slow and hover for a few seconds, I want to get a good read of my drop zone. After that, move out and come in low again, then I'll make my move."

The pilot didn't respond, he just nodded in agreement then lifted the helicopter off the ground and headed toward the theatre. As they approached, York flung opened the door and leaned out for a better view of the roof. He found his target between the main dome and the smaller dome that sat above the ticket office. He signalled for the pilot to pass out over the sea to the south and come back in over the same line, remembering that there were no windows on the back wall near the stage.

As they passed over the bomb site, York got his first proper look at the wreckage since the tide had gone out. He was shocked at the site. Wood still burned on the top. Charred and twisted metal littered the surrounding area. Bodies were still trapped in amongst the rubble. The whole sight was almost heart wrenching.

The pilot turned the Bell back towards the theatre. Having his drop zone marked in his mind, York braced himself for the assault. He attached a rope to the safety handle positioned just above the door the attached it to the clip on his belt. Wrapping the rope around his leg for speed control on the way down, he waited for the right moment before he leaped from the helicopter.

Unclipping the rope once he had landed, he gave the thumbs up to the reporter, who was peering down at him through the opened door; she unhooked the end of the rope from the handle and threw it down to York. He quickly pulled the end up and attached it to the steel bars on the windows which were encircling the roof top, now noticing the windows had been shattered from the blast earlier. Draping the rope down the front of the dome, he gripped tight and began to descend.

So far, the operation was going smoothly, apart from the hundred or so headlights from the police cars almost blinding him when he peered down to check in progress while sliding noticed the hatch the first time he studied the plans for the building, but they seemed to jump out at him the second time. As he reached out and gave the handle a tug, the fear he had from the moment he formed his plan came to life. The hatch had been tightly sealed from the inside; it would have taken more that just a firm kick to open it.

York cursed the fact that his only possible stealth entry had been taken away. He peered up at the windows at the top where he had attached the end of the rope. Taking the measurement of the gap under the set of bars across the window, he gripped the rope again and began to climb.

When he reached the top, he was able to properly take a visual measurement of the gap and judged it to be big enough for him to squeeze through. He took off his belt and rifle and laid them down on the roof. He knew if he was going to fit through the gap, these would have to stay behind.

He un-holstered his handgun and held it tight as he began to squirm through the gap. For a man with a slightly thinner body structure, fitting through would have been easy but for York, it was a struggle. As he finally managed to wriggle through, he lowered himself down to the floor.

The light from the rising sun cast enough rays through the windows to illuminate the room. A walkway encircled a huge dome in the centre of the loft area. A ladder rose up one side then dropped down the other. The room stretched the entire width of the theatre.

He took a few paces to the left until he came to another hatch. This one, unlike the last, wasn't locked. He lifted the hatch door and began to climb down the ladder beneath. As he descended, nerves began to kick in; as they did with every operation he conducted. The fact that the man was armed meant nothing to him, it was the bomb hidden somewhere in the building that alarmed him.

He knew he had to keep his mind focused on the job at hand; Bennett was the only lead to the people responsible for the tragedies of the past few hours. While prepping for the assault, Carter had informed him that the man seen acting suspiciously along the beach at the time of the explosion had been found dead a few miles away. The need to take Bennett alive was greater than ever and York knew this.

As he reached the bottom of the ladder and jumped off, he turned to face a set of stairs leading down. He recognised these to be the stairs for the Gents toilets. To his right was the door to the auditorium. He slowly opened the door, so not to let the hinges squeak. They didn't. He found himself on the left hand side of the sound and lighting booth. Moving through the small walkway under the booth, he ducked down low and crept out to the right side of the room. Keeping low under the small partition between the seating area and the gangway, he peered round the side and looked down the aisle.

The Hostages were still sitting in the same place as before and Bennett was sat in the same chair he had been in all night. York reached into his pocket and retrieved his small communication bug and placed it in his ear. Now was the time to end the siege. He gripped his MK23 and cocked the hammer. Standing slowly and making one last check that Bennett was not waiting to open fire on him, he walked step by step down the aisle until he was just a few feet from where Bennett was sitting. "Miles." York said softly so not to startle the man with the AK.

Bennett turned and stood faster than he ever had before. The call of his name from behind him startled him. He raised the AK-47 and pointed it in York's direction before he even had a chance to notice who was there. His eyes widened as he noticed the handgun pointed at his face. "What the hell are you doing here?"

"It's over Miles. Just put the gun down." York's orders were a long shot, but he thought it couldn't do any harm to ask. He moved slightly closer as he spoke. After one step forward, Bennett tightened his grip on the rifle.

"Not another step Agent York." Bennett ordered firmly "You're just in time to witness the fireworks first hand. Thanks to you allowing the press in close, I am now able to complete the mission I am being paid to do."

York smiled, the whole time he had been asking himself why Bennett had stalled and now he had the answer, he almost kicked himself for not realising. "There'll be no payment Miles. We found a team of assassins at your house who were there to kill your family. Do you call that payment?"

Bennett shook his head and sniggered "There is no way you are telling the truth, he gave me his word." Bennett reached up to take the phone out of the pocket on the front left of his jacket. Before he had a chance to pull it out, York had acted. Two shots were fired. The first ripped through Bennett index finger completely obliterating it before smashing through the phone and into his shoulder. The force of the impact made him drop the AK to the floor. The second hit his left leg sending him to the floor with a thud. York swiftly ran over and kicked the rifle away and kept his gun pointed at Bennett's head.

Looking Bennett straight in the eye he said "I told you it was over."

Upon hearing the first gun shot, Myers, Simmons and the rest of the assault team moved in. They burst through the front doors and swiftly advanced into the auditorium.

Simmons took the initiative to check the sound and lighting booth. He crashed through the door, not bothering to check if it was unlocked first, and made his way up the steps. He stood in the centre of the room and scanned the area. To the front there was a large window overlooking the stage, beneath were the controls. Small dials and leavers littered the control desk. When operational, Simmons guessed, the dials would illuminate the room. Sitting on the chair in front of the desk was what he was looking for. Although smaller than he had originally imagined, he knew he was staring at the explosive.

Myers led the rest of the team down towards the stage area. Two of them picked Bennett up off the floor and dragged him out of the theatre, not really caring if they hurt him in any way. The rest saw to the hostages. None were hurt but all were badly shaken.

Myers sat down next to York who was resting in the front row. He could clearly tell his partner was exhausted. "Mate, you look like hell." He said with a grin.

York threw an unimpressed look at Myers "I feel a lot worse than that. Believe me."

Both York and Myers watched the team escort the hostages out of the theatre. After a couple of minutes, Henshaw walked down the aisle as if he was on a mission. "A Word Alex, please." He said with a stern tone.

York dipped his head and let out a sigh, hoping that a lecture wasn't coming. "What is it Captain?" When he had revealed his plan to Henshaw, his boss was less than impressed. The risks, he felt, were too great. But as York had pointed out, if they had just burst in the front door, or tried to blow the door that had been jammed shut between the auditorium and the diner, Bennett would have had time to detonate the explosives, bringing another unnecessary wave of death and destruction.

"That performance was less than entertaining from on the ground." He paused and changed his expression from a tough frown to an approving smile "But damn you did a good job."

Simmons rushed down the aisle in their direction holding a small black box in his hand. As he approached Henshaw, York glanced at the box knowing full well what was inside.

"I give you the bomb." Simmons said holing the box out to his boss.

Henshaw looked down at it and then looked at Simmons with a confused glare. "So what do I want with it?" He asked handing the box back.

Simmons smiled and turned to York. "I'll give you three guessed as to why I am carrying this around like it was a shoe box."

York looked at him, then realised "It's a dud."

Simmons smiled and nodded "Spot on. The phone Bennett was trying to use to detonate it would have worked if he hadn't missed one vital little thing." He paused and opened the lid of the box. The bomb was no bigger than a cassette tape case. On the top of the device, an old pager had wires protruding from the bottom. There were three wires in total; none of them were connected to the device. "My guess is that whoever coerced him into mass destruction forgot to give him a crash course first."

York looked at the device, it looked small, not nearly enough to destroy a building the size of the pavilion. It looked just big enough to perhaps turn a car into scrap metal. With that in mind, York had a few ideas of why Bennett was there. "My guess is this was a warning, or at least some kind of message."

"What makes you think that?" Henshaw asked

"Because that thing is the one of the most pathetic

excuses for a bomb I have ever seen. I think whoever planned this has bigger things in mind."

11

By day, the Royal Britannia stood proud and tall on the waters of Southampton Harbour. The sun glistened off her pure white hull, giving her the look of pure tranquillity that stopped all passers by in their tracks.

When the night fell, she gave an even more dazzling sight. Thousands of lights were positioned all over the hull and superstructure, illuminating the harbour around her. Over the past five months, since she was transported down the harbour from the building yard, she had attracted photographers from all over the country, all trying to capture the brilliance of the spectacle.

The décor inside was even more exhilarating than the out. Each room had en-suite bathrooms, all decorated with gold taps and shower heads, solid marble counter tops and sparkling granite tiled floors. The spa baths and sauna rooms also made them the perfect place to relax and unwind.

The rooms themselves were just as impressive. Each had a large open fire place with reclining loungers in front. Four poster beds sat under large round port holes, allowing just a turn of the head for the passenger to have a full view out onto the ocean.

The entertainment on the ship was second to none. Big name acts were flown in to perform, from singers to top actors.

The liner also housed three floors of shops ranging from gift shops to top brand clothing lines. There was anything from coffee shops to casinos around every corner. Any one lucky enough to spend time on the Royal Britannia certainly was in for a treat.

Upon leaving dock, she would sail in to the Mediterranean Sea where a group of top ranking government officials from across the globe would board, including the British Prime Minister and the US President. Each had been specially invited to be a part of the liners maiden voyage and all accepted with great pleasure.

From there she would cross the Atlantic to the Caribbean where she would collect her first load of paying passengers once the officials had finished their once in a lifetime treat. For most that had paid for the right to be on the liner, this was definitely a treat. Tickets started at £17,000 per person for the standard rooms and rose to £100,000 for the Presidential Suite. The liner had definitely been built for the super rich.

Once all passengers were on board, the ship would set course around South America and on to New Zealand and Australia. After a week there, they would head for southern Asia and china. From there she would cover Africa, back to the Mediterranean, the UK then back to the Caribbean, totalling a four month round the world trip. For those who paid, they would definitely get their moneys worth.

The man responsible for the magnificent opportunity was a man who appreciated the finer things in life. After spending most of his childhood avoiding gunfire and missiles, his self built fortune, he felt, was well deserved. His motto would always be 'A lifetime of heartache and sorrow should always be compensated by two lifetimes of money'

Having moved to the UK from Iraq when he was just 17, he soon made his name known. Working on a building site as a labourer, he saved every penny he earned to by his first small boat. With that, he began to sell small tours on the Thames. When things began to go well for the teenager, he upgraded to a full size river boat, then two, then three until he built a fleet of river touring boats. Not just on the Thames, he branched out to almost every major river in Britain.

When he sold the company, he raked in over forty four million pounds. His dreams though were far from completed. Every penny from the sale went in to building the largest, most prestigious and luxurious ocean liner ever before seen, The Royal Britannia. Salim Jazir was a name that every one in Britain knew, and admired.

Jazir sat in his chair on the bridge of the liner, looking out over his masterful creation. Just the slightest thought that he had fulfilled his deepest dreams, brought a smile to his face that no one could erase.

The side that most people saw of Jazir, was a kind, gentle and caring man, a man that had given a great deal of time and money to good causes in the past. They always caught sight of the gracious smile he wore whilst in the presence of people. His sky blue eyes were eyes that could be trusted. He was shorter than the normal male, at only 5ft 3in, he was continuously looking up to the friends he would talk to. This was never a hindrance though, when comments were made about his size, he would simply say 'Good things come in small packages'

When he attended functions, he was always dressed to impress. Only the top of the line suits were worn and the most expensive gold chain and rings were chosen, if he could do nothing else, he wanted to impress those who knew him.

The side of Jazir that no one saw however, was a side that only showed itself when the doors were closed. He had been involved in an endless flow of criminal activity since entering the country over twenty years earlier. As far as he was concerned, if it put money in his bank account, then he was up for it. He had been involved in everything from drug dealing to people trafficking and not once had he been caught.

His latest criminal field was one he never knew he would get so much enjoyment from, it seemed strange to him that he could feel no remorse after committing mass murder. He had killed before, the rush he felt when watching the life drain from someone's eyes was overwhelming, the feeling that only a true monster could enjoy and a monster he was. If anyone got on the wrong side of Salim Jazir, they would be given no second chances.

As he sat staring at the open wonder of the ocean, his mobile phone rang. As he answered, the voice he wanted to hear replied. "Good morning sir."

"I trust you have good news for me?" Jazir More insisted than asked.

"I'm afraid not sir." The man came back in a nervous manner "I'm afraid the second device was never detonated. I think I may have made a mistake in my decision."

"Do not panic my friend." Jazir said with a grin "The second device was never planned to explode. I just wanted to make sure that I had the attention of a certain someone, can I assume that was successful?"

There was a brief silence on the other end, one that to Jazir seemed to last for an eternity. "You definitely have his attention; I am counting on your plan working Mr Jazir. Both of us have an agenda and believe me, I plan on seeing mine through to the end."

"As do I, It's time to move on to stage two. I want you to just hold your position until your assistance is required."

"Yes Sir." The line fell silent.

12

The events of the morning played on York's mind for hours after. From the explosion, which brought back memories in itself, to the security officer being killed and through to taking down Bennett in the theatre. It seemed to be like a film repeating itself every time it finished. The images of the young bodies floating on the water were the most haunting ones. It was a sight York wished he had never he had never come across. It was now lodged in his mind, undoubtedly for the rest of his life.

After being sent home by Henshaw to grab a few hours rest, York walked through the door of his apartment, took one look at the glass shattered across the floor and waved away the temptation of calling some one out to fix it. He was too exhausted to care. After a quick shower and mug of tea, he lay down on his bed. His mind turned to the bottle that he had left on the balcony. It had to have been destroyed in the blast, he thought. The urge to go and have a quick look was almost too much to cope with. He knew he didn't really need it, that wasn't the point, he was craving it. When it came to it, he just didn't have the will power to stop himself. He walked back out to the living room and looked out at the table where the bottle was left. He had been right in guessing the bottle had been destroyed. All that was left was shattered pieces of glass covered in whiskey. He walked back to his bed, laid down and drifted off to sleep, unsatisfied.

A few hours later after the same dream he had been having for the past twenty years, he rose out of bed and threw on an ATS polo shirt and a pair of jeans. Over the shirt, he lifted on his double sided shoulder holster then he pulled two Gold Desert Eagle .44 magnum handguns from a box in the cupboard and placed them in the holsters.

As he finished dressing, as if right on cue, there was a knock at the door. He knew exactly who it was; the only person who had a key yet never used it. He walked up to the front door and peered through the spy hole at the tall structure of Myers. He opened the door and let his friend in.

"You ready to hunt down a terrorist?" Myers inquired in a mocking tone. Every time he entered York's apartment, he couldn't help but be bedazzled. It was always perfect, perfectly clean and perfectly organised, the work of a very good maid.

The lounge was big; on the far side were the patio doors, which Myers noticed was now in pieces on the floor. On the corner of the front wall and the right hand wall sat a 50" LCD TV on top of a glass unit. Opposite the TV was a large white leather corner sofa with matching foot stool in front. The other side of the lounge branched off to an open plan kitchen with granite worktops and solid oak cabinet doors and a small hall leading to the front door. To the side of the sofa, was a second hall leading to the two double bedrooms and bathroom.

He always felt slightly jealous of his lifelong friend. Ok he worked harder than anyone, but financial stability had come easy for him since he had been left over forty million pounds in his grandfathers will a little over four years ago. He rarely seemed to acknowledge its existence though, he rarely splashed out, apart from the apartment and the cars, and it had just been sitting in the bank and gaining interest from day one.

Myers walked over to the now glassless doors. Turning

back to York he said "You get fed up with opening the doors every time you wanted to go for a cigarette?"

York laughed "Just wanted to make lighter work for my cleaner actually." He paused a moment to pour two mugs of coffee "They were blown out by the explosion."

Myers looked across to the bomb site "That must have been a hell of a blast to knock triple glazed windows out at this range." He said matter-of-factly.

"Knocked me off my feet too" York replied handing Myers one of the mugs. "My first guess was they used PE4 but now I think about it that was way to big a blast to be anything like that. Even sem-tex couldn't take out my doors at this range. Not unless they filled the whole club with it of course!"

They both moved inside and sat on the sofa. Myers clocked the half empty bottle still sitting on the balcony table, strangely unaffected by the blast. "How's the giving up coming along?" He asked nodding to the bottle.

York shook his head "Don't go there. Every time I try to quit, I have the same bloody nightmare then hit the bottle again. It's like a vicious circle."

The look of genuine concern was painted across Myers face. It was comforting to York to know that his partner cared so much, but at the same time, it was frustrating too. "Stop looking at me like that that." York ordered. "I'll get there, I haven't touched a drop this morning yet and what I witnessed today has bought back some strong memories."

Myers knew he was treading on uneven terrain when it came to the subject of York's drinking and the death of his parents, so he quickly changed the subject. "I looked into the security officer to try and find a next of kin." He informed

York. "Turned out he was a bit of a loner. His parents died a few months back and he was an only child. The rest of his family immigrated to Australia about two years ago. I had the number put on your desk back at the office for when we get back."

"Get back?"

"Yeah, you remember, Henshaw asked us to interrogate Bennett."

York downed his coffee, took the mug to the kitchen and placed it in the kitchen sink. He turned back to Myers and asked "So which one is it going to be today?"

Myers sat and thought for a moment then replied "Definitely the little one."

York grabbed a pair of keys off of the side threw on his ATS jacket and they both headed for the door. After a short lift ride down to the ground floor, they headed for the garages. York had the only double garage in the block, which was just as well. He turned the key in the lock and opened the door to reveal his two most prized possessions.

The first was the 2008 Range Rover sport Supercharged model with a 4.2litre 8 cylinder petrol engine putting out 390bhp. The whole of the car had been modified to York's standard. It looked no different on first glance, but anyone who tried shooting at it would soon learn that the panelling had been made bullet proof as had all the windows. Inside every available space had been turned into weapon storage, ready for any eventuality.

The second car was York's favourite, the Audi R8 4.2 FSI Quattro V8. She could go from 0-60 in 4.6 seconds and had a top speed of 187mph. The car was a head turner normally, but this one was especially attractive. The full custom body kit had been designed by his neighbour and built to spec by Audi. The gleaming silver paintwork made her glisten in the sun and as like the Range Rover, she had been fully bullet proofed.

Myers loved riding in the R8 as much as York loved driving it. No matter what the weather was like, he would roll down the window and try to get as much female attention as possible, even though most of the time the attention was on the driver of such a magnificent machine.

They pulled out of the driveway and headed in the direction of the local hospital where Bennett was being treated for the gun shot wound to his shoulder.

The hospital wasn't far from where York lived, so the journey didn't take long. As they pulled into the car park they passed a Black Mercedes-Benz CLK 500 Sport parked just to the right of the entrance gates. York looked at the car, there was a slight familiarity about this car, he was certain he had seen it before. The sticker on the rear window made him even more convinced, but the more he thought about it the harder it seemed to be to remember.

He cast the thought aside for another time and pulled the car into a parking spot. They both exited the vehicle and made their way to the entrance of the hospital. The receptionist attracted Myers' attention as soon as they entered; she was tall with blonde hair and a bust that would make any man look twice or more.

After a little flirting, they got the ward they needed and headed off down the corridor. As they did, they passed a large, stocky man wearing black bomber jacket and black jeans. He had shoulders like a strong man competitor and even through the jacket, York could tell the biceps were big enough to almost pass as boulders. As he passed he gave them both a cold glare.

"I wouldn't want to meet him in a dark alley!" Myers Exclaimed.

"Don't know what that look was for." York replied. "I never did anything to upset him. I know what you mean though, i wouldn't want to either." They carried on down the corridor. "That bloody Mercedes is bugging me" York persisted with a frustrated look. "I know for a fact I have seen it before."

"Stop fretting about it." Myers said as they passed through the doors to the ward. "It will come back to you after a while,"

They walked through the ward to Bennett's private room. There was something missing. Before Myers left to pick up York, he was informed that an ATS agent would be on guard. There was no one to be seen. As they took a look around, there didn't seem to be anyone on the ward, no doctors or nurses. They looked at each other and then opened the door. Bennett was lying on the bed with a drip bag hanging beside him. Myers looked to the other side of the room to see the guard lying in a pool of blood. While he checked the guard for a pulse, York ran round the bed to find a syringe on the floor. He checked Bennett's pulse, he was dead. "I guess we won't be getting much out of him."

Myers joined York next to the bed "I've seen enough dead bodies today to last a lifetime."

York didn't answer, he thought for a second, and then

the realisation hit him like bullet to the head. Whilst Kirk had been scanning through the video archive at the theatre from earlier that night, he had caught a glimpse of the black Mercedes. The more he thought about it, the more he was certain; the thing that made him sure was the sticker.

He ran out of the room and through the ward into the corridor and through the entrance and into the car park to catch sight of the Mercedes leaving the grounds. He pulled one of His Desert Eagles from the holster and took aim at the rear tyre of the car. He knew full well he could make the shot, but something stopped him. He couldn't quite understand what it was. It could have been the fact that there were dozens of people standing around him watching him take aim. What ever it was he knew that he would come to meet the driver again soon.

13

Henshaw put the finishing touches to his report on the events of that morning. He took a quick glance at the clock sitting on his huge oak desk; the time read 13:45. The day had gone quick. After Bennett had been taken into custody, he oversaw the start of the clean up process. Bodies were still being pulled from the wreckage of the club bombing. The death toll had reached over three hundred and counting. He couldn't help but feel for the families of the deceased. Some of the victims were still teenagers, still kids. What kind of monster would cut hundreds of young lives short? He asked himself, clenching his fist and slamming it on his desk.

Lack of sleep was starting to take its toll on the aging captain. He could feel his eye lid dropping every so often. The will to stay awake was beginning to fade away, he knew he would have to get some rest soon but chance of that was slim.

The phone rang as he began to dose off in his chair, the ring startled him awake.

"Henshaw." He answered

"Sir, its York. I'm afraid we haven't had the chance to interrogate Bennett. Someone beat us to it."

Henshaw let out a sigh. "This is not good Alex; He was our only lead to the responsible parties for this morning's tragedy."

"I know sir, the thing is, the man I saw seems familiar to me, and I am looking at the CCTV footage at the hospital now but can't get a good enough picture of his face to run a trace."

"So where does that leave us?" Henshaw asked, feeling

the chances of catching his man slipping through his fingers.

"His car. I remember seeing a black Mercedes hovering around the front of the pier earlier in the night, I know it is a long shot but I think that could be the only option."

Henshaw didn't reply, he was disturbed by a knock at the door. His secretary peered through. He covered the mouthpiece of the phone "What can I do for you my darling?"

"I'm sorry to disturb you sir, but Joseph Leech has requested you go down to the lab straight away, he has some important information for you."

He nodded his head and spoke to York once more "Alex, I'm going to call you back, it seems Joseph down stairs might have found something. Get the reg' number of that merc' if you can."

"Will do sir." Then the line went silent.

Henshaw left his office and headed for the ATS Laboratory on the third floor of the building. The lab was used primarily for inspection of weapons and explosives but occasionally would double up as a morgue if in depth post mortems needed to be carried out. They had enough computing, science and other equipment in the room to be able to test anything and create anything from narcotics to powerful explosives.

When he entered the room, Henshaw searched for Joseph, the lab technician. He was behind the large Perspex screen on the far right wall of the 3,500 square foot room. Behind the toughened screen was the testing area for explosive devices.
He walked over and knocked on the glass "Jo, What have you found?" He asked in a raised voice, not really sure if the tall,

slim, long haired man could hear him.

Joseph heard and exited the small test area. He grabbed a clipboard from the steel trolley next to the exit and flipped through a couple of pages. "If my tests are correct, we are in deep shit!" he had always been known by the staff at ATS as a bit of a joker but this time, his expression told all. He did not have the usual grin formed under the clump of facial hair he liked to call a goatee. His face was serious.

"What did you find?" Henshaw asked, hating that he had to repeat himself.

"That block of PE4 you had sent in definitely baffled me to start with."

Henshaw shrugged "Meaning?"

"Meaning" Joseph continued "At first glance, it looks like any other piece of plastic explosive. But, when I placed it under the lens, I found that it had been mutated with another chemical. A Gold Powder"

Henshaw looked at the lab tech quizzically "What does the chemical do to the explosive?"

"Intensifies it, dramatically." Joseph turned a few more pages over "My results show that one hundred grams of powder mixed with a kilo of PE4 can intensify the blast up to eight times. If there are more of these out there, like I said before, 'We are in deep shit.'"

"So where did it come from?"

"I did a bit of research and this stuff has come up only once." He flipped the page on his clipboard. "There was one reported incident back in the Eighteen Hundreds where a group of young men were killed after a day in a mine just outside Arundel. One of three survived long enough to write an account of what he saw, he was killed when he tried to seal the mine shut. He called the powder Dark Gold"

"Ok, gather the co-ordinates and patch them through to Alex and complete a report on this a.s.a.p."

Henshaw left the lab and headed back to his office. He pulled a mobile phone from his pocket and dialled York's number. He paused before he pressed the call button. The past few hours seemed to have gone by like a blur.

The line rang twice before York answered "What have you got for me Captain?"

"Jo' found that the explosive we found has been altered." Henshaw explained "It has been mixed with some sort of gold chemical. The mix intensifies the power of the bomb."

"How intense are we talking?" York inquired.

"From the look on Jo's face, I would have to say by a lot. I am having the co-ordinates of the location where the gold is mined sent to you. It's located just outside Arundel, I will have an assault team in the air in twenty minutes, and they should be with you in thirty."

"OK sir." York disconnected.

Once off the phone, York and Myers jumped in to the Audi. York put foot-to-floor and sped off towards the destination marked on his Satellite navigation system. The traffic though town was light, it didn't take them long to get to the dual carriageway, where they would stay till they got to the mine.

York seemed to be as cool as ice as he navigated the road and loaded his Desert Eagles, being one hundred percent certain that they would run into trouble as soon as they arrived.

Myers wasn't playing it so cool. He hated shoot outs. They didn't seem to come up for him as much as York. He was more of the intelligence gatherer of the two, while York would usually be out grabbing the bad guys with a team of ATS' best, Myers would be directing the assaults. Gun fire was something he would sooner do without.

Ten minutes was all the time it took to get to the town where the mine was situated. York pulled the car to a stop a few hundred yards down the road. If there was a welcoming party at the entrance, the last thing he wanted was for them to hear him and Myers coming down the road.

The area surrounding was perfect for an ambush. Trees and shrubbery covered the grounds around the mine, making it easy to sweep in undetected. The only concern on York's mind was the fact that they were sat in a valley of hills, the perfect place for a sniper. He knew he was being paranoid, but that didn't relieve the concern.

They crept through the shrubs and crouched down just outside the entrance to the mine. There were no guards; no one was patrolling the area searching for intruders. It was quiet, too quiet.

They moved forward towards the entrance. York had a bad feeling; something was not right about the whole situation. "This place seems too quiet, if a terrorist group is mining high power explosive chemicals from here, they sure don't care if anyone finds them."

"Maybe" Myers suggested "They don't want to raise suspicion. After all, a bunch of armed guards standing outside a mine that was abandoned over two hundred years ago would certainly raise an eyebrow."

"Possible or maybe we are just too late." York pulled a torch from his pocket and shined it down the mine. It seemed never ending, a void that would swallow everyone who entered, He definitely felt uneasy about entering. "You ready?" He asked Myers.

"I suppose, but I hope you know this place will give me nightmares." The sarcasm in Myers' tone was less than comforting.

They entered the mine and slowly began the two thousand foot decent. The air was damp and cold, they could feel the presence of the miners who had worked themselves to death and been left to rot in the mine. Every step they took they felt they were being watched.

York directed the light towards the floor, searching for anything that might have been left behind by the terrorists. All he saw was the chalk floor of the mine.

What they came across half way down sent chills down the back of Myers' neck. Lying still on the floor was the remains of one of the miners. York studied the remains, the skull had huge crack from one side to the other with a large hole in the centre. The femur (leg bone) had been completely snapped in two. He knew the man had died instantly, he figured he was either the result of a cave in or the victim of a savage assault.

They moved on down the mine. There came a faint noise in the distance ahead of them. At first, they couldn't make it out, but as they progressed further in, they knew it was voices, both male, both with British accents. York pulled his weapons from their holsters first, and then Myers followed.

They crept silently towards the voices and took cover behind a large boulder that seemed randomly placed on the left wall. They peered down into brightly lit section of the mine. It seemed to glow like a treasure cave. They had found what they were looking for.

Inside, two men in white suits were scrapping parts of the gold coloured walls into buckets. They worked slowly, each scrapping was careful. They seemed to fear the substance, the respect they were treating it with was more than most people would offer to another human being.

Myers tapped York on the shoulder and motioned towards two Kawasaki quad bikes parked at the back of the chamber to the left of where the men were working. York noticed both had M16 rifles strapped to the sides.

"You ever heard of scientists packing that type of tool?" He asked, with a sarcastic look on his face, keeping his tone to a gentle whisper. "I bet they have pistols on them too, we need to get out of here. This is definitely the last place I want to be caught in a shoot out, especially if that stuff is as reactive as Henshaw said it is."

They moved back away from the chamber, keeping low and out of sight. As they turned out of view, they both stood and began to walk back toward the entrance. York stopped after a few steps and put his arm out to stop Myers.

"What is it?" Myers inquired

York placed his index finger over his mouth, signalling his partner to shush. He listened carefully. There were voices. He knew they weren't the voices of the two men in the chamber, they had not said a word to each other in the whole time York and Myers had been there. These were further away.

The voices were now drained out by another sound, a louder one. It echoed through the whole mine shaft. Dust fell from the ceiling, covering the two of them as they looked at each other trying to make out the noise.

York knew exactly what it was, he began to feel uneasy. The temperature seemed to rise as if someone had cranked the heating up to full whack. The situation had just become very bad. He turned to Myers. "We've got company"

14

"Our Guys?" Myers asked, knowing the answer.

York shook his head, "When was the last time ATS used quad bikes?" He had to think fast if they were going to get out alive. The situation had spun wildly out of control in a matter of a few minutes. If only he had taken Henshaw's advice and waited for backup, maybe the possibility of them being full of bullet holes in the next thirty seconds would have been avoided.

He shook off all thoughts and concentrated on the matter at hand. "Follow me." He ordered Myers. He peered round the bend to see the two men in the chamber now had their backs turned, working on the rear wall.

They quietly but briskly moved closer to the chamber, the plan forming in York's mind as they moved. He lunged forward and grabbed the first man round the neck and twisted his head with such force his neck snapped, instantly killing him. Myers followed suit a second later but by that time his assailant had reacted. The crushing blow from the man's fist knocked Myers in to daze. York grabbed the man's hand and twisted it round his back until he heard it crack. The man let out a wailing cry as the pain shot through his arm. York took the tool he was using to scrape the dust off the wall and jabbed it in to his opponent's neck. Blood poured down the man's white overalls and spilled on to the floor in front of them.

"We need to move them." York ordered. "Put the overalls on; let's see if these guys are smart enough to know the difference between their guys and the enemy."

They quickly moved the bodies behind the quad bikes

and Myers dressed in the overalls which weren't covered in blood. York made sure he was facing away from the three men approaching on the quad bikes. Myers turned to them as they stopped, turned off the engines and got off the bikes. As they walked towards him, they kept their guns at the ready. He gave them a quick wave "everything ok?"

"Where are the others?" The front man asked. He was taller than the other two and larger built. Myers guessed he spent a lot of his free time in the gym. The other two were fairly short by average male height and seemed very under nourished. The other thing that separated the rear two was the fact that they were Middle Eastern and the front man was most certainly British. "Who the hell are you?" He asked in a raised voice.

York knew there was only one way out of this. To his left was one of the quads with a rifle holstered to the side. He had to move fast if he was win the fight. He reached out and grabbed the rifle. No one seemed to notice for the first couple of seconds, mostly because Myers was standing in the eye line of his three targets. As he pulled the rifle from the holster he flipped the safety off, loaded the barrel and aimed. He gave the signal and Myers fell to the floor to take cover. York fired off five rounds. The first struck the front man on the right side of the neck. Blood sprayed over the two men behind him. The next bullet missed and hit the wall. The next three hit the other two assailants in the torso and they crumbled to the floor.

Myers quickly got out of the overalls "Nice shot; you should be a government agent or something."

York smiled as he climbed onboard the quad bike "jump on the other one. We need to get out of here before anyone else wants to come and spoil our mining adventure." As he turned the key, he found that the rifles weren't the only arms the miners had bought with them. Inside the bag the guns were holstered in were two grenades. He figured they were a safety precaution just in case the mine had to be destroyed. He smiled as a plan came to him. Myers knew the wry smile all to well and after seeing the two grenades knew exactly what York was thinking. "That wouldn't be the best idea ever. Didn't Henshaw say this stuff in here intensifies the blast?"

"We better hope these things are fast then." York replied patting the quad Bike as if it were a stallion. Myers jumped on the other bike and fired up the engine; he kept the M16 rifle one hand, just in case they ran into more friends on the way out.

York looked at the bodies lying around the chamber. The thing that struck him about the three he shot down was that none of them returned fire. All three had their fingers on the trigger ready to fire, but none did. They had ample amount of time to do so. He found it more than odd, it was as if they were ordered to come down here to die, he mused.

He quickly shook of the thoughts and pulled the pins from the grenades. He threw them in to the centre of the chamber and then fired up the engine of the quad. He pulled away at full throttle. The bike was much faster than he expected.

Within half a minute, they were halfway up the mine. Daylight was beginning to appear in the distance. As they drew closer to the entrance, they could just make out the shapes of people standing waiting for them, or waiting for their comrades, which was the more likely. They both lifted the rifles and opened fire as they got to within one hundred and fifty yards of the entrance. As they did, the mine erupted with a deafening roar. Pieces if rock and earth began to fall from the ceiling and the ground shook beneath them. It took just a few seconds before they saw the ball of fire racing up the mine towards them. All they could do was pray they reached the end in time, before they were swallowed up by the flames.

The flames grew closer as the neared the end. The people standing at the entrance dispersed in a panic, some falling over the ones who had been struck by York and Myer's bullets.

As they hit the entrance of the mine, so did the blast. The quad bikes were lifted off the ground and York and Myers were thrown through the air, coming crashing down into a bunch of shrubs a few meters outside the entrance. York shook of the daze of being hurled nearly fifty feet and peered over the shrubs. He noticed just five men remained. All were making their way slowly toward where he and Myers had landed. The front man was the one that took his notice. He was the same man they had seen at the hospital. He looked even bigger now. His biceps were almost ripping the sleeves on his overly tight t-shirt. York hadn't feared many men in his time, but if this man got hold of him; York couldn't even bring himself to think of what might happen.

They got to within ten yards of York. He looked down to see Myers was unconscious, obviously being knocked out by the blast. He closed his eyes, waiting for the first bullets to strike, hoping it would be an instant killer. It never came. Instead of the sound of gun shots, the sound of a helicopter rotor filled the air, closely followed by gun fire in the distance.

The five assailants turned the attention of their gun fire to the aircraft; none succeeded and were shot down almost immediately. York saw the front man and one other run towards the black Mercedes parked just a few yards through the trees. He pulled himself to a stand and followed in pursuit, leaving Myers still out cold.

The two men jumped into the car and raced off, wheels screeching as they did. York ran as fast as his legs could take him and got in to his Audi. As he fired up the engine and put it in to gear, the passenger door opened, Myers struggled in to the seat.

"You finally decided to wake up then you lazy git" York said as he slammed the accelerator pedal to the floor. The R8 sped away down the track and on to the tarmac road. He took a quick look at his partner, who still seemed to be slightly dazed from the explosion. His hair was now ruffled with bits of greenery left in it. His face has small scratches all over from pieces of flying rock and the fact that he had landed in amongst some brambles.

They hit the end of the road and were faced with a choice. As the Mercedes had a good head start, it had now pulled out of sight. York had to choose which way to go, east or west. He turned the wheel to head east when he noticed tyre marks on the road in front of him curving to the right. He knew they could have been left there from any car, at any time, but it was his only lead. The road both ways was clear; he slammed down on the pedal once more and headed west.

After passing over a couple of roundabouts and hitting the dual carriageway, he pulled into the outside lane to overtake the line of traffic in front of him. The speedometer on the R8 hit one hundred miles an hour, Myers held on, just in case the worst happened. As they pulled round another corner the Mercedes came into view. York smiled as he realised his gut instinct had paid off once again.

He accelerated harder to catch up with the Merc'. As he pulled closer, the passenger opened his window and aimed his rifle towards York's car. Bullets began hitting the Audi, bouncing off the bullet proof shell and shooting off in all directions. The passenger cursed as he sat back in his seat.

All of the cars around them ground to quick halt, trying desperately to avoid the carnage that could lie ahead. Cars began to pile into each other, some swerving off the road and into the fields lining the road. People got out of their vehicles and stared in amazement at the spectacle now disappearing into the distance.

Myers returned fire; the Mercedes was much more vulnerable without the armour. The rear window shattered all over the road, bullets slammed into the body leaving holes all along the back of the expensive machine.

The driver knew the situation was far worse for him; he had to think fast if he was going to avoid capture. His choices were limited; he checked the rear view mirror to see Myers reloading. There was only one thing he could do, knowing that there was one target Myers had in mind, the tyres. He slowed down as two shots were fired from behind, one hitting the rear left tyre. The car shuddered as the air escaped with a loud bang. He managed to keep control until York pulled the Audi to the side and shot out the front tyre. The driver lost all control of the vehicle. It wobbled all over the road before pulling hard right, as it did the car flipped in to a hard roll. The passenger, not wearing his seat belt was thrown through the windscreen on to the tarmac then crushed as the car rolled over him. The driver held tight but took a blow to the head by the steering wheel as he was thrown around.

The car eventually came to rest on its roof. York pulled up close on jumped out. He struggled to open the driver's door on his own but managed to pry it open with the help of Myers. They pulled the driver from the wreckage and dragged him away from the destroyed Mercedes which was leaking fuel and at risk of igniting.

They looked down at the huge bulk of a man lying if front of them, Myers bound his hands in cuffs just in case he woke and began throwing his fists around. One blow from him, they knew, would almost finish them both.

They stood leaning up against York's car. York pulled a cigarette from his pocket and lit it. Now he had time to think about what had happened in the last hour, one thing seemed to confuse him. "I have a question." York said to Myers "Why the hell did those guys in the mine not return fire? They had* plenty of time to."

Myers thought about it for a second. York was right. The two smaller men had their fingers on the trigger ready to fire. So why didn't they? Why did they just stand there and take certain death so easily?

15

The ATS building stood at six floors high. The modern style, full glass front gleamed in the midday sun. Amongst the older style properties in the surrounding area, the building looked severely out of place. To the people inside, the views over the English Channel and Brighton Marina were unbelievably spectacular.

York pulled the Audi in to the car park in the basement of the building. He was some what relieved to be back at the office after the day he had had so far. For an hour after the chase, he had been held up by police asking questions and taking statements. The one thing he didn't count on, was one hot shot son of a bitch copper trying to get some extra credit with his chief inspector by claiming he smelled alcohol on York's breath. He wouldn't have minded usually, but the fact that he had consumed well in excess of half a bottle of Jack Daniels only a few short hours ago made him a little nervous as the officer pulled a breath test out of his car. He felt extremely lucky to pass the test until he looked at his watch and noticed the time to be pressing on towards five o'clock in the afternoon. It seemed strange that the officer could smell the alcohol, but since he had not brushed his teeth in the morning, he realised he must have reeked of it.

He parked in his designated space, which he had assigned to himself as it was the closest to the lift, and got out of the car, closely followed by Myers. They walked towards the lift and pressed the button.

"You figured out why you are so special yet?" Myers asked, trying not to laugh.

"I never said I was special." York replied. "I simply can't understand why the fuckers didn't blast us in to the next world. They had plenty of time. The safety catches were off. Their fingers were on the triggers. The only thing I can think of was fright, but for all of them to get scared is highly unlikely. They were nothing short of professional"

The lift doors opened and they stepped inside, pressing the button for the sixth floor as they entered. After a short ride, they exited the lift and turned left out of the doors and in to a small corridor. They walked straight to the end and entered the office on the left, the metal name plate on the door read YORK.

York's office was considered bland and dull compared to the rest of the offices in the building. He had no plant life, no pictures hung on the wall and the colour was a simple cream. All he had in the room was a desk situated just on the right hand wall, with no more than a laptop computer, a clock and a few files sat on top and a weapon cupboard which was full of ammunition. He found no use for anything else; it all just seemed like unnecessary clutter.

He sat in his chair behind the old, slightly damaged and water marked pine desk placed his feet up on it. He occasionally sat a watched the world go by through the glass front wall.

He looked towards Myers, who was standing at the front looking out over the harbour, "So what do you make of the bombing?" he inquired. "You think the guy we caught was responsible?"

Myers shrugged his shoulders, His expression suggesting he was going over the day again in his mind.

"Honestly, I am around seventy percent certain, but then again I have been wrong about these sorts of things in the past. If he isn't the right guy, then we'll find him eventually."

York nodded in agreement "Yeah, I guess these things take time."

Myers turned and walked towards the door "You know we have a meeting in half an hour?"

"No, where did you find that out?"

Myers nodded towards the desk "That note from the boss man under your clown feet. I'm off to the shower room, I am desperate. See you in a while" Then he left the office.

York sat in his chair and momentarily closed his eyes. The day had taken its toll and the couple of hour's sleep he had grabbed earlier in the morning hardly scratched the surface. As he started to drift off, the same images began to appear that did every time he fell asleep. That face had haunted him for years. The terrified expression he witnessed on his mothers face the last time he saw her was heart wrenching. The fact that her father had been taken away by the terrorists when he tried to make a stand, meant she was left to face the situation on her own as he was set free.

The next image was the one that woke him with a jump every time. He could still hear the explosion as if he were there. The noise from the blast was so ear bursting; it left a ringing in his ears for days after.

He woke as if on cue with the vision of the blast. As he woke, he did the same thing as he always did after the dreams. He reached down and opened the top drawer of his desk to reveal a small bottle of scotch. As he reached down to pick up the bottle, he was disturbed by a voice he had been longing to hear all day.

"I hope that's not what I think it is." The voice came with a stern tone.

York smiled as he gazed at the woman standing in the doorway. She seemed more stunning every time he saw her. Her dark blue skirt suit clung to the curves of her body showing off her well formed figure which took a lot of hard work to maintain. Her dark brown highlighted and perfectly straightened hair draped down over her shoulders and down her back. The thing that York found most intriguing about her appearance was her outstandingly bright blue eyes, which he knew was uncommon in dark haired people.

"Just checking it was still there." He replied, shutting the drawer and giving her an innocent look. "How you doing Sarah, you look as lovely as ever."

"Thanks Alex." She offered as she walked towards him and leaned in for a kiss. They had only been on five dates in three months, but the connection they shared was as if they had been an item for years. "I heard about your antics today. You need to be more careful. Rumour has it you came closer to the end than usual."

York could sense the concern in Sarah's voice, then again, since they had got together, she had always fussed over him and he secretly enjoyed it. "Stop your worrying woman; I can take care of my self." He said with a smile. "I like that the first thing you do when you hear I am back is come running to see me."

"Don't flatter yourself." She suddenly seemed to turn serious, she opened the file she had bought in with her and began to scan through what was written. York tried to peak at the contents of the file, but she had it covered.

"I am afraid." She finally said. "I am not just here on a personal level. I was asked by the captain to come and see you."

York knew this day would come; it had been the only wedge in their relationship from the start. It wasn't so much that she was a psychiatrist; he found that an intriguing part of her character, and her insight into people's problems amazed him in a way. The problem here was that Sarah was the shrink for the entire ATS crew, including him.

"So what is it?" He inquired, a slight sarcastic tone creeping in. "The captain afraid of my 'loose canon' tendencies?"

Sarah couldn't help but laugh slightly, and then she went back to serious work mode. She found it surprisingly easy to treat York as a patient, even with their personal bond. "The thing is Alex." She began "Is that he is very concerned about your drinking. He has noticed, as have some of the rest of us, that you have been turning up for work smelling strongly of alcohol. Also, on the odd occasion, not turning up at all. He thinks you need to talk about things that might be bothering you, or eating away at you. Like what happened to your parents for instance."

York looked at her in a way that let her know she was treading on thin ice. "That's not some something I want to talk about."

She let out a sigh and shook her head disapprovingly "Why don't you ever talk about this. I've tried so hard to get you to open up to me outside of work but each time you have avoided the subject. How the hell can I get you to open up?"

He studied her for few seconds, he could see she was reaching out to him, if there was one person who could get to him, it was Sarah, and Henshaw knew that. "OK, but only 'coz I know you won't leave until I give you something to go on." He stood from his chair and walked to the glass wall. "So what do you want to know?"

Sarah took out a pen and opened her note pad "Let's start with the drink. Andy tells me you have become quite dependant on it. What made you start?"

"I wouldn't say I have become dependant on it. Yeah I like a glass or two when I get home but I am in no way addicted."

She scribbled down a few notes "Is that the first thing you do when you get home?" She asked, knowing the answer from previous experience.

"I guess so." He replied sheepishly.

"Then I am afraid there are some signs of addiction or the makings of one." She scribbled a few more notes then turned her attention back to him. "When did this start?"

Strangely, York felt more nervous in this situation that when he was in the field dodging bullets. He took a deep breath then began "It was about a year ago. I hadn't been sleeping very well for a while. I kept having these dreams. More like flashbacks actually."

"How real do they seem? Can you describe them to me?"

York turned to face her "If you stop interrupting I'll tell you."

"Sorry" She said sincerely, she had a habit of doing that.

"As I was about to say. They started off every so often, but they became more regular over time and they never changed. The first thing I would see would be my mothers face. She was crying, scared. Then as I look around, I find myself on the plane we were on that was hijacked. The strangest thing is, is that I'm not me in the dream. I can see myself when I was nine years old. I'm holding my mum as tight as I can and there is a man with an AK-47 trying to pull me away. I can see the fear in my mum's eyes. When they eventually get me away, it cuts to me looking through one of the windows. I am still on board and I can see me and loads of other kids standing in the hanger of the airport looking back at the plane. Then I feel a pain like no other, a burning pain. That's when I wake up in a sweat. The first thing I can think to do is have a drink." He found it easier than he ever thought possible to open up. He wasn't sure if it was the fact that he was opening up to Sarah or not, but he felt almost relieved, like a burden had been slightly lifted. Once he had started, he didn't really want to stop.

    Sarah finished making her notes then she looked at him directly in the eyes. She could see that thinking about what he had been describing had bought slight tears to his eyes, which made her feel a little tearful herself. She stood and walked over to him. She wiped his eyes with her thumbs then kissed him. She knew that his parents had been killed in a terrorist bombing, but she had no idea what had really happened.

    "Why didn't you tell me all of this before?" Sarah asked turning and staring out over the horizon "I could have helped you."

    York smiled, if she had only known how much he

wanted to open up to her before, but he had to be careful. There was only one person he was used to opening up to and that was Myers. "I wanted so bad to talk to you." He finally confessed. "Please understand though I had to be one hundred percent sure I could trust you. This was a big part of my life and always will be. I wanted to make sure you could handle the fact that I might get a little fucked up every now and again."

York sat back in his chair. Sarah stayed standing by the window and turned to face him. She was seeing the side to York she had been searching for. When they had been on dates before, he had always hidden behind barriers. Always showing limited signs of emotion.

"I'm glad you did tell me Alex. It's helped me to understand you better." She walked over to where she was sitting and picked up her file. "I know you can move forward from this, it will take time but I am here to help you every step of the way, both as your shrink and your girlfriend. Ok?"

"Thanks babe that means a lot." Sarah left the room. The thing that York would not let on to was the fact that in his heart and mind there was only one way he was going to move on from the nightmare that plagued his life. Find the man responsible and punish him.

16

Henshaw nursed the first cup of coffee he had been able to grab all day. With all that he had been through, he should have been ready to call it a day and head home to bed, however he felt somewhat energized. He didn't quite know if it was the adrenaline constantly pumping through his body hour after hour as new developments unfolded, or if it was the fact he had pretty much slept through the whole day yesterday in preparation for the stakeout with Myers that night. What ever it was, the coffee would help to keep him on the ball.

While he waited for York and Myers to arrive, he reflected on the day gone by. After returning to the office, he had spent hours on the phone to different people, MI5, Downing street, even the Military officials, to name but a few. The person he spoke to the most was the Prime Minister, as they had been good friends for many years, Whitburn often counted on Henshaw's advice on many subjects, especially talking to the press, which he despised doing. After advising the PM on things he needed to avoid, he tuned in to the news on the television in the lunch room and listened intently at what Whitburn had to say about the club bombing. It had been, Henshaw decided, the best press conference his good friend had ever given. For a while, he was even convinced by the story, although he knew a gas leak would not cause an explosion of that magnitude. Lying to the people of Britain may well have been frowned upon by the members of Whitburn's constituency but there was no doubt in Henshaw's mind that it was the best thing to do, so as not to cause upheaval.

He finished his coffee then sat behind his desk and pressed a few buttons on his computer. The Mercedes' drivers' picture, with all his information, popped up. Henshaw read the info intently then looked at the picture. He was younger when it was taken but the features were still the same. He had a thug type look about him. A strong, cold expression seemed to be permanently mounted on his face. The defining thing about him was the small scar just under his right eye. Henshaw examined it for a second, and then read how he had come to get it.

York and Myers entered the room and sat on the sofa. There was silence for a short moment. Henshaw tried to gather his thoughts while the other two sat looking at him expectantly. York finally broke the silence. "So what's up boss? You wanted to see us?" He noticed the look on his boss' face and instantly recognised it.

Henshaw nodded "I wanted to say well done for your efforts today." He began. "You both excelled yourselves. You actually managed to bring down the man who was responsible for the death of Bennett and we think he may be responsible for the bombing as well."

York and Myers smiled to each other then gave a high five. Then York looked at Henshaw and noticed he still looked somewhat displeased. "You ok boss?" He asked

Henshaw turned the computer monitor round so they could see the picture of the man they caught then began to explain. "The man you captured is Danny Reign. He is a former SAS soldier who was kicked out around ten years ago." He pointed to the scar below Reign's cheek then continued "The scar was a flesh wound from a bullet fired by a twelve

119

year old boy who had found his dads gun and decided he was going to play soldiers with it. The wound impaired his vision thus ending his career. My sources say he was one of the best soldiers they ever had, as tough as they come."

"So why has he ended up in a cell down stairs?" Myers inquired, speaking for the first time.

"Around six years ago." Henshaw continued. "Reign was employed by MI5 on a one off operation to flush out a terrorist cell in North London. Let's just say they paid him enough money to spark an obvious interest in is mind. A week after the operation was over, He disappeared off the radar. He hired a few other ex servicemen and started his own group of mercenaries. To date we believe he has over four hundred men working in Britain. They hire themselves out to the highest bidder, whatever they are asked to do; they do with no questions asked."

"Ok." York said while examining the picture "If Reign disappeared off the radar, how is it we know so much about him and his organisation?"

"Simple really, various government agencies both here and in the states have used him for different operations over the last three years. About six moths ago he refused to do any more. This is the first we have heard from him since then."

The thought that the same government he worked for, hired ruthless thugs to do the dirty work, scared York slightly. These guys had obviously lost all respect and remorse for human life. Although Henshaw had not mentioned the type of missions they were paid to undertake, he had had some experience of these types of groups in the past. He knew that they were only hired for jobs no-one else would do, even professionals. "Why the hell would a soldier fight for his country one minute then turn against it the next. It doesn't make sense."

Henshaw could see York was having trouble processing the facts. Reign was a hero; he had achieved one thing all British soldiers strive for, The Victoria Cross. Henshaw was thinking on the same level as York now; this man loved his country enough to risk his life for it, there was no way he could now hate it. "I guess the only explanation." Henshaw suggested "Is that he is now driven by money. When he was at war for the country, he had motivation to succeed for the well being of the British public. I guess now his only motivation is the large amount he gets paid to do what he does best, whether that be committing crimes against us or not."

York stood and walked over to the window. The view was similar from his office. "Ok, maybe I can just about come to terms with the reason. If he is as good as he is made out to be, how was it so easy to catch him?"

"He messed up." Myers interjected. "When we were in the mine, he expected us to come out either gagged or dead."

York knew Myers had a point; it was the only logical explanation. If they really wanted them dead, they would have done it in the beginning. "So what do we do with him?" He asked

Henshaw let out a sigh, one that gave York and Myers the impression they weren't going to like the answer to the question.

"I am afraid I have been ordered to let him go."

York was shocked by the revelation. He had risked his life to capture this murderer and now his efforts were being thrown back in his face. "How the hell can we let him back out on the streets? You said yourself that he was the one who killed Bennett. That makes him a murderer."

Henshaw shrugged his shoulders and said "It is out of my hands. The defence secretary gave me the direct order to cut him loose. Something to do with him being too valuable an asset to have locked up. Please understand Alex there is nothing I can do about this"

York understood, although Henshaw was the head of ATS he still had to answer to higher powers. What angered him the most was this sort of thing was all that was wrong in the world. Crimes were committed more regularly than they were many years ago. The simple reason for this was that the justice systems, not just in Britain but the rest of the world too. Guilty people were left to walk the streets and innocent ones were locked away. On the odd occasion that the right man was prosecuted, he would be safe in the knowledge he would be free to carry on his rampage in a few short years. Punishments were not nearly severe enough and for those who committed the worst crime, York believed, should be punished with their lives.

"So what happens now?" York asked as he sat back down on the sofa.

Henshaw looked at him; he looked tired as did Myers. There was not really anything that could be done until all evidence had been processed and crime scene investigations had finished. Henshaw had been like a father to the both of them since they started at ATS, but more so to York.

He looked out for them and occasionally gave them harsh advice on situations that needed some outside intervention. All he ever wanted was the best for the both of them.

"The best thing you can do." Henshaw said to them both "Is go home, get some sleep and we can start afresh in the morning. It's been one hell of a day and we could all do with some rest."

"When will Reign be released?" Myers inquired

"First thing in the morning, we will give him a small taste of what life would be like behind bars, just as a warning. Now go home you two and make sure you are here for eight AM."

They both stood and headed for the door. York turned back to Henshaw who was watching them leave. "Can I ask you something Captain?"

"Go ahead." Henshaw replied

"Do you really think it is a good idea to release Reign?"

"Only time will tell my friend. Only time will tell."

17

Jazir sat in the back of his Rolls Royce Phantom staring out into the night sky. The time on his watch read 21:56, he was right on schedule. The day had gone almost to plan, apart from his hired help being taken into custody but that was simply minor inconvenience. He knew Reign would be out by the next morning; at least that's what he hoped.

The driver pulled the car onto St James' Street and pulled up outside Jazir's apartment block. He got casually out checked the surroundings then opened the door for his passenger. Once happy he had performed his tasks to the best standard, he got back into the car and headed down the road.

Jazir greeted the young, attractive female porter as he walked into the building and headed for the lift. The lobby area was decorated in a neutral stone colour. So many times Jazir had been in to hotels and high class apartment blocks and been taken back by the bright, overpowering décor. He wanted to create a tranquil area where residents could sit and read the morning papers while they waited for their cars to be brought round by the valet. He had a few cream leather sofas placed in a small area to the right of the reception desk with a coffee machine and a snack bar, where foods such as croissants and pastries would be served all throughout the day.

The floors were made of solid granite and the lights were pure crystal chandeliers. The whole place was exactly as he wanted it. Although the designers didn't really see eye to eye with him when it came to taste, but they were being paid a lot of money to do as he asked.

He had never invested in property before; he was more

interested in things that moved, such as boats and aircraft. Something sparked in him when heard the plans for this place though. The designs were immaculate and he fell for them straight away. The only condition to him investing; he would occupy the penthouse suite.

He got into the lift and rode it until the door opened into his apartment. The reception room was decorated in smooth cappuccino colours. The furniture accented the neutral walls whilst lamps and ornaments brought slight colour to the room. Jazir was not one for fancy decoration, not when it came to his own accommodation. He liked to be able to sit and be in a complete meditative state from time to time. If the room became too busy and bright, that would become an impossible task

He walked through to the large kitchen/ breakfast room and pushed the button on the stainless steel kettle. The units were all made of solid oak, so he had decided to go for stainless steel appliances, which he thought went well but was unable to convince the interior designer. Atop of the wood cabinets lay a smooth, sparkling black marble worktop which encircled the room and island breakfast bar in the middle. The whole kitchen seemed almost unused. He rarely ate here, most of the time he ate out at his favourite restaurants. For breakfast, he always stopped at the same roadside service station and enjoyed scrambled egg on toast with mushrooms. It wasn't the most upmarket place for him to eat breakfast, but he loved the food and spending time in the presence of less fortunate people made him feel lucky to be in his position.

Once the kettle had boiled he pulled a mug from the cabinet above, placed a herbal tea bag in, then filled it with water. He grabbed a packet of digestive biscuits off the counter then headed for the terrace beyond the French doors across the reception room. Outside, he had a large sun lounger and a garden table with chairs in the centre. Placed around the edge of the terrace were pots filled with some of his favourite plants and shrubs. He sat down on the lounger and sipped at his tea while enjoying the warm summer evening.

As he drank his beverage, he felt something, a feeling he wasn't alone. He often had the urge to check the apartment for uninvited guests but this was different. He could hear the faint creaking of the floor boards behind him in the living room and they were getting closer. He remained seated so as not to startle the intruder in case he was armed. He pulled a Glock 17 handgun out from inside his suit jacket and cocked the breech ready for firing. He waited until the footsteps, which had stopped by the terrace doors. He then he leaped to his feet and twisted towards the intruder,

He was shocked when he had realised he had company but nothing could have prepared him for this. The face in front of him was one he had not seen for many years. The face was similar to his only slimmer and far more weathered. He had the same thin black hair and dark mysterious eyes as Jazir but they seemed to be troubled. The structure of the man in front of his was far from healthy. Then again Jazir could not pass judgement as his over indulging manner was starting to get the better of him.

He had not seen his brother in over ten years and after he had shaken off the initial shock, he was pleased to see him. He reached out his arms for a hug "Mohammed" he said in an overjoyed manner "I can not believe it is you."

He released Mohammed from his grip then looked him up and down "You look terrible, what has happened to you?"

Mohammed moved towards the table and sat on one of the chairs "I have been well my brother" he replied "I feel better than I look anyway. How are you? You have a great place here."

Jazir told Mohammed to wait and he ran to the kitchen and poured a drink for his unexpected guest. When he returned he said "This is nothing but bricks and mortar, or however they say it here. My real pride and joy is my ship."

Mohammed nodded knowingly "Yes, I have seen the pictures; she is a fine ship indeed. Allah has treated you well my brother."

Jazir could see the sincerity in his brother eyes, he was genuinely please for his success, even though he knew there had always been a little bit of jealousy there. The word 'Allah' was not one he was used to hearing these days. He had turned away from his faith many years earlier. As his empire started to grow, he became a man of luxury and materialism. Religion never had a chance with his lifestyle.

"What's made you come here?" He asked, suddenly realising he hadn't asked yet, not that he needed an excuse to visit. Jazir had made it quite clear that his home was his brother's home, which is why he had a key flown to him when the apartment was built.

Mohammed's face suddenly tightened and he looked to the floor "I have come here because I have heard of your plans." He didn't continue. He saw his brother's expression change from one of joy to one of anger, instantaneously.

"That is of no concern of yours. I have left you out of

it for a reason." Jazir was protective of his younger sibling and always had been.

"I am not here to get involved brother. I am here because I disagree with the measures you are taking. I know you feel strongly about the situation in our country but this is no way to react."

"How dare you come into my home and question my judgement. This is my fight and has absolutely nothing to do with you. If you only knew the real reasoning behind it, then you would be fully supportive" Jazir was becoming more infuriated with every second. Mohammed had never been told how their father had come to perish; he was only a baby when it happened. His mother had decided it best to keep him from the truth to protect him. Especially after witnessing first hand what the truth had done to his brother.

"I am sorry Salim, but the killing of innocent people will not solve anything. Think of the families of those who died this morning. After all of that, you can just come home at the end of the day and sip on tea as if nothing is out of the ordinary? What sort of person have you become? I used to look up to you."

"Do you think the people of this country give a damn about the innocent lives lost in Iraq over the years? That far out-ways the lives lost this morning. I can not believe that my own flesh and blood is against me. How dare you. How dare you Mohammed."

"I see that you are not going to listen to me. I was afraid of that. I am sorry brother, but I am going to have to do something about this myself." Mohammed stood and headed inside towards the lift. Jazir took a moment to think of what

Mohammed might do. He had come too far to be stopped now. This had to be seen to the end and no one could be allowed to stand in his way. Not even his own flesh and blood.

Jazir suddenly became aware of the gun still in his hands. The thought of killing his own brother scared him. It was not like anything he had felt before, but it was necessary. He stood and walked inside. Mohammed was waiting for the lift. Jazir grabbed a cushion from the sofa and walked towards the lift.

"I beg you brother." Jazir pleaded "Think about this for a moment."

Mohammed shook his head, he didn't look at his brother, and he simply replied "I have thought about this enough. I must do what I must do."

"So must I" Jazir came back. With that he lifted the pillow and covered the end of the barrel. The pillow silenced the pop and he fired twice. Both bullets hit Mohammed in the back of the head. He was killed instantly and fell to the floor.

Jazir felt a tear roll down his face as he stared at the body of his baby brother lying in a pool of blood. It was the hardest thing he had ever had to do. He felt dirty, evil. He knew though that desperate times called for desperate measures.

Gavin Connors walked in to the conference room as Whitburn was just pouring himself a mug of coffee from the machine just behind the doorway. The PM poured a second mug and handed it to him. To his surprise, it was just the two of them. In usual meeting of this nature, there would be members from all areas of the country's defence network.

He sat down on the chair opposite the PM and pulled out a file from his bag. He handed it over and waited patiently and quietly while Whitburn read through it.

As he waited, he scanned the room. He hated it with a passion in here, the walls were painted in magnolia and the floors were covered with simple grey carpet tiles. The coffee machine was the only other object apart from the large, rectangular cheap wood table and chairs. It felt as if no one really cared. Then again, he thought, there wasn't much that went on in here that required décor which would make you feel warm and fuzzy. On many occasions, tactics of war and destruction would be discussed in the room, so the plain feeling was all that was needed.

Although there had always been a mutual respect between the two of them, they didn't always see eye to eye. In fact they had been conflicted more in recent months than ever before. Connors was a firm believer in harsh punishment. He always maintained that if someone committed the capital crime, they should be given the capital punishment.

Whitburn however was a little more forgiving and trusting than that. He strongly believed that the right treatment could help any criminal to change his or her life, what ever crime they had committed.

He finished reading and placed the file on the table. "I can see your point in the matter Gavin." The PM began "But I think at this stage, planning retaliation strategies is a little premature."

"I thought you might say that." Connors replied. "But if you could just hear me out. This country has been fighting the war on terror for many years now. We have lost many soldiers and so have other countries' military forces. It is time to put a stop to it once and for all."

Whitburn shook his head "I am sorry Gavin, the answer is no. This has failed in the past and it will fail again. I can't risk it."

"Sir, we need to retaliate. The people of this country are expecting it. If you just sit back and do nothing, they will lose faith on your ability to remain in charge."

Whitburn stood and leaned in towards Connors. His tone changed from calm to aggressive. "I will not risk the lives of innocent people just to get payback for an attack. We don't even know who is responsible. I don't care if terror groups are coming forward, it was to be expected. There is no way I am going to change my mind Gavin, that's my final decision."

Connors grabbed the file from off the desk and slammed it in to his bag. Then he walked out of the door, making sure he slammed it behind him.

Whitburn couldn't believe his defence secretary had just acted like a five year old just because he hadn't accepted his drastic plans. Then again, he should have put some serious thought in to it before presenting it, he thought.

There was nothing that was going to persuade him to change his mind though, the repercussions would be too great, and the loss of life would be even greater.

18

It had been the first full night sleep York had had in months and he felt unusually refreshed. Sharing how he felt about his parents death and the dreams he had been having for longer than he could remember, made him feel like a great burden had been lifted from his heart. The thing that annoyed him the most when he woke up was that he still woke to a hangover. After leaving the office, he headed straight for the off-licence where he replaced the bottle of Jack Daniels that had been destroyed in the blast.

Although he had the same nightmare when he first fell asleep, it was not nearly as severe as normal. All he saw was the explosion this time, which seemed easier to cope with. The hard part was seeing that look on his mothers face. The dream didn't seem as clear in his mind when he woke up this time; the details were shady, which after so many years of waking up in a puddle of sweat, was a relief. He was on the road to recovery now and he had Sarah to thank for that.

He sat in the driver's seat of his Range Rover across the road from the ATS Headquarters. The night before he had got into a steamy phone debate with Henshaw about how bad an idea it was to let Reign go free. Eventually he came to terms with the fact it was out of his hands, but he couldn't let it go. Henshaw informed him that Reign was due for release at 6am, so York had set his alarm for five, giving him enough time to get ready and out the door by twenty past.

He didn't bother to go in to the HQ, he simply sat and waited. At five past six, Reign left the building and got in to the Taxi that had pulled up in the driveway. York let the cab get far enough away before pulling away in pursuit

He followed for well over half an hour up the A23 before the Taxi hung a left on to the slip road towards Crawley, York followed close behind. At times he had gotten to close and wondered if Reign might have spotted him, but he figured a night in the cell would have left the huge man tired and out of sorts.

They headed through the town centre and continued north towards the Manor Royal industrial estate. As they pulled into a unit on the north side, York brought the Range Rover to a stop a few hundred meters back. He took a small pair of binoculars out of the glove compartment and watched as Reign left the taxi and walked in to the unit.

For a few minutes, all remained quiet and still. A few cars had driven passed him, but nothing else. Around the perimeter of the unit he was watching, he spotted two men circling the grounds and one standing in a small cabin at the gates. He focused the binoculars on the men, noticing they were carrying firearms under their coats.

As he watched for a few more minutes, he witnessed Reign leaving through the front doors carrying a large black holdall. York was in no doubt that this was the base of operations for Reign's group of mercenaries.

They had hidden the real use of the unit perfectly. Sections of the grounds were covered in mounds of sand, shingle, bricks and other materials giving the look of a regular builder's yard. Large grab trucks were parked along the right side of the unit and a fork lift sat dormant near the mounds of sand.

The other thing that made the area perfect for their

operations base was that the unit backed on to Gatwick Airport. With the sort of activities the group seemed to take part in, they would possibly need to get out of the country fast.

The guard in the cabin was the only sign of life York could see now. The other guards had walked behind Reign and disappeared around the back of the unit. York knew if he was going to get an idea of what was at the rear, he would have to get closer.

He pulled the car up to the front of the unit; he got out and walked up to the guard's cabin. When the guard inside spotted York he quickly placed his coffee on the desk in front of him and turned away from the morning news he was watching on a small fifteen inch in the corner of the desk.

"Can I help you sir?" He asked politely.

York was surprised by the man in front of him, he was small. He seemed as if he had been starved for months on end and deprived of sleep for well over a week. He had unusually pale skin and his hair had long since thinned out. He was in no way fooled by the look though. If this was in fact the base for Reigns group, then this man was a highly trained killer.

"I said can I help you sir?" the guard asked once again, his tone becoming slightly less polite

"Sorry" York replied, "I was wondering what time you open."

"I am afraid we are not open to the public sir, this is private property."

"Oh, sorry." York said taking a step back to gain a view of the rear side of the unit. He noticed two black four wheel drive vehicles parked up by the rear fence with their engines running. If he had to guess he would say that Reign would not be hanging around for much longer.

"Was there anything else, I'd hate to have to personally remove you from the grounds."

York could sense the guard's patience was being tested and considering he had left his desert eagles in the car, he figured he should respect the guard's wishes. He jumped back in to the car and drove off down the road.

Once out of sight of the guard, he turned the car around and parked facing back towards the unit. He pulled his phone from the pocket of his jeans and dialled the number. After four rings Myers answered.

"I hope you have a good reason for calling me at this hour." Myers said obviously being awoken by the call.

"It's time to rock and roll partner, we have work to do. Get Simmons to gather a few guys and meet me at the Manor Royal Industrial estate in Crawley."

"Hold on, what the hell are you doing in Crawley?"

"I'll explain when you get here. Just hurry up." With that York hung up.

While waiting for Myers and the team, York scanned the visible area for somewhere to get some breakfast and a coffee. All he could see was a burger trailer a few yards down the road. Although it would not be his first choice for fine dining, the need for a caffeine fix was too great.

After grabbing a coffee from the van, he got back into his car to find his phone ringing. He looked at the screen to see who was calling then answered. "Detective Carter, to what do I owe the pleasure?"

"Morning Alex, how's it going?" Carter asked

"More sleep would be nice but that's life. What can I

do for you?"

"My team have been doing some investigations into the guy you arrested in the Theatre. I found some interesting facts about him."

York couldn't really see why Carter was calling him about the matter. Things like that were usually dealt with by Henshaw or one of the office staff. "What did you find?"

"We interviewed his wife who told us that a large sum of money was deposited into their account a few days before the attack. She had no idea where it had come from so she went to the bank to find that the transaction had been approved by Bennett himself."

"Sorry to interrupt detective but I fail to understand why you called me with this." In reality York wasn't that sorry about interrupting. There was nothing worse to him than wannabe hero cops butting in to anti terror matters.

"Well I was about to get to the point." Carter responded, slightly annoyed at the interruption. "I took a look at the CCTV footage for the day he was at the bank. He came in with the same guy you took in to custody yesterday. Not only that, the funds were paid in by account transfer. The paying account belongs to a Mr Mohammed Jazir."

York thought for a moment, trying to remember if the name had cropped up before. Although it did seem familiar, he couldn't quite place it. "So do you think he could be a good lead?"

"Well he might have been, but he was found with his brains blown out in his brother's apartment in Mayfair last night. His brother was nowhere to be found."

"You know you could have just said he had been shot,

but thank you for the mental image. See if you can track down the brother, he is our prime suspect. Good work Carter."

"Thank you Alex. Before I go, the brother's name is Salim Jazir."

After hanging up the phone, he took a sip from his coffee which tasted like it had been made from toilet water, then switched on the radio, hoping to hear something about the shooting in the news.

He could see what carter was getting at but if Salim Jazir was the mastermind behind the attacks then surely he wouldn't have been as careless as to kill someone in his own apartment. Then again, criminal masterminds seemed to be lacking in common sense these days. He did now remember why the name seemed familiar. Jazir had been in the news a few times over the past few months. He was a rich man, and York knew that with rich criminals came the best in security. He could tell the day was about to get a lot messier, though it had only just began.

19

Myers turned up with Simmons, and the rest of the team, twenty five minutes later. Myers pulled the Toyota Land Cruiser up behind York's car and jumped out, followed by Simmons and his team of six men. While waiting, York had got in to his combat gear and readied his MK23 for action. "What took you so long?" He asked Myers with a wink.

"Shut it." Myers replied with a smile. "So why have you got us all out of bed at the crack of dawn and had us come all the way over here?"

York explained the events of the morning, following Reign, witnessing the armed guards and the phone call from Detective Carter. "If we are going to bring down the scum bag behind the bombing yesterday, we need to up the game. I strongly believe the information we want is in that building and we need to get it."

"Ok so what's the plan?" Simmons asked.

York opened the boot of his car and pulled out a laptop computer. He waited a few seconds for it to boot up then punched in some commands until he had what he wanted on screen.

The satellite image showed the area all around them. It took just a little zoom to focus on their target. York began by pointing Reign's unit "This is our target, as you can see any attempt at entry from the front or sides on foot would be suicide. That's why I want you to enter from the rear." He refocused on the rear of the building for the team to view "As you can see some good sized trees line the back fence so you will be well covered. Once you are in, be vigilant. These men are highly trained and will take you out if you give them a chance. I want you to be better and faster than them. Have grenades at the ready and keep that finger on the trigger at all times. Are there any questions?"

One of the team members, a tall black man who looked as if he had been body builder from birth raised his hand. "What exactly are you going to be doing?"

York smiled at the obvious dig "Me and Andy will be coming in from the front. There is a guards hut by the front gate and I am driving a fully bullet proofed car. Basically by the time I am finished the hut will be no more than rubble."

No one else spoke, at York's command they simply piled back into the Toyota and waited for the mission to begin.

York looked at Simmons who seemed uneasy with the plan "What is it?" York asked

"I'm not sure this is going to work." Simmons replied with a frown etched on his face "I mean do we even know how many of the fuckers there are in there?"

"I did a quick count when I arrived here and there is around nine on site. That includes Reign."

Simmons sighed then said "I guess it's the best option we have unless you think they will open the door for us."

"Afraid not my friend, this is it." With that Simmons studied the image on the screen, to get an idea of how to approach the rear of the building, then jumped in to the Toyota and pulled away. York turned to Myers who was loading his rifle. "What about you? You got any doubts?"

"Just one." Myers replied. "I'm not convinced by the whole road rage part. I'm bad enough in a car as it is."

York laughed at the joke. In reality Myers was a maniac

when he was behind the wheel. The number of speeding fines he had built up had almost filled the glove compartment of his BMW. If he hadn't have been made exempt by the government from being penalised by points on his licence he would have surely lost it a long time ago.

York sat behind the wheel of the Range Rover a minute later and awaited the word from the team that they were in position and ready. The apprehension of operations like this one always got his heart pumping. Even though he had been fully trained for it, he still felt the same nervous tremble he had felt on his first mission.

He had only been in Iraq for three days when he was given his first assignment. Two British soldiers had been taken prisoner in an office building in Baghdad and he was a part of the rescue team. He had only four months of combat training behind him prior to receiving his orders to serve in Iraq, but with the help of his fellow soldiers he managed to keep his nerves under control enough to complete the mission successfully.

It took only ten minutes for Simmons and the team to locate the target and get in to position. When the call came York started the engine and edged forward enough to gain full view of the target. He looked through the binoculars and made a full scan. There was something different now than before. The two vehicles that were parked at the rear of the building were no longer there. He couldn't believe it, the whole time he had been sitting in the car waiting for the team to arrive, he hadn't taken his eyes off the place. Then he remembered leaving the car to grab the coffee. It had to have been then that they made their escape unnoticed.

He cursed himself for letting them escape. It was unlike him to be outsmarted by the enemy, it rarely happened. When it did, he didn't take to it kindly.

He cast the thought out of his mind and concentrated on the task at hand. Now was the time to do what he did best. This was what he had joined ATS for and he wasn't going to let anything spoil the adrenaline rush he was about to get. He radioed through to Simmons. "Let's roll."

Simmons team had grouped at the rear of the unit behind the fence. After a quick motivation talk they were ready to go. When the signal came they needed nothing else.

Simmons pulled a pair of wire cutters from his assault vest and began rapidly cutting though the chain link fence. Once a large enough hole had been made, he barged through, followed closely by his team. They ran over the muddy terrain and took position up against the rear wall of the unit by the doors.

At the same time, York slammed his foot down on the accelerator. The engine roared and the wheels screeched as the car pulled away sending a cloud of smoke trailing behind. As they approached the gates and the hut, York could see the hut was now empty. The guard who was there earlier had now gone. He pressed hard on the brakes just in time to stop the car from crashing in to it.

York looked at Myers, who had the same confused look upon his face as he did. There were only two reasons in York's mind why the guard had been pulled from his post. Either they were about to be ambushed or the unit had been vacated.

Without another thought, he accelerated through the

slightly open gates and pulled up alongside the large front doors. Both him and Myers jumped from the car and ran to the doors. Taking a few seconds to listen for any sign of human life on the inside, they heard nothing. Not knowing what was waiting for them on the inside made the adrenaline increase though York's body. When he thought they were making a surprise attack, he was able to keep himself calm, but now it seemed the element of surprise was no longer there. York was in no two minds about it, Reign's crew knew they were coming.

"Are you ok for entry?" York asked in to the communication radio on his vest.

"Ready and waiting for the command." Simmons came back.

With that, York signalled for them to enter. They burst through the doors at exactly the same time. The room was filled with crates and boxes from floor to ceiling. York moved with stealth and alertness, checking around every corner for signs of enemy presence, there was no one in sight. Apart from the foot steps on the other side of the unit, which he guessed belonged to Simmons and his team, the room was basically silent.

He walked along the outside of the stacked crates to the left of the room. A few yards in front of him, he saw a staircase leading to the first floor. He slowly walked towards the stairs, rifle pointing in the direction he was heading. As he reached the stairs, he peered round the side; he could see Simmons at the other side of the room directing his men. "You found anything yet?" he inquired.

"Nothing but boxes." Simmons replied. "If you saw

people in here, I'd say they new we were coming and did a runner."

"I'm thinking the same, I'm going to head up to the first floor with Myers, see what's in these crates before you clear the room." York turned to Myers and signalled to him to follow, he simply nodded and did as he was asked.

York had never been placed in a position at ATS that out ranked his friend but when it came to situations like these, York took charge. Myers didn't have a problem with that. The only reason he ever tagged along was because York always insisted he was the only right hand man he could trust.

They made their way slowly up the stairs to the first floor. The top opened up to a single corridor which ran along the entire length of the unit. York looked down the corridor to the left and the right. There were four doors, two each side of the stair case. He signalled for Myers to take the right while he took the left two.

They rarely split when on operations like this but occasionally the situation required it. York opened the first door he came to. Inside was filled with labelled file boxes on steel shelving units. He entered the room and read the labels. Some were marked with a stamp that read COMPLETE in bold read letters. He tried to make out what was underneath but the handwriting of whoever wrote it was too bad for even an encryption specialist to read. He took one of the boxes down from the shelf and lifted the lid, it was empty. He pulled another down, which was again empty. Pulling them off one by one and coming to the same end again and again. He soon realised in the time he had been waiting for the team to arrive, Rein had managed to pull off one hell of a clean up job.

York began to wonder if he should have made a move when he first arrived. Taking on an army of fully trained killers wouldn't have been the craziest thing he had done in his life but it would have definitely been suicide.

He left the room and walked to the door at the end. He slowly opened the door and had only taken one step inside when he was forced to make a quick exit. The barrage of bullets came as if from nowhere followed by shouting. "Get out you stupid mother fuckers. GET OUT."

York recognised the accent straight away. Reign had picked this one up from somewhere in Russia. He waited for a moment before he made any sort of move. Myers joined him as he sunk to the floor and poked a small telescopic mirror round the corner of the door.

The room was an office and a small one at that. There was only room for a small desk at the rear, which was where, York mused, the man was hiding.

"Cover me, I'm going in low." York ordered Myers. "Try to keep him shooting at the door; I will close in on him from the right."

Myers nodded and stepped into the doorway, opening fire on the back wall to give York enough of a chance to get far enough in to be covered from sight by the desk. As he stepped back in to the corridor, the man returned fire. Oblivious to the fact that York had now made it to the side of the desk and had his Desert Eagle aimed at his head.

"Drop it." York ordered. The man froze on the spot, instantly recognising he was in a situation that he couldn't control. He made one final attempt to escape by swinging the AK-47 round towards York. He hadn't counted on his assailant having read his mind and already going for the block. York grabbed the barrel of the rifle slammed the butt of his pistol in to the side of the Russian's head. He fell to the floor, being instantly rendered unconscious by the blow.

"Target acquired." He shouted to Myers who was still outside the door. Myers soon joined him and looked down at the shaven headed man on the floor.

"Nice hit. He should be out cold for a while."

"Get him down stairs and see if you can tie him to a chair or something. We'll get to him when we have finished our search."

Myers nodded and dragged the man out of the office and along the corridor to the stairs where he radioed for help in getting the large Russian down to the ground floor.

York looked through the drawers in the desk, all were empty. The computer on the desk had been completely destroyed and the hard drive was missing.

The room hadn't been decorated in the slightest. There was just a faint layer of white primer paint slapped on the plaster board which would have made any interior designer cringe.

He had been adamant that they would find some sort of information inside as to who was behind the bombings. The feeling of admitting he was wrong had not come up many times but when it did, he hated to accept it.

As he walked towards the door, he was stopped by the ringing of the telephone on the desk which he had neglected to take notice of. He walked back to the desk and lifted the receiver. "Hello?'

"Good morning Alex, It's nice to finally speak with

you."

20

The voice sent a shiver through York's body. Although the voice had been altered, a sense of evil could still be found in the tone. "Who is this?" He asked.

"I am the man you are looking for," The voice came back, "I felt it just that I should make the effort to contact you, especially since you have gone to so much trouble trying to track me down. I felt, however, it would be best to wait until I had your full attention."

"If my attention was all you wanted, you went the wrong way about it."

The comment was met by a sniggering laugh "I highly doubt that you would have agreed to speak to me if lives hadn't been lost. What made it more spectacular, was that it happened right under your nose and there was absolutely nothing you could have done about it."

York could feel the rage rising throughout his body. He clenched his fist and brought it crashing down on to the centre of the desk, "You listen to me you crazy son of a bitch. Not one of those kids in that club deserved to die yesterday. They had never done anything to you."

York's angry tone was matched, "The entire population of your country are all guilty of the crimes committed throughout the world. All I have seen over the past few years are your precious soldiers who have been killed in Iraq and Afghanistan spread all over the news papers. What about those innocent lives of that are lost in the same Taliban attacks. The lives of men women and children who are not part of the war. What about soldiers from other nations, who fight for the same cause and place their lives at risk for your people. You British have only one concern and that is yourselves."

York leaned against the desk and contemplated what he had just heard. Although the man on the other end was in no doubt crazy, he actually had a point. It was the one thing that he had grown up hating about the world; it was every man for himself. Blaming Britain alone for the problems in the world was slightly harsh, York thought. Yes the people of the U.K had their selfish tendencies but he could think of worse countries. When the rest of the world needed them, Britain was always there. The entire population would give money, if it was needed. They would lend a hand when something needed to be done. At least that's what York really wanted to believe.

York could feel himself gaining a slight glimmer of respect for the man he was talking to, in a strange kind of way. Then the mental images of the club bombing came flooding back and all respect was instantly erased.

"Do you really think that blowing up three hundred innocent people is going to change anything? If you do, you are crazier than I thought."

"I don't take kindly to personal criticism and name calling Mr York, so please, unless you want to be pulling more bodies from rubble I suggest you keep your comments to yourself."

York took a deep breath, realising he was pressing all the wrong buttons. If he was going to get anything out of this man, he was going to have to be civil "Ok, I apologise. We need to get something straight though. Our policy on terrorism is strictly non negotiable. I am ordered to use any force necessary to bring justice to those who attack our country."

The statement was met with the same laugh as before "I am afraid that you will be unable to bring justice to someone you can't find Mr York. Perhaps I need a new approach, lets try this. There is an explosive device, armed with in excess of five kilos of the substance you call Dark Gold, heading for the centre of London. As you are aware, I am more than willing to detonate it unless you, and only you, complete the mission I set."

The shock hit York like a punch to the stomach. He couldn't begin to imagine what sort of damage five kilos of that stuff could do but he knew it would be catastrophic. "What do you want?" York asked in a much lower tone.

"I thought that would change your attitude." The man replied. "There is a man I am interested in having a discussion with. What I want you to do Mr York, is bring him to me, so that I may talk with him in private."

He couldn't understand why this psycho needed him to do the job for him. If he wanted to talk to someone then there were other methods of going about it. York figured the person he was after would be less than willing to come quietly "Ok, Who is it."

"Before I tell you, let me lay some ground rules. First of all, I am setting you a time limit of twelve hours to complete the mission, if you are a second late, I will detonate the bomb. Second, if you tell any of your friends at ATS, the result will be the same, and third, when you bring this man to me, if I even smell the police anywhere near I will detonate. Do we have an understanding?"

The urge to tell him to fuck off was so appealing to York, but he couldn't let thousands of people perish at his ignorance. He checked his watch, it read 09:30. He figured, there was no choice. "I agree, so who is it?" He asked for the second time.

"James Whitburn." Then the line went dead.

York almost choked on his own saliva as the shock hit him like freight train. Of all the things he had been asked to do in his life; of all the missions he had been set; he had never branded any of them impossible, but he felt this one was. Even if he could get in to see the Prime Minister, there would be now way on earth of getting him to go anywhere without proper security, especially not after the bombing.

He stood silent and for a while, thinking about what his next move would be. There was no way he could complete the task he had been set. In his mind, there were only two options open to him. Find the bomb or find the man with the detonator.

He fell in to such a trance trying to figure out a plan, he hadn't noticed Myers walk through the door.

"Hey." Myers said as he approached York. "Did I hear you talking to someone?"

York snapped out of his daze and looked at Myers, who could see the confusion in his eyes. Although he had been told not to inform anyone, York had to tell Myers, he needed help and if there was one person he could count on it was him." He went through the whole conversation from start to finish, explaining the mission he had been set and the rules he had to stick to. Myers looked almost as stunned as York felt.

"It can't be done." Myers stated "Any one else would be do-able, but the PM, no way."

"You don't think I know that?" York replied. "To be

perfectly honest, I think he knows it to, he is just dicking me around."

"So what are you going to do?"

York contemplated the question for a second. It was the ultimate question. On the one hand he could do what he had been asked to do and probably get killed trying. On the other hand, he could try to find the bomb and disarm it and again, get killed trying. Which ever way he went, the result would ultimately be the same.

"The first thing we need to do is find out what that damn Russian knows." York stated as he headed for the door.

Jazir's car pulled up outside the run down council town house in the coastal town of Littlehampton. The driver beeped the horn once then sat back and waited.

From the door of the house came the man Jazir wanted to see. He wore a tacky pair of denim jeans and an old T-shirt that looked more grey than white. His chin was covered by a thick, curly beard and his black hair had been recently cut. He looked out of shape. His rib cage could be seen through the T-shirt. Jazir could see under the beard that his face was drawn in slightly.

"Have you been under nourished Ahmed?" Jazir asked. "Have my men not been looking after you?"

"They have sir." Ahmed replied. "I am most grateful for the opportunity you have given me. It is a real honour to work with you sir."

Jazir pulled a bottle of chilled water out of the built in refrigeration unit under the side of the seat and handed it to Ahmed. "Here my friend, Hydrate yourself. You will need strength for the mission I am to set you. Now let us enjoy the ride, when we arrive at our destination, I will reveal all."

The car cruised along the motorway towards Southampton and Jazir's ship. It took them only forty five minutes to reach the harbour where the liner was moored, ready for her maiden voyage.

As the car pulled up to the portable stairwell placed against the side of the liner, Jazir opened the door and climbed out of the car, closely followed by Ahmed. They made their way up the stairs and on to the deck of the ship.

Jazir opened the door to the inside and motioned for Ahmed to take the lead. The corridors seemed to lead on for miles. Ahmed was awe struck by the sight of the luxury rooms and exquisite dining areas he passed on the way to the private elevator leading to Jazir's room.

They rode the lift all the way to the top. The doors opened to a small hallway. At the end, a door lead to the reception room. On the right hand side; another door lead to the only bedroom and bathroom in the suite. On the left hand side, there was another door, which Ahmed figured lead to the kitchen.

Jazir lead him to the reception room then disappeared for nearly ten minutes. Ahmed took the time to admire the room. The view from the window was mind blowing, looking out across the whole of the harbour. The room itself had been well decorated. The walls were separated by a golden dado rail. Above the rail, the colour was a deep red, below it, a very dark gold. The colours just didn't seem to fit together very well in Ahmed's mind. He was no interior designer, but he did have an ounce of taste.

The room was well filled with antique looking cabinets and display units. Each unit had some sort of china or crystal ornament displayed inside. In the centre of the room, two large black leather sofas and two matching armchairs encircled a pine coffee table. Ahmed sat on one of the sofas and inspected it further. The wood detailing had been crafted from solid oak and the leather felt soft. If he had to guess, he would have said the whole room would have cost a small fortune to create. To Ahmed, it was the closest to royal luxury he would ever get.

Jazir returned as Ahmed was enjoying the view. He placed a large black case on the oval coffee table. He carefully opened it, revealing two large metallic canisters attached to wires. The wires lead to a digital display, which had buttons numbered from zero to nine along with one red and one green button at the bottom. In between the canisters was a small black box.

"This is the package I need you to deliver for me. As you can see, the timer has a numerical key pad. All you need to do is enter a code which you will be given when you reach the target. Once the code is entered the timer will begin countdown. You then have one hour to get yourself out of the blast zone before detonation. Do you understand?"

Ahmed studied the device for a second. It was a similar design to some he had used before. Before he had been moved to Britain, he had successfully completed many missions for many different terror groups throughout the world, all with a one hundred percent success rate. He had come highly recommended for the job and Jazir knew he would come with a high price tag.

Jazir pulled a brown envelope out of his jacket pocket

and handed it to Ahmed "This covers half of what we agreed. When the mission is over, I will give you the rest."

Ahmed closed the case and lifted it from the table; he offered out his hand to Jazir "This is the last we will see of each other. I will notify you where to send the final payment."

Ahmed shook Jazir's hand, the left the room.

21

Myers led York down the stairs and passed some of the stacks of crates in the main area of the unit. They walked into an area in the centre of the room which was free of the crates. The Russian was tied to a chair, surrounded by Simmons' men.

York spotted Simmons at the back of the unit and walked towards him. "Hey."
Simmons turned and walked over to York "What's up boss?"

"I need the outside perimeter secured. See if you can find anything in the rubble outside. There must be something that can help our investigation."

Simmons nodded and ordered his men to follow, knowing exactly what York was really saying. When they had vacated the building, York took off his rifle from over his shoulder and placed it on one of the only single crates on the edge of the open area. Then he took off his bullet proof vest and his holster and placed them down, taking one of his Desert Eagles out and took the magazine from the base of the grip. Satisfied it was fully loaded, he pushed the magazine back in and pulled the slide back to load the bullet.

He turned and stared at the Russian, who had been gagged so couldn't speak but had the distinct look of extreme fear in his eyes. York couldn't imagine why Reign would hire such a wimp. It was quite obvious that this man was no trained killer.

York walked over and stood in front of him, not taking his eyes away from the captive for one second. The fact that he was scared would make York's job even easier. He needed what ever information this man had and he would go to any lengths necessary to obtain it. Getting the info out of someone trained to keep quiet was a near impossible task, but someone who seemed close to wetting themselves could never last long under torture.

There were certain measures that York needed to take in order to get the result he needed. If this man was over scared then over doing the interrogation could lead him to suffer a heart attack, especially since his pulse rate was probably sky high already. Yet if he went easy on him, he probably wouldn't give anything away.

York scanned the room, searching for some chairs. He spotted a couple of fold up stools over by the door. He walked over, grabbed one and carried it back, placing it a few feet in front of the Russian. He sat down and spent the next minute in silence staring in to the eyes of his captive, trying to read him.

The Russian finally broke the silence "What…What do you want with me?" His speech was slow and stuttered.

"What's your name?" York asked.

"Sergei."

York smiled, trying to calm Sergei's nerves "My Name is Alex York. I am an Agent with the National Anti Terrorist Service. What is your position in Reign's unit?"

Sergei took a deep breath "I am the communications and technology sergeant. I take care of things like radio equipment and other devices. I am not trained in combat so there is no need to keep me restrained." He knew the attempt was a desperate and useless one, but he was scared and had to try.

"I'm sorry Sergei, I am afraid I can't let you go just yet. I think you may be able to help me in my investigation." York kept his tone soft and spoke each sentence slowly making sure the Russian understood exactly what he was saying. "Do you know the name of the man Reign has been working for?"

Sergei shook his head "I am sorry, I do not. He took the job on his own. We were ordered to clear the building of all trace of out presence here."

York was impressed with Sergei's English, he spoke it fluently. Many of the people he had interrogated in the past had never been taught the language. "Ok, I believe you." He lied. "Maybe Reign has mentioned the bomb to you."

Again Sergei shook his head, this time keeping quiet.

York stood and walked over to Myers who was sitting on the crate where he had put his weapons. "This is getting me nowhere. I'm not sure if this guy is telling the truth or not."

Myers nodded "I know he is lying," Myers stated, keeping his voice to a whisper. "Remember back in the mine, those guys were all Reigns men. If they knew about the mine, they knew about the bomb. I think you need to change the questions slightly, or perhaps the way in which they are delivered."

York nodded in agreement and walked back over to Sergei. He sat back down on the chair and took a cigarette packet from his pocket. As he lit one, he offered the pack to Sergei who shook his head "People always told me smoking would kill me." York said. "I don't know what the fuss is about. The only time it has ever harmed me was when I burnt myself." He looked at Sergei and smiled. "You seem like a smart man Sergei, so I am going to give you another chance. I would like the truth this time please. Who is the man Reign is answering to?"

"I told you before, I don't know."

York stood and walked behind serge. He took a drag from the cigarette then pressed it against the underside of Sergei's arm. "It won't take long to burn through your jacket. I suggest you tell me now."

Sergei said nothing; he simply sat still and closed his eyes preparing himself for the sting. When it came, he let out a wailing scream. The sting was like nothing he had ever experienced, it shot through his body like a lightning bolt. When the cigarette was taken away, the sting remained. The smell of his own flesh burning only added to the pain

York stood up and walked back to Myers to give Sergei a chance to calm down.

"That was a bit harsh." Myers stated "I was thinking we should just ask the questions in a slightly harsher tone, not brand him for life."

"What good would it do? I have dealt with these characters in the past, pain is the only way."

He walked back over and sat down "I'm going to ask you one last time. Who is the man Reign has been dealing with?"

"I have told you" Sergei shrieked, trying his best to block out the pain. "I have no idea."

This time, York took his desert eagle and placed the barrel against Sergei's shoulder bone and pulled the trigger. The echo of the shot was drowned out by the Russian's screams. Myers walked over to York, who seemed to be enjoying the torture. "What the hell are you doing? Your gonna kill him."

Myers looked dead in to York's eyes. They seemed

completely void of all emotion. "I think it's time we ended the interrogation."

"Not until I have the info I am looking for." York turned back to Sergei and pointed the gun towards his knee, as he was about to pull the trigger, he was stopped.

"No." Sergei pleaded. "No more, I will tell you. Please, just don't put me through any more."

York sat back down on the chair and stared at the quivering man in front of him, waiting for him to start speaking.

"The man Reign is working for calls himself Mr Jazir. He is some rich man from the Middle East. That's all I know about him I swear"

"Ok, I believe you." York assured him, not expecting the Russian to take his word for it. "What about the bomb?"

"Reign made some sort of reference to it but he never said where it was heading."

"I hope you are telling me the truth Sergei."

"I am, I swear."

York nodded and stood, walked over to his gear and began to put his vest back on. Myers gave him a disapproving look.

"Don't look at me like that Andy; I got the information didn't I."

Myers nodded "I guess you did. So what now?"

York finished getting his gear back on and turned to Myers "I need you to go looking for the bomb."

"What about you?" Myers asked.

"I have to try and track down Jazir. If I find him, I find the detonator."

York was disturbed by Sergei laughing; he turned to the Russian still strapped to the chair. "What's so funny?"

Sergei looked York dead in the eyes He seemed to have changed from a quivering wreck to a mad man in a split second. "Do you really think he will let you find him? He knows everything about you Alex. He knows how your mind works. He knows what your move is going to be before you do. The only thing you can do is complete the task he has set you."

York looked at him for a few seconds. He was right, if he really wanted to stop the bomb, the simplest solution would be to complete the mission, but he needed a plan. There was no way he could walk in to Downing Street and just walk out with the Prime Minister alone.

He began to run over different plans in his mind, each time he cast it aside as impossible. The situation he was in was definitely one he would struggle to win. But if there was one thing he was certain of was that he was no quitter. It was then that he realised there was only one way of truly preventing the worst attack the country had ever seen. He walked over to Myers and ran through it with him.

"You're crazy." Myers stated "Even if it does work, you won't be able to avoid the trouble it will bring."

"Don't you think kidnapping the Prime Minister of Britain is trouble enough? I don't think I could actually do any worse."

Myers shook his head "If it's the only way, then so be it. But I'm not happy with it in the slightest."

"Go get Simmons and tell him to meet me in here."

As Myers left the building, York turned to Sergei. "I

hope you've told me everything. That 'you'll never find him' comment is telling me you haven't."

Sergei laughed as he did before "Of course you won't find him. You have failed to catch him so far, what makes now any different?"

York looked at his captive trying to work out what exactly what he meant. He knew the Russian had been holding out on him from the start. "What do you mean?"

"My god. You don't know do you?"

"Know what?"

Sergei felt an overwhelming sense of security flood over him. "You have been searching for this man for longer than you realise."

York suddenly knew what Sergei was telling him. He could hardly believe it a first but after a few seconds; the rage that had driven him for so many years came flooding back in one hit. He grabbed Sergei, who was still tied to the chair and forced him on to his back. He slammed his foot down on the Russians chest and pointed the gun at his face. "I want to hear you say it." He ordered in a low and hateful tone.

Sergei laughed through the pain of the bullet hole in his shoulder, now being trampled on by York's size eleven trainers. "You don't need me to say it. You know exactly what I am talking about."

York jammed the barrel against Sergei's forehead. "Tell me, or I pull the trigger."

Sergei looked his straight in the eye "Jazir is the man who killed your parents."

22

Reign stared in awe at the sight of the Rolls Royce phantom as it pulled up in front of him. Since he was a child, his passion for cars had been his only one. It had stemmed from his father, who was a mechanic for many years. If he had been granted the chance to become a collector of fine vehicles such as the Rolls in front of him, he would be able to die a happy man.

He opened the door and climbed in. He offered out his hand to the man next to him "Morning Mr. Jazir. I trust that I have done everything to the standard you required."

Jazir looked at Reign and smiled, not accepting the hand shake. "You have certainly lived up to your reputation. I'll be the first to admit that I had my doubts when your leader came to me, but I have been proven wrong and that does not happen a lot."

"Thank you sir, that means a great deal to me."

Jazir reached in to the inside pocket of his jacket and pulled out a brown envelope. He passed it to Reign who opened it and counted the money inside.

"Have no fear my friend." Jazir assured "It is all there. That concludes your mission for now. Like I said, I am very impressed with your work, so you can count on a call from me for future ventures."

"It will be a pleasure to work with you again." Reign held out his hand once more. This time Jazir returned the gesture.

As Reign opened the door and got out of the car, he turned back to Jazir "There was one more thing I needed to discuss with you sir."

"What was that?" Jazir asked, slightly frustrated with being held up for longer than he needed to be.

"The explosive device destined for London. You won't really detonate right?"

Jazir looked at Reign, trying to understand the motives for the question. He felt the large man leaning against his overly expensive car was trying to over tread the line slightly, but he had nothing to hide. In a few hours, he would be a distant memory in the minds of those involved. "As long as Alex York does as he is told, then no. However, I am more than willing to do what is necessary to complete my mission"

Reign didn't respond, he simply closed the door of the Rolls and watched as it pulled away in to the distance.

Connors sat at his desk rifling through the tonne of paper work he had come in to find. This was the worst part of his job, even though it took up probably over sixty percent of his day. The thing he loved about his job was the pressure. He was the man who was responsible for all aspects of the countries security and defence. He was also the man in charge of the armed forces. When things really began to heat up, he could always be counted on to step up a pace with it. He was well respected as one of the hardest working men in parliament.

He checked his watch and realised he had been hard at work for over an hour now. He gulped down what remained of his coffee and headed for the door to go to the staff kitchen and pour another.

As he held out his hand to push the handle down, there

was a knock at the door. He opened it to see the slender frame of his secretary. "I'm sorry to disturb you sir." She said courteously. "I have some information for you."

He looked down at his cup and shrugged off the thought of getting another, it would have to wait. He motioned her in to the room towards a chair. He remained standing in front of her.

"I have just received word from ATS. They have taken one of Danny Reigns men hostage in Crawley sir. They are about to interrogate him."

"Have they managed to find anything out?" Connors asked.

"No sir. They are going to keep us up to date."

"Thank you" Connors said as he moved towards her. She gave him a provocative smile as he approached.

"Has it been a stressful morning so far sir?" She asked, keeping the smile in full bloom.

"The hardest." He replied

She stood in front of him and he leant in for a passionate kiss. Then she walked over to the door and locked it. When she returned, she gave him another kiss. He picked her up and flung her on the desk, still covered in paperwork. He looked down at her and smiled "I love this job."

As he was about to lean on to her, he was disturbed by the phone ringing. He picked it up though he was in no mood to talk. "Connors." He barked

"It's done. We have completed our mission."

"Good. I will be in contact for your next assignment."

"Thank you sir. I trust the funds have cleared."

"Yes. That will be all." He slammed the phone down

and turned his attention back to his secretary, who had now removed her clothing from the waist down.

The news took a while to digest. For years he had spent his entire free time trying to track down the man who was responsible for the bombing, now he was within reach and he had no idea what to do.

While Simmons had one of his men take Sergei to the hospital. Myers ran down the road and grabbed coffee for everyone. When he returned he handed them a round then walked over to York, who was just sitting, staring in to oblivion. Holding out a cup, he said "Coffee?"

York took the foam cup from Myers and sipped. He didn't say a word. The words were spinning in his mind like a whirlpool. He could hardly believe that after all the years of searching, he finally knew who was responsible. The problem now was finding him.

"Alex." Myers said trying to distract his partner.

York shook off the day dream and turned to Myers "Sorry, I was miles away."

"I understand." Myers always tied to stay as patient and as understanding as possible when it came to the subject of York's parents. Now, he had to be a lot more so. York was going to need all the support he could get and Myers was ready to give it "We need to get moving. If we get back soon, you may well catch Sarah before she goes."

"Goes? Goes where" York asked.

"It turns out she pulled an all nighter trying to find something that may help you in your search. She came up with nothing though."

He could hardly believe that someone could do that for him. He had only told her a few hours before and she must have got right to work on it. Their relationship had never progressed much, but the feelings they had been having for each other were growing slowly and this helped heighten York's feelings for her greatly.

He shook off the thought of Sarah, saving it for later and went back to concentrating on the information he had just been given.

"What do you know about this Jazir guy?" York asked as Myers turned to walk to the car.

"All I know is he has just had a huge cruise ship built. It's docked in Southampton. Why?"

"No reason." He paused for thought then said "You go back with Simmons. I have a couple of things I have to take care of."

Myers nodded then turned and jumped in to the Toyota, then drove off.

York stared at the pavement in deep thought. This was it, this was the moment he had been waiting for his whole life. If he was going to do this, it had to be done right. He needed a plan and he needed one now. Anything he had been planning to do before was now out of the question. He had a new mission. The question was; what would he do with Jazir once he found him? Killing him would be easy, York thought, but he wanted the bastard to know what pain was really about.

He pulled his phone from his pocket and dialled the number. After two rings, Kirk answered.

"Kirk. It's York."

"Hey man, what's up?" Kirk replied

"I need a favour. The warehouse I'm at. If I give you the address, can you find out the phone number?"

"Sure, easy stuff."

"Ok. Find out the number of the last person who called and then tell me where it came from." This was where York was expecting Kirk to say he couldn't do it. Just to make life more difficult.

"No problem. I will need a couple of minutes though."

"Ok call me back." Then he hung up the phone.

While he waited for the call back, York opened the boot of his Range Rover and checked the ammunition. He was fully loaded with both .50 calibre bullets for his desert eagles and 9mm bullets for his assault rifles if he needed them. All he really needed was the location. He would go in unarmed if necessary as long as the job was done.

Kirk phoned back while York was in the middle of the first cigarette he had enjoyed all day. "I got the location. It was from a Mobile." Kirk explained.

"Are you able to use the signal to locate where it is now?" York asked.

"I knew you would ask that so I am already running the search."

There was a brief silence before Kirk spoke again. "Ok, your friend is not far from you actually. He is at the Pease Pottage service station about twenty minutes from where you are. "

The vengeful look he had become known for by those who new his situation seemed locked in his eyes. He had only one thing on his mind now. Get him.

"Is everything ok Alex?" Kirk asked.

"Yeah." York responded in a low, hard tone. "Call me if he moves." He hung up the call, jumped behind the wheel of the Range Rover and sped off towards his target.

Kirk heard something in York's voice he definitely didn't like. He could sense the hateful, murderous feelings, so he knew he had to act. He left his work room and headed for the lift. He rode to the top level then walked down the corridor towards Henshaw's office. He tapped on the door and waited to be beckoned in.

Henshaw was lying on his sofa when Kirk walked through the door.

"Sorry sir." Kirk offered. "I had no idea you were sleeping."

Henshaw sat up and took a quick sip of his now cold coffee "Not to worry young Kirk. Not to worry. What can I do for you?"

Kirk stepped fully into the office and closed the door behind him. Following Henshaw's request, he sat in the chair by the desk. "I have just had a call from Alex." He explained. "He asked for a number to be traced then he asked for the location of that number. I wouldn't usually take it as anything other than routine but he sounded agitated. I could be wrong but I felt that I should let you know."

Henshaw frowned, if York was simply following up on a lead he would have called in as he always did. York had never led an operation without keeping him updated. As he thought about it more, the last person he spoke to was Simmons and that was over an hour ago. "Did you find out who the call came from?"

Kirk fumbled though some papers in the folder in his hands and found what he was looking for. "The call came from a mobile phone belonging to a Mr Jazir."

Henshaw looked Kirk directly in the eye. His eyes widened and his face turned pale. He grabbed the phone and dialled York's number. The phone rang but no one answered. He decided the next best person to ring would be Myers, if any one knew what York was thinking it would be him.

Myers phone rang twice then he answered. "This is Myers."

"Andy." Henshaw had a sense of urgency in his voice. "Where are you?"

"I'm on my way back with Simmons and the team. We should be...."

"Forget that." Henshaw ordered. "Where is Alex?"

"He said he had something to take care of."

Henshaw stood from the chair and slammed his fist on the desk. "Andy. Listen to me very carefully ok. Alex had Kirk trace a phone call which led back to a man named Salim Jazir. Did you hear that call?"

"Yes sir. If it's the call I'm thinking of then he is the one who is responsible for the bombing yesterday." Myers felt it best not to discuss what was really said on the phone.

"Andy you need to go back for him." Henshaw ordered. "The man he spoke to is Salim Jazir. He is also the man who was also responsible for the death of Alex's parents."

There was a brief silence as Myers digested the information. "Where is he?"

Henshaw looked at Kirk expectantly. "Kirk, where did you send him?"

"Pease Pottage Services." Kirk informed.

Henshaw relayed the location to Myers then hung up the phone. He had known for many years that Jazir was the bomber on that disastrous day which changed York's life forever. He could never bring himself to tell York though, for this simple reason. York had been so consumed by hate and revenge that he would have gone after him immediately. The result would be murder and considering there was never any evidence to suggest Jazir's involvement in the bombing; York would have been arrested and prosecuted.

The events that Henshaw had been trying to stop for so many years were now out of his control. He just hoped one thing, that York would show mercy on Jazir for one simple reason: If there was no evidence was found connecting Jazir to the club. York would be branded a cold blooded killer.

23

York pulled in to the Pease Pottage Services and parked towards the back of the car park. He checked his gun was loaded then placed it in the back of his jeans and covered it with his t shirt. He reached down in to the glove compartment and pulled out the binoculars. Although he wasn't entirely sure who he was looking for, he scanned the area anyway.

Everything seemed normal. People were sitting in their cars tucking in to burgers or light snacks before continuing on their journeys. Truckers were stretching their legs and having smoke; this was the only time they could get their nicotine fixes.

The car park was busy, as it usually was on a hot summer day like today. The number of cars parked up made it difficult to narrow down which one was Jazir's but he remembered one thing he had learned about him, he was Rich. As soon as he thought of that, a car jumped out at him.

The Rolls Royce looked strangely out of place parked in amongst all of the common cars. The expensive motor almost added a touch of class to the surroundings. York got out of the car and keeping himself low, made his way towards the Rolls.

When he approached, he saw it was empty. There would be no way of getting inside. With the alarm system it was probably packing, he would fail before he even got close. The only thing he could do was wait.

Patience had never been York's strong point, if something had to be done, he wanted it done immediately. He always said waiting wastes time and time is something that can never be replaced.

He got back in to his car and waited for over half an hour, keeping a close eye on the Rolls. He hadn't really thought through what he was going to do when Jazir showed his face. With all the people around, he couldn't just walk up to him and pull the trigger. He needed a plan and fast.

Jazir and his driver came into view. York expected to be in his fifties, most people with his level of success and wealth were at least mid to late forties. But this man was a lot Younger, more in his late thirties. He soon shook off the thought of the man's age; he was here to kill him no matter how old he was.

As the driver got in to the car after holding the door open for Jazir, York fired up the Range Rover and pulled away quickly. His aim was to reach the exit before they did. As he pulled out of the exit and headed for the roundabout, pulled the car up on to the verge and waited for the right moment.

This was it, he was about to come face to face with the man who ruined his childhood, ruined his life. He still had no idea how he was going to handle the situation, but he didn't care now. This was something he had been waiting for, for many years.

As the Rolls Royce pulled in to view in his wing mirror, he pulled the Range Rover out in to the centre of the road, blocking the exit. Jazir's driver slammed on the brakes to avoid collision.

The driver stepped from the car and walked towards the car blocking his exit. York didn't move right away, he needed to wait until the driver was in the right position to cut him off from Jazir's view.

At the right moment, York got out of the car. He aimed his gun at the driver, who froze instantly. "Don't even think about running or yelling." York instructed the driver. "Just look as of you are talking to me."

The driver nodded "Please don't hurt me, we will give you what ever you need."

York could see the fear in the driver's eyes. He could hardly believe that all of his years of good work with the army and ATS had boiled down to holding an innocent man at gun point.

"What is it that you want?" The driver asked.

York took a few second to think up his next move. "I want you to turn around and walk towards the car, when you get there get in to the drivers seat then unlock the rear doors. I will be right behind you every step so if you try to run I will shoot you." York wore a serious expression to add to the threat, even though he had no intention of shooting the driver if he ran, but he needed him to believe he would.

The driver nodded "OK." Then he turned and began to walk slowly towards the car.

York walked close behind, keeping low and out of sight of Jazir. He followed the driver all the way to the car. As the driver got in to the driver seat, York rushed for the rear door and jumped in the back with Jazir. He pointed the gun towards the front "Drive." He demanded.

He pulled the gun away from the driver and pointed it at Jazir. He said nothing; he just held a long hard stare at the man who killed his parents.

"What the hell is the meaning of this?" Jazir asked in

an authoritive tone.

"If I were you Mr. Jazir, I would keep quiet."

"What ever you say, Mr York. What ever you say."

There were two things that Ahmed could guarantee would happen on every trip to Britain. The weather would be wet and the trains would be late.

The sound of the announcer's voice was beginning to get on his nerves, especially since every time he spoke, it was to say his train was further delayed. The longer he sat watching the crowd go about their business, the more his nerves intensified. Police patrolled the station in pairs; they spread themselves out across all eight platforms, walking up and down looking for any signs of suspicious behaviour.

The officers who patrolled his platform had barely given him a look, they simply walked straight passed. He had to concentrate hard on not attracting attention, which was harder than it seemed. Here he sat with the power to take the lives of the hundreds of people, parading around paying no thought to anyone else. The thought that all these men, women and children from all walks of life saw him as nothing but another commuter made him smile. But why wouldn't they? He asked himself. They had no reason not to trust him. They all felt perfectly safe in the knowledge that nothing bad could happen. Maybe it was the police patrol that gave them a false sense of security. Maybe it was ignorance. What ever it was, Ahmed knew in a few minutes, he would get on his train and head for his target.

As the train pulled in to the station, he let out a slight sigh of relief. Once he was on the train, he was on the way to completing his mission. Just a short taxi ride at the other end and he was there. That was the easy part though. He had stipulated when he took the job that it was not a suicide mission. Once the bomb had been placed in its correct location, he had to get out of London.

He waited patiently for inbound passengers to leave the train then he stepped on, found him self a seat and placed the case on the floor next to his feet. He stared out of the window over the other platforms at the same people he had been watching for the past hour. He felt something that was foreign to him as he saw two young children playing. He felt a slight sense of sorrow for the innocents that would loose their lives in the next few hours. It wasn't so much the adults, it was more to do with the children than anything. He had always loved kids and the fact that many children would die in the attack almost put him off the whole idea.

The feeling didn't last long; a few seats down he noticed a bunch of teenagers giving an old man some grief. He realised why he had taken the job in the first place. He hated the attitude of the British, especially the youth. He blamed the government; they were the reason young people believed they could get away with anything. Parents were no longer allowed to use discipline. Not like in his country. Where he came from, children respected their elders.

There was now nothing that could be done about all the problems he saw in the British. They had sealed their own fate in his mind. Their intrusion in to Middle Eastern affairs on a number of occasions; enraged him. They were stepping in to a conflict that was not their own, then wondered why retaliation was necessary.

Even after taking everything in to consideration, he still felt slightly sorry for those who just lived their lives as best they could. It was not their fault at all. They had just fallen victim to poor leadership and that was what the whole fight was about. He knew he had to make a stand. Not only for himself, but for the rest of the world and in a short few hours, he would make his stance known.

24

York kept the gun pointing firmly at Jazir as they headed for the location York had given them. They were no longer on the dual carriageway. They were now heading down narrow countryside lanes. York kept his eye on Jazir while watching where they were heading. Not far now, He thought.

When they reached the end of the lane, York ordered the driver to make a right, then turn immediately left on to a dirt track. The road was uneven and York struggled to keep the gun fixed on Jazir. About half a mile down, once they had entered a woodland area, York told the driver to stop.

"Get out." He ordered Jazir. Then he pointed the gun at the driver. "Turn the car around and head far away from here. If I get even the slightest sense that you are nearby, I kill your boss. Do you understand?"

The driver nodded and York stepped out of the car. Jazir was standing a few yards away. He seemed calm as if this was nothing he hadn't expected. It was a strange sight for York to see. Usually when he took someone at gun point, for whatever reason, they had some level of fear in their eyes. But not Jazir, he remained cool and focused.

"Move." York said sternly as he motioned further in to the woods. Jazir obeyed and walked slowly through the over growth.

"What are you going to do to me Alex?" Jazir asked in a nervous manner.

"Shut up and keep walking." York replied. He had a look in his eye that Jazir had noticed earlier, the look of a cold killer.

After walking for a few minutes, York ordered Jazir to stop. "Down on your knees." He Ordered. "Hands behind your head."

Jazir did as he was asked. "If you want to find the bomb." He advised. "Then you are going about it in completely the wrong way. I will not give in to bullying."

York walked around so he was facing Jazir. That killer look was still burning in his eyes. He didn't talk straight away. He just stared deep in to his captive's eyes. Reading them like a book.

Jazir decided there was one reason he had been brought here, to be executed. It didn't make sense though. He thought the best thing that York could do was use him to stop the deaths of over a million people. There was hatred in York's face that Jazir recognised instantly. It was a hatred that he had felt in the past. This was nothing to do with what had happened over the past couple of days. This was personal.

"Do you know why I have brought you here?" York asked, breaking the silence.

"I would assume it has something to do with the explosive device heading for London." Jazir replied, knowing full well that wasn't it.

York kept the gun pointed directly at Jazir's forehead. He could sense the slight arrogance in his captive's voice. Here he was at the receiving end of a .50 calibre weapon and he was talking like he was still in control.

"You know full well that's bullshit." York said angrily. "Let me give you a clue, it has something to do with an attack you made on a passenger plane twenty years ago."

Jazir couldn't help but smile "I see you Brit's like to hold on to rubbish stories and rumours. I was cleared of that at the time. Your government realised it would be hard for a boy of fourteen to organise a terrorist bombing."

York stood and thought about the statement. He was right; no boy he had ever heard of had been able to run a mission like that. It required the 'know how' of someone with experience. If that was the case, then why would the Russian have told him Jazir was the one? He had no reason to lie, none at all.

York shook off the thoughts and turned his attention back to Jazir. "You're lying. I have strong intel that you were the one behind the bombing, which means you are the one who killed my parents."

"You know, revenge is a very dangerous motive Alex. But I can fully understand. I know exactly what you are feeling."

York lifted the gun up and smashed it down across Jazir's face. He fell to the ground and let out a painful shriek. Once the initial shock had subsided, he raised himself back up to his knees and looked up at York again.

York leaned in so he was just inches away from Jazir's face, which was now bleeding from a cut on his cheek. "What the hell do you know about what I am feeling you son of a bitch?"

"I know more than you think Alex. Do you think you are the only one who has ever had to endure the pain of loosing people close to you? Are you really that selfish?"

York could feel the rage building inside. He could feel his hands starting to shake; the temptation to pull the trigger right there and then was hard to resist. There was something in what Jazir was saying that struck a nerve though. For years he had been so consumed with revenging his parent's death, that he had lost the concept of what it meant to be a decent human being. He no longer knew what the right thing to do was. The same question began to run through his mind. Did he really need to kill this man?

He let his arm holding the gun fall to the side, then took a step back. "What happened to you that was so bad?" He asked, keeping the hateful tone up.

Jazir's head dropped, digging up the painful memories seemed hard for the tough, ruthless businessman. "It was twenty five years ago. My Father was a well educated chemical scientist. He had done a great deal of work for many countries throughout the world. He was working on behalf of the British Government at the time. I don't quite know what it was he was working on, but I know it was big. Secrecy was an absolute must." He paused to take a deep breath before continuing.

"He told me that the assignment had been a successful one and that he was expecting a team of British military escorts to transport him and his findings to London for final analysis. Two days later, the team arrived as expected. What we didn't expect, was for them to open fire on us. They killed my mother and my father, and then they turned his laboratory upside down searching for the work he had carried out. When they found it, they took my brother and me away with them. We were held for a number of weeks before being let out in to the world again. We were told never to tell anyone what we had learned from our father, or what had happened to him."

York looked at him. A strange thought came to him. Here he was with the only person he had ever met who could really understand what he felt and it was the man who made him feel like it in the first place. He felt sorry for Jazir, for a moment. In the years since the attack, there had been times when he wished he had died that day. The pain never seemed to go away, or get easier to cope with. He lifted the gun back up and aimed it towards Jazir once again, snapping out of the slight trance.

"Do you really think that killing a bunch of innocent people can be justified as revenge for your family's death?" York asked the hateful tone back in his voice.

"You don't understand Alex. I targeted that plane because it was carrying one of the three men who made up the team."

"Why not just take him aside. Why did so many innocents have to die?"

"I never planned for the bombs to go off. But as I said earlier, I was just a boy. The men I hired had planned all along to help me with my mission then complete their own."

"Who was the man you were targeting?" York asked, knowing it made no difference what so ever.

"Ask your boss." Was all Jazir said.

York grimaced "What?"

"I said ask your boss." Jazir's face seemed to harden. "Enough questioning now. If you are going to kill me then get it over with."

York readied himself to pull the trigger, but something inside him was stopping the action. This was what he had wanted for so long and here he was with the perfect opportunity; but he couldn't. He simply stood over Jazir with the gun pointing down towards him. Then he realised why he couldn't do it. He suddenly thought of all the lives that hung in the balance if he didn't find the bomb in time. He looked down at his watch, which read 12.17pm. Time was ticking by. He knew the more time he spent going over old wounds, the less chance he had of finding the bomb. For now he had to put his personal fight with Jazir to the back of his mind and concentrate on the matter at hand.

Myers sat in the front seat of the Land Cruiser, trying desperately to get in touch with York. Every time he called, it just put him straight through to voicemail. He knew exactly how York thought. And he knew if he didn't get to them in time, then it would be too late. York would have killed the only lead to the location of the bomb.

The car sped up the A23, swerving round every car that got in the way. Myers hated high speed driving; an accident at these speeds would likely kill all of them instantly. He had always had trouble in cars though, ever since he was little. He just didn't trust them. He couldn't understand why people treated them with such disrespect. He saw it every day on the news, people dying as a result of reckless or dangerous driving. Yet after hearing of a fatal crash people would get in to their cars and drive like lunatics. It made no sense to him and it never would.

He was disturbed from his deep thoughts by his phone ringing. He looked at the screen to see who was calling. It was Henshaw "Yes sir." He answered.

"Andy, where are you?" Henshaw asked.

"We are one junction away from the service station sir."

"Turn around, I've just heard of a call made to the

police about five minutes ago. The man claimed he was Salim Jazir's driver and they had been hijacked by a crazy man in a Range Rover."

Myers almost laughed; the man had made York perfectly 'Crazy'. "Where did the call come from sir?" He inquired.

"It was the car phone in Jazir's roller. He wasn't exactly sure where but he notified us that the car had a tracker. I'll send the location to the car's computer. Just get there fast, before the cops do."

"You got it sir. You got it."

Myers pressed a few buttons on the screen of the onboard computer after hanging up the phone. He checked the incoming message tab, which had the number one next to it. When he bought up the message, the screen was filled with a map of the local area. On the map was a small red blip, pointing out the position of Jazir's car. Myers noted the location to be around five minutes drive from where they were. He signalled for Simmons to turn around at the next available location and head towards the blip. If they were going to stop a disaster, he had to get to York before he took away their only lead.

25

The Rolls Royce came in to view a few hundred yards ahead. The driver was sitting behind the wheel waiting patiently for Myers and his team to arrive. As they pulled up, the driver got out of the car and ran towards them.

"Help." He cried. "Please help."

"Sir, are you the man who made the emergency call?" Myers asked, walking towards the driver, who seemed to still be shaking.

"Yes, they are at the end of this trail." He replied, pointing down the dirt track where York had led him.

"Ok, stay here with one of my team members and he will debrief you."

Myers signalled for Simmons and one of his team members to join him as he walked briskly down the track. He could only imagine what to expect when he found York. With the way he had been over the last few years, with all of the sleepless nights he had endured, just thinking about what he would do if he found the man responsible was too much to comprehend.

"So everything that has happened over the past couple of days, all those innocent kids who have lost their lives. They all died because you wanted revenge." York was becoming more enraged the longer he thought about it. All of the earlier thoughts he had after hearing Jazir's sob story had now gone. He actually thought the monster in front of him had a heart.

For a moment he had forgotten the explosion at the club. He had been too wrapped up in revenge, that he had lost sight of everything. It was all back now though. Now he had a new agenda. He didn't want Jazir dead, he needed him. The problem was, as far as he knew, Jazir had come to the same conclusion. He knew he had gone about the whole situation wrong. Jazir was a resourceful man. He had what ever he needed at his helm. Yet it had been easy to find him, too easy perhaps.

"Don't judge me Alex." Jazir said, catching the disgusted stare York was giving. "We are not that different you know."

"How the hell can you even try to compare us? For a start, I don't go around killing hundreds of people to get back at someone who wronged me over a quarter of a century ago."

Jazir sniggered "You really are a gutless man Alex. Sometimes when you have something which needs to be done, collateral damage can not be avoided."

York moved in close to Jazir. Close enough to feel his breath on his cheek. He lowered his voice to a whisper, more because seconds before, he had heard the sound of people walking through the woods. He figured it could only either be Myers or the police. Who ever it was he had two choices, kill Jazir now or drive fear in to him. "Do you know what Salim, you're right. Collateral damage is un-avoidable. That's why you are going to help me find this bomb, or you will be mine."

With that, He was disturbed by a familiar voice "Alex, put the gun down and step away from Jazir."

York looked up to see Myers and Simmons a few yards away, both aiming their weapons at him. After every thing all of them had been through over the past three years, it had come to this. He didn't blame his partner though; his actions over the last few hours had not exactly been by the book.

Myers repeated the request; again York simply gave a quick glance and ignored it. He looked back down at Jazir, who still seemed calmer than ever. "Tell me where the bomb is and we can all just go on with our lives."

Jazir looked up at York with disgust pasted all over his face "You stupid man." He cursed. "The last thing I want is for things to go back to normal. The whole point of this action is to make a change. And that can only be accomplished by you completing the task I set you earlier."

"At least tell me what sort of bomb it is. Is it nuclear?"

Jazir laughed "It a product of your own stupidity. You know exactly what sort of bomb it is. There is enough Dark Gold to put a sizeable whole in the earth. That's all I am telling you."

York smiled; he had exactly what he needed "Thank you Mr. Jazir."

Jazir looked up at him again, this time he looked puzzled. He hadn't given him anything to go on, not really. All he had told him was how powerful the bomb was and he hadn't even really gone in to much detail about that.

York holstered his Desert Eagle and signaled for Simmons to come over and place Jazir under arrest. Then he walked over to Myers, who was looking as confused as Jazir.

"What the hell was that all about?" Myers asked "I thought you were going to kill the poor bastard."

"I was never gong to kill him." York replied. "Yeah, I wanted to, you have no idea how much I wanted to. When I signed up for ATS, I'll admit the only driving force behind my decision was revenge. Something changed yesterday though.

When I saw all of those kids' bodies all over the place, I realized that I can make a difference in what I do here. We are entrusted to stop shit like this happening. That's exactly what I got from him."

Myers still looked confused "So why the hell did you go dark?"

"I had to. I didn't want you and the rest of the team to be involved if my emotions got the better of me. To be honest, there were a couple of moments where they very nearly did. But I kept it together."

Myers began to understand a little now; it was actually a normal thing for York to do. He couldn't understand why he hadn't thought about it before, instead of panicking. On a few occasions in the past, York had decided to work completely alone without the knowledge of anyone in the team to protect them. York could be called many things, crazy, immature at times. But the one thing no one could ever call him was selfish.

"So what did you get from him?" Myers inquired, hoping it would be something good.

York pulled out his phone and threw it in the air for Myers to catch "I got us a bargaining chip." Then he walked off up the dirt path to where he figured the car and the rest of the team was waiting.

Myers looked at the phone. The voice recording screen was open. He pressed exit then opened up the files, choosing RECORDED CLIPS. There was only one file on there, it had no name. He opened it and listened intently to everything that York and Jazir had said since they got to the woods. There was only one thing that stuck out in his mind about the whole conversation though. Only one question came to mind. "What the hell did Henshaw have to do with anything?"

Fifteen minutes later they were on the road back to HQ. Before they had left, York searched Jazir's car, finding nothing of interest apart from one thing. Jazir's diary. The list of names and contacts seemed endless. Jazir was a reputable business man and his connections in so many areas were invaluable. York found it amusing that even with all of those contacts, some of whom were members of the justice system, there was no one who could help him out of the trouble he was in now.

He recognized some of the names in the book but not all of them. He would have to pass it on to Kirk and his team down in the tech rooms, so they could check each and every name for criminal records or known terrorist connections.

After scanning the diary from front to back, he pulled out his phone from his pocket and pressed the speed dial button for Henshaw's office. The line rang ten times then went through to divert. There was another ring then Henshaw answered. "Yes Alex?"

"Sir we're about five minutes away." York informed him. "Is the interrogation room ready?"

"Yes, I have raised the temperature slightly as you requested. Let him mull over his options for a while before we grill him though. I'd like you to come to my office when you get back for your debriefing."

York remembered the words Jazir had said 'Ask your boss' He had every intention of doing just that. He couldn't believe that his captain was involved some how, but if he was York was determined to find out how.

"I will come straight up after dropping Jazir off sir." York finally answered "I have something I need to discuss with you anyway."

Henshaw didn't question York about what it was he wanted. He knew full well that discussing important matters over the phone was the biggest mistake any Government Agent could do. There was no way of telling who could be listening in.

Once he had hung up the phone, he gazed out of the window. He suddenly realized that he hadn't eaten all day and the puckish feeling was growing. They couldn't stop though, he would have to wait.

He turned and looked at Myers, who seemed as if he was in utter amazement as he drove the Rolls Royce through Brighton and on to the sea front road. When York had decided that they were going to transport Jazir's car while Simmons took Jazir, Myers had pretty much begged to be the designated driver. When York agreed, He seemed as excited as a child on Christmas morning.

"Nice drive is it?" York asked, feeling slightly jealous.

"You have no idea." Myers came back. "This is as luxury as they come. I still don't know why you haven't bought one."

York shook his head "If I'm honest, the only people I see driving these things are fat, bald City Slickers with no respect for anyone other that themselves and their bank balances. No thanks."

"I see your point." Myers said with a smile. The smile faded and he looked round at York "What the hell do you think that Jazir meant when he said ask your boss?"

York bowed his head, not really sure how to answer. He wished he knew. "I have no idea." He finally responded "But I am determined to find out."

26

They arrived back at HQ ten minutes later after getting stuck in a line of traffic caused by road works. York got out of the car and dragged Jazir out of the back. He led him to the lift at the end of the car park, closely followed by Myers. The doors opened as soon as York pressed the button. The ride to the fourth floor, where the interrogation rooms were situated, was short. No words were exchanged, although York had many more questions to ask. Really, the more he thought about it, he actually just wanted to put a bullet in Jazir's head more than anything. He hated that they needed this scum bag, without him they would never find the bomb.

They stepped out of a lift and turned right down a narrow corridor. There were two doors on either side at the end. York led Jazir through the first door on the left.

The room they were in bore no decoration. The walls were simply concrete and the floor was covered in shabby carpet tiles. There was a steel table and two chairs in the centre of the room. York sat Jazir down on one of the chairs facing a large mirror window in the centre of the wall.

He said nothing as he left the room and joined Myers in the next room, which was the opposite side of the mirror window. There were various computer monitors placed all around the room. Some could measure heart rate, body temperature etc. One of them was simply for the technician to make notes and file his reports.

The technician was a tall, wiry man with a well looked after bald patch on the top of his head. His glasses seemed to York as if they could be used for star gazing. He had a thin face with no facial hair. To any one who didn't know him, he looked more like a serial killer than a government agent.

York and most of the rest of the team at ATS would agree that Gary Clancy was one of the best in his line of work. He had started out in the police force, sitting in on interrogations and brining in high tech equipment to try and read suspects, or just to give them a fright so they confessed. When he was hired by ATS, he was thrown straight in at the deep end. A notorious Terrorist cell leader had been brought in by MI5 for interrogation on his first day. He had to familiarise himself with the computers in just ten minutes before the interview started. From then on, he had never looked back on the decision he had made.

The past few years had also given Clancy a knack for detecting signals of lies and suspicious behaviour. When he stared at the face of Jazir however, he could see no signs of nervousness. In fact, he could tell of no emotional signs what so ever.

"I see you have a challenge for me." He said to York as he entered.

York laughed, sensing the sarcastic tone in Gary's voice. "He will be a tough nut to crack that one." York informed him. "He shows no signs of fear at all. I would take some extra measures when you speak to him."

"How far would you like me to go?" Gary asked

York looked at Jazir; the hate for him was as strong as it had been earlier. He wanted this man to suffer. "Do what ever you need to. We need him to break. I'll be back down in twenty minutes to check on progress."

York left the room and made his way back to the lift.

He rode up one floor to the operations and investigations floor. The lift opened on to another corridor. This time, the door he wanted was straight ahead. He walked through in to a room filled with a dozen people working at computer screens; all of them part of the investigations and operations team. On the right hand side of the room, there was a separate office with whitewashed glass frontage. On the door the name tag read Kirk Stevens.

He walked over to the door and knocked before he walked in. Kirk was sitting at his desk, working hard on his computer. His office was kitted out with mostly Star Trek memorabilia. York always thought it bordered on obsession, but Kirk simply called it a passion.

"Alex, what's up my friend?" Kirk asked with a strangely happy grin painted on his face.

"I need a favour." York answered, getting straight to the point. "It's a bit of a delicate matter. Very hush, hush."

Kirk sat back in his chair; he gave York an intriguing look "Ok, sounds interesting. I like those sorts of favours. Actually, I like the return favours better."

York smiled, even in the worst of circumstances Kirk's sense of humour could always bring a smile to his face. "I need you to look in to all the calls the captain has made and received in the last few days."

Kirks enthusasm seemed to drain away in a matter of seconds. His grin turned to a worried frown. "Do you really think I can do that without him noticing?"

"I'll be honest, if my hunch is correct, it will be a difficult task and it is more than likely he will have taken certain measures to ensure no one is doing exactly what I am asking of you. So if you choose to do it, you will have to be careful. Just remember, you do have a choice. If you're not comfortable, then I won't hold it against you."

Kirk sat in silence for a few moments, contemplating his options. He had known York for a long time and he had never asked for anything unless he had a very good reason. Whatever he had found or been told, Kirk mused, he obviously needed the right evidence to tell anyone what it was. It all came down to trust and he trusted York with his life.

"Ok." Kirk finally agreed. "I'll do it."

York let out a sigh of relief. For a moment, he thought he would have to find his own way of getting what he needed "How long before you can get it for me?"

Kirk tapped a few commands in to his computer and waited for a few seconds. "How about in, oh say, ten seconds time." He said confidently. He tapped a few more buttons then turned the screen so York could see it.

There was a long list of numbers running from the top of the screen to the bottom. Each of them had call time, duration and date next to them. York scanned the dates and found yesterdays. He looked at the phone numbers beyond that point. Henshaw had received a lot of calls, but York knew he would have being the head of a government agency. There was one number that stuck out. There had been over ten calls made to and from it throughout the day and nearly double that today. He wrote the number down on a scrap of paper from Kirk's desk and stuffed it in his pocket.

"You're a diamond in disguise Kirky. I owe you one." York said as he headed for the door.

"Actually." Kirk replied before York walked out of the

door. "I think you owe me a lot more than one."

York turned and looked at Kirk with a big grin on his face "Who's counting." He said, and then he left the office.

He took the lift up to the sixth floor and walked through to his office. He dug the piece of paper out of his pocket and opened it out on the desk. He stared at it for a while, hoping that it would lead to absolutely nothing. The last thing he wanted was to find out that his boss and good friend had been playing against him throughout the past two days. But there were things that seemed to fit with his theory. Like the fact that Henshaw had arrived on the scene of the club bombing so early. Then again, he thought, maybe the stakeout he said he was on was real. It wasn't just that, he couldn't understand why Reign had been released. The defence secretary knew this. The evidence against him was enough to have him thrown in prison for the rest of his life, yet he was still cut loose. It was a perfect example of how messed up the British justice system

Then there was the fact that Reign had cleared the industrial unit of pretty much all trace of their existence. He had to have been tipped off. Could it have been Henshaw? He asked himself.

He picked up the phone and dialled slowly. He could feel the palms of his hands begin to sweat. He was shaking slightly too. He couldn't help but wonder if he was just being pathetic or if his feelings were completely justified.

The line rang six times then went over to answer phone. As the recorded message kicked in, York almost dropped the phone. He was trembling harder now. A sick feeling began to rise in his stomach. All the suspicions he had about Henshaw, which hadn't come about until Jazir had mentioned his name, were now confirmed.

This was it; there was no going back now. No undoing what he had just done. No way to erase the voice of the message from his mind. The words of the man kept repeating in his head. He tried so hard to connect the dots, but every time he thought for a few seconds, that voice would pop back up.

They were such simple words, an introduction. Yet to York, at that moment in time, they were more than just words. They were life altering. They destroyed every thing he had ever been taught by Henshaw. Those simple Words "This is Danny Reign. Leave a message."

27

York composed himself for a moment before leaving his office and heading down the corridor towards Henshaw's. He had not even thought about what he was going to say. It was all too much to take in. He couldn't imagine Henshaw turning against his country, he had been a true patriot all his life and for him to suddenly work with the likes of Reign seemed unreal.

He stood outside the door to Henshaw's office for a few seconds before knocking, taking a deep breath as he waited for a reply.

"Come in." Henshaw finally answered.

Henshaw was sitting at his chair staring out over the English Channel. He loved to watch the people enjoying the hot summers on the beach and watching ships pass every so often in the distance.

"Sit down Alex." He ordered.

"I'd rather stand thanks." York replied with slight attitude.

Henshaw turned his gaze from the window view to York. He was standing just inside the door with his arms folded. He could clearly tell something was bothering him; he had an idea what it was.

"Alex I know the memory of what happened to your mum and dad is still fresh in your mind. But I will not condone you taking it upon yourself to punish Jazir. That was a stupid move and one that could have cost you your career."

York laughed, he knew as soon as he was out of ear shot someone would be on the phone to Henshaw giving their interpretation of the events. He also knew that person was none other than Agent Simmons.

"Sir, my actions today, I will admit, were less than perfect. But I did get the result we needed. I found the man responsible and I caught him."

"Maybe so. But your methods weren't exactly standard procedure. Since when have we allowed torture to gain information?"

York knew this rubbish could go on for a while. Here he was getting a grilling about what's right and what's wrong by a man who, unless he was very much mistaken, was involved with the whole thing in some way. It wasn't right, he had to act now.

"That's a good question. How about this one though. Since when do we allow back stabbing, two faced traitors to run ATS?" York tried to think of ways to put his point across politely, but he couldn't think of a single way to do it.

Henshaw stood and slammed his fists on the desk "What the hell do you mean?"

York placed his phone down on the desk and played the recording of him and Jazir. Henshaw seemed to calm down slightly until he heard the part that incriminated him.

"You can't actually believe this nonsense?" He asked his voice slightly shaky.

"I refused to." York stated.

Henshaw let out a long sigh.

"That was of course until I decided to get Kirk to check up on your recent calls."

"What gives you the right to check up on me?" Henshaw spluttered, his blood pressure obviously rising to boiling point again.

"It's my job sir. If I suspect anyone, no matter who it might be, I have to check it out. You taught me that when I first joined. Funny how your own teaching can backfire on you isn't it."

Henshaw sat back down. He knew exactly what York would have found. He cursed himself for not being more careful, he never expected to be the one under surveillance. That was his mistake though. He knew how good York was at his job. There was always a risk that he would find out but he just simply decided to ignore it. "What exactly did you find?"

"I know that you have been in constant communication with Danny Reign." York stated. "As you can tell from the tape, I can also assume you have something to do with Jazir and everything we have been through in the past two days."

Henshaw bowed his head. He was a caught man and he knew it. There was only one thing to do now, he had to confess everything. He looked at York "Please sit down. This may take a while."

York sat on sofa and waited patiently for Henshaw to begin, hoping it wouldn't take as long as he made it seem.

"When I was just a rookie in the navy," Henshaw began. "I was approached by a man from the Defence secretary's office. He told me I had been picked to join a secret team of soldiers. We would carry out missions which needed to be completed under the strictest discretion. I was young and naturally I accepted. The team was made up of six men but we were divided in to two. Our first mission was to take out Allad Jazir, Salim's Father. We were told that he had been working for the Iraqi government developing chemical weapons. We completed the mission as asked and that was it. It wasn't until a month later that I found out what Jazir was really doing. He was in fact working for the British as Salim told you."

"You see Alex; someone had uncovered a new chemical which had disastrous effects. There were only a few people who ever knew about it. Our team was created to ensure it didn't fall in to the hands of terrorists. The thing was; we had not been told about the chemical. As far as we were concerned, we were nothing more than just another special forces group."

He paused to take a sip from his glass of water sitting on his desk "At least, most of us didn't know. There was one of us who were fully aware of what was going on. In fact, he was the man who set the whole thing up. Back in those days, Whitburn had climbed through the ranks of the marines faster than anyone could have imagined. He decided out of the blue to quit the corps, that's when our team was built."

"I take it he was one of the members." York injected.

"That's correct. Apparently, he was the one who found the chemical and took his findings to some top government officials and they financed the whole thing. Killing Jazir was our only mission though. We were reassigned straight after."

"So who were the rest of the team members?" York asked.

"The three who weren't with me were sent in first, but they were all killed by a random land mine. The other two who made up my team were Whitburn." He paused again to take a deep breath "And your Father."

York couldn't believe what he was hearing. His dad

was once a Special Forces operative. There was one thing that didn't fit "Wait a second. How the hell did my dad end up on a Special Forces team? He was never in the army or anything."

"You're right, he was never a soldier. He was though a government spy and a damn good one. That's why he was chosen."

York could hardly believe what he was hearing. He was learning things about the man he looked up to the most that no one had ever taken the time to tell him. Why? He wondered. His father was no longer here, it would not have hurt any one if he had just been told the truth in the first place. "Ok, so my father was what MI5?"

"MI6 actually, mostly foreign operations. Anyway back to what I was saying. I found out that Whitburn was planning to use this stuff in the future. He was going to provide soldiers with access to grenades filled with it and use as an interrogation method. If the captive didn't speak, he would be injected with it. From what I can make out, it is a pretty horrible way to die."

"So that's why Jazir bombed the plane we were on and why he wants me to abduct the PM." York mused out loud.

"What?" Henshaw winced.

York was surprised that Simmons had left that part out. Then he realised that no one had heard of the phone call, only of the conversation they had in the woods. "Back at Reigns base he called me and told me I had to bring the PM to him by nine thirty pm or he would detonate the bomb."

Henshaw took a moment to process the new information. "What did you tell him?"

"Nothing. Of course I had no intention of actually doing it. What about the other thing? The calls you have made to reign, what are they about?"

Henshaw sighed "I can't tell you Alex."

York's face hardened, "Bullshit." He scorned "I think that I have more than earned the right to know why the fuck you are in communication with a man who yesterday blew up a club and committed mass murder."

"We had nothing to do with that." Henshaw blurted out.

York took a moment to take in what Henshaw had just revealed. "What the hell do you mean by 'We'?"

Henshaw hung his head and let out another sigh. He hadn't meant to say it, but he couldn't help himself. York had been right in the fact that he had earned his right to know what was going on. He had been like a son to him for many years, he owed him.

"All paperwork to do with team that was set up to take out Jazir was thrown to the back of the cabinet as soon as we finished the mission." Henshaw explained "It remained there for a lot of years, until Whitburn became Prime Minister. He realised that the team could play a vital part in clamping down on global terror. So he found the best men from all over the world to join the team. He came to me to run it, more because I already ran this place so I could do it all discreetly from here. We work mostly for governments all over the world."

Suddenly, everything started to make sense. For as long as York had worked for ATS, Henshaw had times where he would disappear for days at a time with no word on where he was going or when he would be back. He didn't for a second think this was the reason for it.

He knew he had seriously misjudged Reign; he was on

the same side. But the more he thought about it, the more he couldn't understand why they were working for Jazir.

"There is just one thing I need to ask. If you are really on our side, why the hell did you let Jazir bomb the club and why did you allow him to get a weapon of mass destruction in to London?"

"We had no idea what was going on. All we were told was to deliver Bennett and a small package to the destination. As far as we knew, it was just supposed to be a hostage taking with no casualties"

York was trying to read Henshaw's eyes as he spoke; he seemed to be telling the truth. "Who gave you your orders?" He asked.

"The orders came from the Secretary of State for Defence"

"The Defence Secretary? What the hell has he got to do with any of this?"

"The Prime Minister placed him in charge of the unit. He is my boss" He paused for a second to wait for a response, none came. "Please understand Alex, this has to be kept classified. No one and I mean no one can know about this."

"Of course, I understand. I am sorry I doubted you sir."

Henshaw smiled, he knew he had made a great agent in York "You did your job Alex. You did it very well."

"I do have just one more question sir. Why were you doing things for Jazir?"

"I have no idea. One of the rules of the game is we don't ask questions. It means we can maintain full deniability."

Silence filled the room as they both concentrated on

their own thoughts. York could not quite come to terms that his boss and good friend had been living this double life.

Henshaw was beating himself up inside over what he had just revealed. It was highly classified information and it had just rolled off his tongue so easily. Maybe it was because he knew he could trust York. He knew things about the agents past that could never be repeated to anyone. Maybe it was just because he felt some level of responsibility over what had happened to all those young people, he couldn't tell for sure. But there was one thing he was sure of, His secret would be safe with York.

"So where do we go from here?" Henshaw asked breaking the silence.

York shook his head "I have no idea. I don't think we will be able to break Jazir in time. I also know there is no way I will abduct Whitburn."

"There is only one thing left to do then." Henshaw stated "We have to find that bomb."

28

York left Henshaw's office and headed back down to the interrogation room where Jazir was being held. The new information he had just been given was hard to take in. He still couldn't believe that Henshaw had been heading up a secret unit. He felt some what proud of the man. He had enough work on his hands with ATS, let alone taking on the responsibilities of the other lot. He was doing it for his country though. York told himself.

He walked in to the room next to where Jazir was being held. Myers was watching intently as Gary was performing the interrogation.

"How's it going?" He asked, knowing it was not going to be good news by the look on his partners face.

"He's not going to give us the location." Myers replied, frustration showing in his voice. "He keeps saying he will give us what we want if you do as you have been asked."

"Has everyone else been notified about the bomb?"

Myers nodded "Yes, I called up to Kirk a little while ago and gave him an up to date report. His team is searching high and low for Intel. What happened with Henshaw?"

York didn't answer. He hated lying to Myers but he had given his word, he couldn't say anything "Not much, he just wanted to give me a bit of a grilling over the whole Jazir incident."

York stared trough the glass and looked directly in to Jazir's eyes. They seemed fixed, emotionless. "I want to talk to him." He said, and then he walked out of the door and in to the room. He signalled for Gary to leave. It was now just him and Jazir again.

Strangely, Jazir seemed a lot more fearful about being alone with York than anyone else. York noticed the beads of sweat falling down his face. If there was going to be a time to break him, it was now.

"You comfortable Salim?" York asked

"Don't patronise me Alex. I know you are here to do the same as that man but I can assure you I will never tell you what you want to know."

York leaned in close to Jazir's ear and lowered his voice to a whisper "I'm not here to ask you anything Salim. I just want you to know when this is over; I will be coming for you." Then he left the room.

He walked back in to the room where Gary and Myers were watching.

"That will put the wind up him for you; try your best with him." He said to Gary.

"Do you think he will break with the right persuasion?" Myers asked nodding towards Jazir, who seemed a little more nervous now.

"Let's hope so." York answered. He looked at his watch; it was almost 15:30. They were running out of time fast, he knew there was no way they could break Jazir, get to the sight and disarm the bomb in the space of six hours. It was likely to be a highly populated area, in which case they would need to evacuate the area which would take more time.

"It's no good, we need to find that bomb and fast." York stated "Gary can keep pressing Jazir. We can have Kirk and his team looking in to who Jazir has been with in the passed few hours."

"So what do we do?" Myers asked.

"We're going to London my friend."

Henshaw sat and listened to York's plan, then gave him the go ahead. Once they had left, he picked up the phone and pressed 3. The line rang a few times before there was an answer.

"Defence Secretaries office, how may I help you?" The female voice answered.

"This is Tom Henshaw. I need to speak with Mr Connors right away."

"Yes Mr Henshaw. I'll put you straight through."

Henshaw couldn't help but wonder what she meant by straight through. He was put on hold for at least ten minutes. He hated that music everyone played these days when they put you on hold. The household amenities companies were the worst, especially gas and electricity companies. They would play the worst possible music down the line in the hope it might persuade you to hang up. He never did though.

When Connors finally answered, he sounded different than usual. Under these circumstances, he would usually sound upbeat, but today he seemed quiet and fed up.

"Hello Tom. What can I do for you?" Connors asked.

"Hello sir. I thought I better mention we have Salim Jazir in Custody."

There was a brief silence on the line; Henshaw could hear Connors' long, deep breaths. "Ok Tom, we need to make sure he doesn't talk. He can not expose our unit. If he does, Whitburn's term in office is over and we will be goners."

"Yes sir, I agree. I can't imagine that he will talk. There

is one more thing."

"What is it Tom?" Connors asked, sounding a little more frustrated.

"I take it news of the bomb has reached you." Henshaw replied.

"Yes it has. We are taking the Prime Minister to a safe house. I am staying put though. I can work better from here. Will that be all?"

"Yes sir. Thank you." Then Henshaw placed the phone back on the receiver.

York and Myers walked through the doors in to the O-I room. Kirk was standing in the doorway of his office looking through some paperwork with another techie. He seemed almost engrossed in the information.

York walked up to him and tapped him on the back "I hope that's a good read." He said with a smile.

Kirk looked through his ridiculously strong glasses at York. He didn't look impressed. "I have these guys working their butts off to find possible locations for the bomb." He paused and motioned them in to his office. He walked round the desk and sat in his swivel chair.

"I took in to account the time he gave you." Kirk continued. "I have to say, it seems odd. Most work places are closed by that time. The subways are no where near as busy as earlier in the day. In fact, I would say the best place to put a bomb would be a residential area."

York noted what Kirk said and nodded "So do we have anything?"

Kirk let out a laugh "That's the thing; there are so

many housing estates in London that we wouldn't know where to start."

The three of them sat in silence for a second, trying hard to think of possible high casualty areas. It was Myers who spoke first.

"What about arenas?" He asked with a slight bit of excitement in his voice. He wasn't used to being the first to come up with something.

"I haven't looked in to that area. It can't hurt I suppose. I don't think there is much going on but it is worth a shot."

"Do the best you can Kirk." Said York, trying to egg him on. "We are heading up to London to start the search. The minute you find anything, call us ok."

Kirk nodded as both York and Myers stood and walked out of the door. He hated when things like this came up. Working at a fast pace was not his best asset. He like to be thorough, he knew full well how many mistakes could be made if he rushed his work. This was no time for mistakes though. Now the stakes were higher than they had ever been in the time he had worked for ATS.

York and Myers left the O-I Room and took the lift down to the car park. When the doors opened, York saw a face he had been longing to see since yesterday. She seemed much more striking every time he laid eyes on her. She was wearing a long black dress that seemed to gracefully flow over her curves. Her hair had been perfectly straightened and her eyes seemed to glisten under the lights.

She rushed up to York and threw her arms around him, then pressed her lips against his as tight as she could. "What the hell happened to you this morning?" She asked as she pulled away. "I had a call saying you had gone crazy and kidnapped some one. Is that true?"

York sighed "Yes, but I was in complete control the whole time. I knew what I was doing."

She shook her head at him. Her expression seemed to change from concern to anger in a blink. "Don't you scare me like that again you bastard. I thought you were in trouble."

York smiled; no one had really had as much concern over him as she did since his mum. Sarah reminded him of her a little. She was as caring and gentle and they both had a fiery temper when he did something they didn't like. He felt almost safe when he was around Sarah, like nothing else in the world really mattered.

"So what's with the fancy dress?" York asked, looking her up and down. "I hope that wasn't just for my benefit."

She gave him a look that suggested 'wishful thinking' "Actually I have a seminar to go to in Southampton tonight. I would have invited you, but given the situation I can't see you being available."

York looked over at Myers, who was standing by his Range Rover. "I tell you what." He said pulling her close "How about I go and save the country from bad guys, then I will join you after that. I'm thinking a posh Hotel; Champagne; maybe a nice Jacuzzi bath. What do you say?"

She leaned in and kissed him passionately then said "I say, perfect. I don't think I will be able to concentrate on the seminar now." With that she walked in to the lift. As the doors closed, she blew him a kiss.

Wow, was all that went through York's mind. He had

never had anyone like her before. His dating history had been short. Whilst he was young, he never went out to pubs and clubs, it wasn't his scene. Instead he spent most of his time in the gym or reading. His friends called him boring, he called them foolish for thinking partying and drinking would ever get them any where.

No one had ever really understood him except Myers, until Sarah came along. She had always known there was more to him than met the eye and slowly she was being proven right.

He walked up to the car and suddenly it dawned on him, he had left the car at the Pease Pottage services. "Care to explain?" He asked Myers.

"What?" He replied. "I couldn't just let it get stolen now could I? It's a nice car, if you don't want it, I'll have it."

York smiled, Myers was always looking out for him "I'll let you drive then."

29

The journey had been crowded, stuffy and all round horrible. He hated public transport everywhere, not just in Britain. It amazed him that some people, usually the fat business men, refrained from ever buying anti-perspirant deodorant sprays. They all seemed to think that a can of body spray was always enough. The smell that they gave off was sickening. Not one of them seemed to be wise to the fact though, they all seemed ignorant.

When Ahmed arrived at Victoria Station, he kept his head down and simply walked with the crowd. If the authorities had become wise to the bomb, they would have armed police crawling all over the stations. He saw none as he walked through, a sigh of relief was needed.

It wasn't far to go now, just a short ride on the underground Jubilee line to Canning Town then two stops on the DLR (Docklands Light Railway). It wasn't quite over then though, his target was well guarded. When he entered, there would, without doubt, be bag searches. He had to come up with a plan to get in. One look in the case and the mission would be over.

He stepped off the DLR train and looked directly at his target. It was a lot larger than he had imagined. Having never stepped foot into London in his life, he had never really come to understand the magnitude of the attractions.

He walked off the station and made his way down the path towards the main entrance. There were a few cars in the car park, which he knew would belong to the staff as the centre didn't open for another few hours yet. He too would have to wait for the place to open before he could put the final part of the mission in to action.

He found himself a seat which overlooked the river Thames. The docklands were busy; Cargo ships sailed up and down the river all loaded with containers. Crewmen were hard at work and the dock workers were scurrying about in a never ending, fast paced mode.

He looked down the river, either side was packed with buildings and work sites. He felt the beauty of what Allah had created had been ruined by the commercial living that drove the western communities. It was places like this that destroyed the earth. The pollution that the factories were creating disgusted him. It seemed to Ahmed that none of the people who worked in these places gave a damn. This was one of the reasons he had agreed to take on the assignment. Slowly but surely the world was being overtaken by commercialism and he felt it was his responsibility to take action.

The hours passed slowly as he sat in his own thoughts. The car park began to fill slowly behind him; men and women dressed in suits were beginning to queue up at the main entrance. He suddenly realise another problem had arisen. If he walked up in the Jeans and t-shirt he was wearing, he would stand out like a sore thumb. He had to do something soon.

He had to get the choice right; he had to find someone who was the same size as him. He walked through the car park and watched the people arriving. Judging the size of the men was not as hard as it seemed and soon he found a target. The man drove a brand new Ferrari 575. Perfect, Ahmed thought, if he was like the rest of the self indulgent pricks that drove these sorts of machines, he would come running when the alarm goes off.

He let the driver get to the queue before he made his way to the car. He kept low and out of sight. As he got to the car, he searched around for something he could use to cave the window in. There was nothing, he had to come up with another plan. He looked down at the briefcase in his hand, perfect. He held the case tightly and swung it at the window. For an expensive car, he thought it would have taken at least two attempts to weaken the glass. It offered no resistance though. On the first swing, the glass shattered and the sound of the alarm silenced the crown by the building.

He crept a few cars down and waited for the man to arrive to investigate. Now came the second phase of the plan. He had to take the mans clothes. The fact he had arrived alone meant no one would miss him and go looking for him, the problem was he was in a busy car park and it was still light.

The man approached and seemed frantic at the sight of the damage to his car. It was obviously his most prized possession, which seemed incredibly sad to Ahmed. The man looked around, searching for the culprit responsible for the damage. He didn't see Ahmed coming at him; He felt a sudden pain shoot through his head as Ahmed brought the case smashing down on to the back of his skull. The impact immediately knocked him unconscious and his body fell to the floor. .

Ahmed checked his pulse, he was still alive. He quickly undressed the man and threw the clothes in to the super car. Then he jumped in to the driver's seat and began to change. No one had noticed the struggle; they all just carried on with their conversations, which suited Ahmed down to the ground.

The suite actually felt pretty good to wear. The fabric was incredibly soft and light. The shoes were slightly big, but not enough to make any sort of difference to him. He picked up the unconscious man and placed him in the car. Then he locked the car and threw the keys away.

He walked over to the entrance where people were now being let in to the building. He joined the queue and did his best to simply blend in to the crowd. Five minutes was all it took before he was at the guard's station.

"Invitation please." The guard demanded.

Ahmed felt around his pockets, trying to buy some time, he had to think of something fast. He was unaware he needed an invitation. Suddenly a slight hatred towards Jazir came over him. He had not been properly prepared for the mission and that angered him. He had no idea what he was going to do now, he knew if he had no invitation he would not be going in.

Luck seemed to be on his side today, as he felt in the inside pocket of the jacket he found what he was looking for. Allah was on his side for this one, he mused. He handed the invitation over to the guard, who looked at him questioningly. Ahmed began to feel nervous, this was the last hurdle he had to jump and it seemed ever more difficult.

The guard folded up the invitation and handed it back to Ahmed.

"Thank you sir, enjoy the conference." he said motioning him through.

Ahmed walked past the guard and as soon as he was out of ear shot, he let out a huge sigh of relief.

Henshaw made his way down to the holding room to where Jazir had been transferred to. After two hours of interrogation, nothing new had been revealed. The frustration could be noticed in everyone's faces. All had been hoping for an easy end, but all hope had now faded.

He opened the door to the cell and walked in to find Jazir sitting on the small bed in the left corner. The room was cold and damp. There was an awful smell in the room that made him retch. Even blocking his nose didn't help, it was as if something had died and begun decomposing in the air vent. He knew exactly what it was, to make the surroundings as uncomfortable as possible for the detainee, especially if they hold needed information.

"I see you have made yourself comfortable Mr Jazir." He said.

"I am far from comfortable." Jazir fired back in a harsh tone. "You assured me this would not happen."

Henshaw walked over and stood in front of him "I apologize for this; I must admit I didn't think it would." He sat on the bed next to Jazir "I have to say though, the fact that you were working against us leads me to believe this is the best place for you."

Jazir threw Henshaw a hard stare "What the hell do you mean. I told you what was involved when I hired you. There was no reason for you to know about any bomb that I planned to detonate. The fact is, it is you who has betrayed me."

"How do you figure?"

"Well," Jazir said as he stood and walked to the small window opposite, "You never told me you were working on behalf of the government."

Henshaw smiled, he loved it when the bad guys played the victim "You have been on the British Intelligence watch list for years now Salim. You didn't really think you could hire a unit who have worked for the government without us turning against you did you?"

Jazir didn't answer. He just gave Henshaw the same hard stare he had retained for the last few minutes.

"Anyway," Henshaw said to break the silence. "I will be transferring you to another location in a few minutes. I have made the arrangements and am just waiting for the papers to be drawn up by the holding officer so I can sign them."

Jazir's stare changed now, he was no longer looking angered. Now he was just confused. Where he was going to be taken, he wondered. Knowing the sort of people Henshaw was associated with; it wouldn't be a holiday camp. Where ever it was, he had to prepare himself for the worst.

Henshaw left the room, then returned a few minutes later. He was holding a pair of handcuffs which he roughly placed around Jazir's wrists. He grabbed him by the arm and forcefully led him to the door. They walked through the corridors then rode the lift down to the parking floor. Henshaw pretty much dragged Jazir over to his Jaguar.

"A little short of standard procedure today I see." Jazir stated. "Since when do prisoner transfers get made in the boss's car?"

Henshaw opened the rear passenger door and pushed Jazir inside. "Since now." Then he slammed the door.

Jazir sat in silence as they drove west. This was not part of his plan; he had trusted people today and had been betrayed.

He was however, very impressed with the fact that Henshaw and Reign were double crossing him and they never gave even the slightest hint. They must have worked extra hard to keep him from finding out, he mused. Being captured didn't bother him much, there was plenty they could hold him on sure, but he had a good team of lawyers who had a knack for making evidence disappear.

They drove for an hour solid before Henshaw pulled the car over in to a lay by in a quiet area. There were fields all around; they were empty, which could only mean there were no farmers around. They were alone and now Jazir was beginning to panic.

Henshaw turned and looked deep in to Jazir's eyes. "Why did you not tell me about the bomb?" He asked in a deep hateful tone.

Jazir looked at him. The rules had changed now; Henshaw was no longer under the tight reigns of the office. Here he could get the answers out of him any way he wanted. There was not much point in lying about anything anymore; there was no recording equipment around, no one taking notes. Whatever he said here, he knew, would stay here.

"I'll ask you again." Henshaw repeated, this time slightly more impatiently.

"I neglected to tell you because you didn't need to know." Jazir's voice was slightly shaky. "All I hired you to do was deliver the item and destroy any evidence that linked me to the crimes. I guess I was wrong in thinking that you could possibly undertake such a task."

Henshaw laughed "Do you really think that I had any intention of destroying that evidence. You knew when you hired us we worked closely with the government. So yes, you were wrong in thinking that." Henshaw paused and stared at Jazir for a moment. He seemed to be taking in what was said and realising his mistake. "Now I need you to tell me where the bomb is."

Jazir looked at Henshaw; he knew all his cards had been played. It was obvious he was not going to get what he wanted. The truth was he was not a monster. The killing of hundreds of innocent people would not heal the wounds set in place by Whitburn. The whole thing had just been a way to coerce York in to doing as he asked. That was his next mistake. He had underestimated York greatly and now he was regretting his actions.

"The bomb is at the Excel centre. It is set to go off at nine thirty." He bowed his head as he spoke as if he was ashamed of what he had done. Although most thought of his as an evil man now, the true side of Salim Jazir was slowly showing; the side that had gained him many friends and business associates.

Henshaw nodded. It had been easier than he thought to get the location out of him. That made his job a lot simpler. "Get out." He ordered.

Jazir looked at him with confusion written all over his face. He didn't argue though. He had seen these types of situations in the past. He simply opened the door and got out.

Henshaw pulled his phone from his pocket and dialled the number he wanted. There was an answer right away.

"Yes?" The voice on the other end said sternly.

"I have the location. It's in the Excel centre."

"Good. Let York know as soon as possible. We need

him to wrap this up quickly. He is still our strongest asset."

"I agree." Henshaw stopped to think for a second. He looked through the window at Jazir, who was walking slowly down the road. "What shall I do with Jazir?"

There was a short silence before the question was answered "Dispose of him." The voice finally came back

"Yes sir." Henshaw said, and then he hung up the phone.

He threw the Jaguar in to gear and slammed down on the accelerator. As he approached Jazir, his target suddenly launched himself out of the way and in to a ditch at the side of the road. Henshaw stopped the car and got out. He walked up to where Jazir was now struggling to his feet. He stretched his arm out; in his hand he held a fully loaded pistol. Jazir stared down the barrel of the gun, fear filled his hold body. He didn't have a chance to plead for his life before Henshaw pulled the trigger. The bullet smashed in to his forehead and exploded though the back of his head. Henshaw watched the man die instantly and crumble to the floor. He rolled his body back in to the ditch then turned and headed back to his car.

30

Sheldon Murphy pulled his car up to the front door of 10 Downing Street. The day had been a long one and was far from over. His team had been working every lead to find the man responsible for the attack on the club and the news that ATS had beaten him to it had been hard to swallow. All of his years of hard work to make it to the Director General position had almost been for nothing the day ATS were formed. They seemed to steal all of the field work leaving MI5 with nothing but desk jobs.

He still had his share of action though. ATS were nothing to do with London security. In fact, they seemed to just stick to the south coast mostly, leaving him with the rest of the country. Every now and again however, they ignored the rules by taking on cases that were out of their jurisdiction, much like tonight.

He had been getting ready to take an early finish when the word came in about the possible bomb threat on London. It wasn't so much the threat that angered him; he had a team who could take care of that part. It was the fact that Alex York had taken it upon himself to come to the city to track it down that really pushed his buttons. This was his area and he wasn't about to stand by and let ATS take all the glory.

There wasn't much he could do legally to stop York from coming, he could try his best to make sure MI5 found the bomb first though and then it was finder's keepers.

The years of hard work for MI5 had taken their toll on Murphy. His hair was now fully grey and the lines on his face seemed to become more noticeable as time wore on. At fifty five, he was in good physical shape though. He attended all kinds of fitness classes and worked out in the gym at least twice a week. It was essential for him to be in good condition, especially since he still loved to get his hands dirty out in the field. It was a part if him that would never die, the love of a little action now and again, he felt kept his love for the job alive.

He sat patiently in the car waiting for the Prime Minister to come out; he scanned the area for possible threats as he did every time he came here. It was an old habit he had acquired after a crazy member of the press tried to attack the PM a few years earlier. He had been placed on the right hand of Whitburn when he had taken office and had formed an immediate bond from there on.

When the door of No. 10 finally opened, the man heading towards the car was the man he had been expecting. The passenger door opened and Gavin Connors slipped in to the seat.

"Can I help you sir?" Murphy asked.

"I wanted an update on the search for the bomb. I understand your team is working hard to find it." Connors tone seemed slightly patronising.

"My team are the best in the country." Murphy barked not taking lightly to the sceptical tone the Defence Secretary was using. "If anyone can find it, we can."

Connors held up his hands "Hey, I'm just asking, there is no need to get defensive."

Murphy let out a sigh, then spoke in a calmer manner "I'm sorry sir, it has been a long couple of days, and what's more, Alex York is on his way to London to try and do the hero bit himself"

Connors looked straight ahead as if he were searching for something, some legal way to keep York from finding the bomb first. "There isn't much I can do, you know as well as he does that the jurisdictions were set in place as more of a moral agreement than anything else. The best that we can hope for is that you find it first."

Murphy nodded in agreement "That's exactly what I figured sir." He turned and looked at the Secretary "Are you planning to go with the PM to the safe house sir?"

"I wasn't going too originally." Connors replied, "But I think I will. If the bomb goes off, I am going to be needed to form a retaliation plan, I can't do that if I am dead now can I." He paused to laugh a little "That brings me to my next point. I have been in contact with a man who has been able to create the type of device we talked about. I believe you should be receiving it soon."

"I have already. I will keep it safe until you get the approval you need. To be honest, I don't think you will. The Prime Minister is a stubborn man; he knows that hitting an enemy country this hard could start World War Three."

"I sort of agree from that respect." Connors stated. "I feel that the risk is worth it though. We have many enemies and I think with the right method, we could bring our allies to feel the same way if we use the right method of persuasion." He paused for a moment to check his watch. "Anyway, back to the problem at hand. I wasn't aware the Director General had taxi service in his job description."

"It was sort of a last minute thing like yourself sir. Let's just say I may be of some use at the house, especially with the security strategy."

Connors agreed, who better to have running security than the DG himself. "I came out to make sure you were ready, as all is clear, I shall bring the PM out. Don't go away." With that he stepped out of the car and headed back inside.

While he waited, Murphy checked all was ready, he pulled his gun from its holster under his suit jacket and checked it was loaded, the placed it back. It was at least an hour's drive to the safe house and although they had a three car police escort, all of whom were armed; he knew you can never be too careful.

The journey took longer than Murphy had anticipated. The traffic through London was heavy and the constant road works didn't make it any easier. Once they were out of the city, the tension in the car seemed to drop, not for him though. He knew |York would soon be on the trail of the bomb and he didn't like it one bit. He had checked in with his team on a few occasions throughout the drive, but they had learnt nothing new.

He had always been in such control throughout his career that when things like this happened, it made him nervous. He always liked to ensure he knew exactly what was happening at every point of any operation. He hated being shut out, which was how he felt now. The more he thought about it though, the more he realised that it didn't really matter who found the bomb, as long as it was found. Here he was sitting thinking about how angry he was that ATS were going to get the glory for this one when there were potentially millions of people's lives at stake. He cursed himself for thinking like that.

He looked in the rear view mirror at the two politicians

sitting in the back. They had hardly spoken a word since leaving Downing Street. When they did speak, it was simply work orientated, there were no friendly words between these two and there never would be.

Shortly after Whitburn had taken office, the problems between the two of them started. Connors was unhappy with some of the actions and policies the Prime Minister had put in to action and he wasn't afraid to say it.

The conflict of strategies continued for some time until, during a press conference, Whitburn stood up in front of the entire nation and aired his disgust and anger at Connors for certain actions he had taken in the past.

Connors was often asked why he didn't just resign as Defence Secretary. He simply responded 'It's my job and I love it.'

Although they had their differences, they eventually managed to find common ground. They began to agree with each other on various tactics and actions and soon they were starting to make some great progress. Then over the past couple of days some of the arguing had started again. Especially when it came to the press conferences, Connors wanted to lie, Whitburn didn't.

Murphy pulled the car in to the drive way of the safe house. The house was big, at least five bedrooms, he mused. His security team were already there. He spotted one of them standing at the front door. He was a stocky man with short hair and a firearm strapped to his belt.

Murphy stopped the car, stepped out and opened the door for Whitburn, which was greeted with a thank you. He didn't bother to open the door for Connors as, to be perfectly honest; he had the same feelings towards him as Whitburn did.

They all walked inside and headed for the reception room. The room had been kept nicely. There were two three seater cream leather sofas sitting opposite each other in the centre with a large walnut coffee table separating them. They all made their way over and sat down, all partaking in the coffee that had been made ready for their arrival.

"So what is me being here actually going to achieve?" The PM asked bluntly. "I can't work form here."

"I am sorry sir" Murphy replied sincerely. "I am afraid it is protocol. If there is an immediate threat to London, we are to remove you until the threat is taken care of."

"We can't exactly have the Prime Minister killed in an attack" Connors interjected "It would take too long to get the replacement in and we would need to make plans for retaliation."

Whitburn sensed what Connors was really trying to say 'If you weren't the PM, we could have left you to die.' He didn't mind though, the truth was, he sort of felt the same way.

There was silence in the room; none of them knew what to say next. The situation over the last couple of days had been the worst for Whitburn since taking over office and the lack of sleep was starting to take its toll. He was so tired he could hardly think straight. He laid his head down on the arm rest slightly and shut his eyes for a second then he fell in to a deep sleep.

Connors sat silently and sipped on his coffee while Murphy went to check in on the surveillance team. When he arrived back, he was joined by one of the guards. He looked different to rest of them. There were a couple of them who looked like the sorts you would see guarding the doors of a night club. This man was different though. He had a real hard look about him. There would definitely be no way anyone would dream of standing in this guy's way, he thought. But as he looked closer, the man had small cuts on his face and a bruise on the top of his almost fully bald head.

He looked back to Murphy "Who the hell is this great lug?" He asked with a smirk on his face.

"This Gavin." Murphy replied. "Is the man who is going to ensure we are kept as safe as possible. I'd like you to meet Danny Reign."

Connors merely smiled and went back to his coffee, staring across at the other sofa where Whitburn seemed to be dead to the world.

31

When the call came through, York and Myers were only about ten miles away. York put the accelerator to the floor. The Range Rover kicked in to full speed down the busy motorway. York moved the car in and out of the traffic with ease. During his time in the military, he had under gone intensive driver training. He had been told to drive a four wheel drive vehicle through a forest in the dead of night with no headlights. Compared to that, this was easy.

Within twenty minutes of the call, he pulled in to the Excel centre car park. He had never been to the centre before and was amazed at the sheer size of it. The design of the place was simple, he thought, it was simply a huge rectangle with what looked like decorative steel piping along each side of the roof all forming triangular shapes. He figured the beams had some sort of structural purpose and if that were true then the whole building would also be made of steel framing. This made his objective slightly simpler.

He saw a few police cars surrounding another car parked a few meters away and headed straight for them. As he approached, an officer walked up to the driver's door. York wound down the window.

"I am afraid the car park is being closed off sir." The officer informed him.

York pulled out his ATS ID from the glove box and handed it to the officer "What's going on?" He asked.

The officer nodded towards the Ferrari "Security found a man unconscious in the driver's seat. He had been stripped. When we got here, he had come to and said a man had attacked him."

York looked around; the victim was still there, sitting in the back seat of a police car. "I am going to need to speak to him."

"He is pretty shaken up. I guess you could though."

As the officer began to walk away, York got his attention again "I think you better get your superiors down here. If my intelligence is correct, the situation is far worse than a mugging."

York and Myers stepped out of the car and walked towards the car where the victim was sitting. York immediately noticed he was still wearing an expensive Rolex watch on his right hand. And he had what looked like a real diamond stud in his ear...

York crouched down so he was at eye level with the victim then offered out his hand "Hi, my name is Alex York. I work for the National Anti-Terrorism Service. Are you fit to answer a few questions?"

The victim looked at him questioningly. "Sure." He replied, shaking York's hand. "But what the hell has this got to do with terrorism? I was mugged for crying out loud."

York shook his head "I don't think so sir. In fact, I think the man who attacked you was trying to gain access to the conference."

"Why?" The victim asked holding his head in slight pain.

"I am afraid I can't answer that. What I need is for you to try and describe the attacker for me."

The victim shut his eyes to try and visualise what he saw. It was hard, the whole thing had happened in a matter of seconds. "I never really got a good look at him. It all happened so quickly. I do know he was Middle Eastern though."

"Are you sure?" York waited for the nod, which he got. "Was there any other defining features about him. We need to try and identify him on the CCTV."

The man shook his head "I am sorry, I was knocked unconscious almost immediately."

"Thank you" York said then stood up and walked away.

He pulled his phone from his pocket and dialled the number. Kirk answered almost immediately. "ATS. Kirk speaking." He said in a posh manner.

"Kirk, its Alex. I need your help."

"Shoot." Kirk offered.

"I need you to access the surveillance footage for the excel centre. I haven't got a clue how to go about it; I know I just need it ASAP."

"It's a good thing I know exactly how to go about it then isn't it." Kirk gloated. "What do you need from it?"

"There is a Ferrari 575 parked in the outside car park. There was an attack here, the man we are looking for is definitely a foreigner, Middle Eastern I think."

Kirk laughed down the phone "That doesn't really narrow it down very much. Aren't there like millions of Middle Easterners in London?"

York didn't reply to the obvious racial remark. Although Kirk was no racist, he did have some strong words to say about the immigration laws over the years and usually, not very good ones.

"Ok, I can make a call and get the surveillance. I

should be back in contact within ten minutes."

York looked at his watch, it read 1958pm. He only had an hour and a half left, time was running out. "Ok, no longer though." He ordered.

"Hey." Kirk replied, in his usual sarcastic tone. Nothing ever seemed to faze him, even in the direst of circumstances; he could always keep the sarcasm going. "You do know I have been at your beck and call all day and haven't let you down yet."

Again York didn't reply he simply hung up the phone to allow Kirk to get on with it. He stood for a moment staring at the huge building in front of him. He felt seriously unnerved about the fact that inside, was a man who could wipe-out everything within a mile radius.

The chances were, that Jazir could have been in contact with his bomber at regular intervals early on in day, as he was in custody now, he couldn't have done that. He wondered what the bombers orders were in that instance. Was he to abort the mission, or was he to detonate.

York had been able to read Jazir pretty well by now. He knew that he was no ordinary terrorist bomber. Most of the attackers he had come across had been religion fuelled. Their mission was destruction, to kill the people they called infidels. They believed that what they were doing was the work of Allah. Jazir was different though, he was not fuelled by religion, he was fuelled by revenge. Was that more dangerous? he asked himself. His argument was not with the all of the people in the country, just with three of them and one he had already taken care of. York had a decision to make now, go in hard or try to talk him down.

He realised the man inside, although hired by Jazir, would not necessarily have the same views and motives. He knew he had no real choice left. There was only one option he had and that was to go in hard.

The chief inspector of the local police didn't take long to arrive. He looked slightly pissed though and York knew it would be at a couple of action junkies coming in and taking over his crime scene. He seemed as if he was on the final stretch of his career now. His hair had long greyed and his belly was putting his belt under severe pressure.

"Who the hell do you think you are? Coming down here and ordering my officers about." The CI barked at York.

York didn't let himself sink to the fat fuck's level; he remained calm even though inside he wanted to knock the fucker out. "I think you will find I have given them no orders." York informed him. "Yet." He added to dig the knife in a little deeper.

"On what grounds are you taking over this scene?" The CI Asked not changing his tone.

"On the grounds that there is a nutter in there with a bomb that could wipe out every thing within a mile of here." He hadn't meant to go in to so much detail, but he just could help but break. So much for calm.

The CI stood silent in complete shock. He was speechless. The news seemed to hit him harder that York thought it would. He seemed to be shaking slightly; obvious to York he had never been in such a dire situation before.

"What do you need?" He finally spoke, this time in a low nervous tone.

"I need you to close off the entire grounds." York

explained. "No one goes in and no one comes out, is that clear?"

The CI nodded then went back to his car to radio for back up as York's phone rang. He instantly recognised the number. "That was fast." He said as he answered.

"Once again I come through." Kirk replied smugly. "The man's name is Ahmed Atul. He is an ex Iraqi military fighter. He is good with explosives so if he has built this one, it will be tamper proof."

"I doubt he was the one who built it, he would have to be a chemical weapons specialist. Thanks Kirk, you did good again."

As he was about to hang up, Kirk stopped him. "Alex, you need to know something."

"What's that?" He asked

"A few hours ago Henshaw took Jazir from the building. He said he was transporting him to another location."

York couldn't understand why but he thought his captain must have had his reasons. "Ok." He said.

"Jazir was found dead in a ditch a little while later."

York could hardly believe it, he had no care for Jazir but it was a strange occurrence. "What about the captain?" He asked

There was a silence, which York knew meant bad news "There was a witness who said she saw an older man in a Jaguar shoot Jazir point blank. I think we can assume that the Captain is no longer on our side."

The news struck York like a fist to the gut. All the years he had known Henshaw, he would never have guessed him to be a traitor. Now all of the cards had changed. He realised that

Ahmed was now on his own; he now had the opportunity to try and talk Ahmed down. But a thought crossed his mind, he was treating this as if Ahmed had taken full control of the building and as far as he knew, he hadn't.

"Are you able to get me access to the live feed?" York asked.

York could hear Kirk's fingers tapping away on his keyboard. "I can't send it to you but I can tell you that it seems as if everything is as normal. The conference is still going."

"Thanks Kirk." Then he hung up the phone.

York looked around for Myers, who was busy trying to entertain the Chief Inspector. He walked over and grabbed him by the arm, pulling him away. "We need to talk." He said firmly.

He explained what Kirk had said about Jazir and Henshaw. Myers looked as stunned as him. "We need to get this over with quickly. I say we go in there now.

"Do we know where this Ahmed is?" Myers asked hopefully.

York shook his head "My guess is he would have edged his way out of the conference and planted the bomb by now. My guess is, as he got here so early, he is going to make a run for it."

Myers looked at the entrance "I think you're right. We need to go in now."

32

They didn't bother kitting out in their usual assault gear. They simply loaded their weapons and headed for the entrance. Once inside, they stared in amazement at the size of the inside. In front of them was a long corridor which made up the back bone of the centre. It stretched from one end to the other and was at least forty foot wide.

On either side of the corridor there were various different eating establishments and shops. On the right, there were doors that lead to the underground toilet areas. In between the shops and toilets, there were giant steel doors that lead to the two halls that, when opened up, stretched the whole length, but had partitions to separate them in to different areas.

They walked along the corridor to the centre of the building. In front of them was a set of stairs that led to the downstairs car park. Behind them was another set of stairs that led to an upstairs restaurant. The place was so big; they had no idea where they were going to start first. In the end they chose the conference room. If Ahmed was in there, they would find him, or at least that's what they thought.

When they entered the partition where the conference was being held, they realised that the chances of actually spotting him were somewhat slim. There were thousands of people, all dressed in smart suits.

"This is going to be hopeless." Myers said matter of factly.

York nodded in agreement, and then he had an idea. "Go and wait for me in the main entrance, I know how we can find him."

Then York headed towards the front of the hall. He walked up to one of the security officers standing by the stairs leading to the stage and whispered in his ear. Then he headed back out through the huge door and down the corridor. All he had to do now was wait for the right moment.

After a few moments, he heard the announcement being read over the microphone, 'Mr Ahmed Atul, you have a telephone call at the front entrance'. This could go one of two ways, He thought. Either Atul would realise he had been made or he would think it was Jazir. That was if, of course, he was still there.

As he waited for Ahmed to show his face, he watched the men and women from the meeting walking around, buying refreshments and heading for the lavatories. He couldn't help but feel slightly sorry for them, if he failed, they would all die today. Then again, he thought, so would he. Failure was not an option for him. He had to find that bomb and disarm it.

He knew he could evacuate these people from the building once he had located Ahmed. Until then, he could not. If the bomber got wind that they were there, he would definitely detonate.

Ahmed finished arming the device then placed it carefully in its spot. This was it now; this was what he had been building up to for weeks. All the preparations he had made. All of the dummy bombs he had built, all perfect replicas to the one he had just armed. Now he had to get away.

He could hear the noises from the conference in the background. It was hard to make out what they were talking about but in any case, it would not matter in a short time. Their pitiful lives would be nothing more than a memory to those who seemed to cherish their existence for reason he could not fathom.

He checked the case was in its rightful position then he made for the door. As he walked through, he heard the thing that he had been dreading throughout the whole mission, those words seemed to pierce right the way through his skin 'Mr Ahmed Atul'.

The worst had happened now, he had found. The message said he had a call, but no one knew he was here and there was no way it would have been Jazir, not this late on in the proceedings. He had been quite strict on the fact that once he had left with the package, there would be no more contact.

He began to run through in his mind what to do next. He couldn't run, the upstairs and the outside would be, he knew crammed with cops. There were two choices now; both were not good for him. He could either get caught or die. Neither one of them he particularly liked.

York waited patiently for over ten minutes before he decided give up. It was obvious to him that Ahmed was no longer in the building. If he was, he would have heard the announcement and if he was as smart as York was betting on, he would have realised they were here for him. It was obvious to him that Ahmed was not here.

He pulled the small communication radio from his pocket and pressed the button "Chief Inspector White. This is Alex York. We are clear for full search and evacuation."

As soon as he said the words, police burst in from both entrances at either end of the corridor. York raced to the room where the conference was being held and rushed up to the stage. He didn't waste any time explaining to the man at the microphone what was going on, he simply barged him out of the way.

He had to be as careful as he could when explaining to the people what was happening, the last thing he wanted was to create mass panic. He stared at the crowd for what seemed like a minute but was actually only about five seconds.

"Ladies and Gentlemen, I am sorry to interrupt your meeting." He paused to take a breath. One thing he had never really been good at was speaking in small groups let alone thousands of business men and women. "I am afraid that we have to ask each and every one of you to exit the building with immediate effect. Please ensure that you do this in an orderly fashion."

As he continued, people had already started to get up and head for the door. He was quite impressed with the way they were whilst exiting the room and heading down the corridor. Even the armed police, now scattered all over the building, didn't faze them. If this was Brighton, he thought, there would be pandemonium.

York stepped down from the stage where he was approached by the CI. After the tense way that they had met, he realised that he had not yet asked the fat mans name. "How is the search going Inspector?" He asked whilst stretching out his arm to make a proper introduction.

"Inspector Wycombe," He informed. "I don't believe I had the chance to learn your name."

"My name is Alex York."

The two shook hands. All tension that was there before

had now vanished. They could now work together without any hold backs "Have your men started the search?"

"Yes, they are searching the entire building. If your guy is still here, we'll find him."

York nodded and shook Wycombe's hand once again. Then he headed back out towards the corridor. There was hardly room to move in and out of the crowd. It was then it dawned on him, if Ahmed hadn't yet escaped, now was the perfect chance. He ran along the side of the corridor and through the glass doors at the end. Outside, the police were rounding up every one who came through and checking them for ID. There was no way Ahmed could chance going this way and all the other exits would surely be covered.

York thought for a moment. There were so many places he could be hiding. Only a few were open to the public. There was only really one place he thought he could be and that was the downstairs toilets. He ran back in to the building and along the left side of the corridor, barging passed anyone who gets in his way. The first toilets door came up a few meters in. He crashed through the door and flew down the stairs almost missing his step a couple of times. At the bottom he came to another door and the he was at the toilets. He checked the men's, nothing. Then he checked the women's, again nothing.

He rushed back up the stairs and along the corridor to the next door. He ran down the steps and checked both the ladies and the gents as before, again nothing. He was beginning to think he was barking up the wrong tree, that perhaps he had really done a runner.

He didn't rush up the stairs this time; he had lost hope

of finding Ahmed. As he walked through the door at the top, which took him back out in to the main corridor. He scanned the area. People were still making their way through the doors at the one end of the corridor. The other end was clear.

He was starting to loose hope of finding the Ahmed and the bomb. He walked down the corridor. To his left there was a set of stairs leading up to the seating area of the restaurant. He walked up the steps slowly, as he reached the top he looked to the left side, it was clear. To the right there was a door that seemed to be slightly open. He walked up and pushed the door open after grabbing his Desert Eagle that was tucked in to the back of his jeans.

The room behind the door was one of the smallest kitchens he had ever seen. It had been a recent addition to the centre after a costly makeover but in the short few months since it's re-opening, the restaurant had attracted a huge customer base and built a good reputation for good food.

He walked through the kitchen slowly with his weapon drawn and ready to fire if needed. The units were the cleanest he had seen in a long time, he was impressed. Cleanliness seemed to be at the bottom of the priority list with most restaurateurs these days. Here however, it seemed to be high on the list.

Adrenaline was racing through his body now. Usually in these situations, he remained calm. This was different, the thought of someone holding such a powerful weapon at their fingertips scared him and fear was something he was not used to

At the back of the room he came to another door, above was a sign that read cold storage. He opened the door and looked in. It was almost half the size of the main kitchen and was full with all sorts of cold foods from fish to vegetables. He walked in looking on each of the shelves. Nothing seemed out of place, except one thing at the back. On the top shelf, which was just above York's eye level, was a large black brief case. He looked around it and saw nothing that indicated the case was attached to anything such as a weight sensor. He slowly lifted the case and lowered it to the floor, treating it with the utmost respect. Although he didn't know for sure it was what he was looking for, he had a strong suspicion.

He placed the case on the floor and tried to open it; it was locked and required a code to open it. He took his gun and held it by the barrel the smashed it down on the catch. It took a couple of attempts to break it open but it finally gave up the fight. He lifted the lid and stared at what would usually send most people in to a panic but he remained calm.

The bomb it self was a strange set up. There were two blocks of PE4 (C4) placed on the left side. The explosives were attached to some wires which led to a mobile phone. He moved his hand to pull out the connector from the explosives. The device made a high pitched beep as his hand passed over the case. It had been well set up with some sort of anti-tamper sensor. If he had been a bomb expert, he might have found a way round it, but he had never taken any interest in bomb disposal. There was only one man he knew for sure could disarm it, Myers.

He pulled the comm.-radio from his belt and hit the talk button "Andy, this is York; I need you in the upper restaurant kitchen immediate…."

He couldn't finish the sentence. A fear took over his whole body the gun was pressed against his head. He hung up the phone immediately, and then he threw his gun to the floor. "Nice to meet you Ahmed." He said, assuming it could be no one else.

"Alex York." Ahmed Replied. "It's nice to finally meet you. Where I come from, you hold a certain celebrity title."

York smiled as he turned to face his opponent. "Celebrity huh. I've always wanted to be famous."

Ahmed screwed his face at the sarcasm "The only thing you are famous for is being the most hunted man in Iraq. You have put to death many influential people in your time Alex. Especially in those two years where no one can seem to place you any where. I wonder if they would look at you differently if they knew the sort of missions you undertook."

York looked at him for a moment. He didn't recognise the man standing in front of him, but he was talking to York as he knew him. "Have I wronged you in some way Ahmed?"

"When you agreed to take on those assassination missions, you wronged more people than you could ever imagine."

Ahmed's voice was turning hateful now, if he was going to stay alive, then he had to turn this conversation around. "So what happens now Ahmed? You kill Thousands and go home a hero, is that it? I don't thin k so. In fact, what you are going to do, is disarm the bomb, then go to prison where you will undoubtedly get beaten and butt fucked by every inmate who has a thing against terrorists."

Ahmed laughed, "And what makes you believe that I will do anything you say?"

York didn't answer and Ahmed knew exactly why when he heard the clicking of what he knew was the hammer of a pistol. He turned to find he was looking down the barrel of a Heckler and Koch MK23 pistol. On the other end, Myers was wearing a smile that suggested he was very pleased with being the one to get his partner out of trouble, not the other way around as it usually was.

33

Once Ahmed had been cuffed, York led him out of the kitchen and sat him on a chair in the main dining area. It was larger than it looked from downstairs. There were tables and seating for at least sixty people. The bar was edged with blue neon lights which gave a tranquil feeling to the surroundings.

York pulled up a chair and sat opposite Ahmed. They sat in silence for a while; this was a usual technique for York. He liked to get a read of the person he was about to verbally rip apart. Ahmed was unlike most he had questioned in the past, especially since there was so much at stake. He thought the Iraqi would have more signs of emotion in his eyes, perhaps a level of fear. There seemed to be nothing though. He seemed not to fear the thought of his own death and he would be well aware that's what would happen now he had been captured. If the bomb went off, the blast radius would bee large enough to make sure he was vaporised.

There was another reason for him taking his time to ask questions. The reason for the interrogation was simply to find out how to stop the bomb from going off. He had to give Myers a few minutes to start working on it, and then he would know for sure whether Ahmed was really needed.

He sat and looked at Ahmed square in the eyes, he moved in close enough to smell the sweat starting to seep from the pours of his captive who was obviously starting to feel a slight wave of fear flow though his body. "Sit tight Ahmed." York said in a hard whisper. "I'll be right back."

He walked towards the kitchen and opened the door. The entrance to the walk-in fridge had been covered by blast sheets now and an armed officer was keeping guard out side. York walked straight pass the guard and through the sheets. Myers was crouched over the bomb; he seemed to be deep in concentration.

Clocking the fact that York had entered the room, Myers sat up and looked at his partner. "It's not looking good mate." He explained "I can't find any sort of control panel anywhere. There is definitely no abort switch either. I don't think I can do it."

York looked down at the device, remembering the beep that happened when he went near it. "What about that noise I heard earlier? What was that?"

Myers pointed to four little round buttons in each corner of the case. "Those things there are temperature sensors. They're the reason why the device is in here. I can't say this for certain, but I think the device would have needed to be kept in here for at least an hour before it was able to be armed."

York looked at him; he had never taken any interest in bomb disposal; that was Myers gig. When he was in the police, Myers had agreed to undertake an intense level of training after his fifth year on the force. There were a number of elements in the programme, such as weapons training, hand to hand combat and explosives. In fact he often bragged that he was more qualified to be an anti terror agent than York was. He was never too fussed that York was the one to gain all the credit though, he was a great agent and a lot more courageous than Myers would ever be, although sometimes that could be a hindrance.

"So how do they work?" York asked, trying to show

some level if interest in the device even though all he wanted to know was 'can it be disarmed?'"

"The sensors set themselves to the temp of the room." Myers began. "My guess is he chose this place because the restaurant has been closed for a week due to some hygiene issues and he knew it would be a great place to conceal the device. Anyway these things regulate the temperature of the device. If anything with a higher temp penetrates the perimeter of the sensors, they trigger the bomb."

"Why have I never heard of this method before?" York asked

"Because it has only ever been used once before," Myers replied. "I only know that because I had to do a case study on it."

"When was sit used?"

Myers didn't answer; he looked away as if trying to search for a believable answer. York had worked with him for too long though and had learned all the tell tale signs of avoidance Myers had to offer.

"Hey," York said in a raised vice to get Myers attention. It did. "When?"

Myers looked at the floor for a second then back up at York "It's an exact replica of the bomb used to blow up the plane you parents were on."

A silence filled the room, York was overtaken by the sudden need of a few hits of scotch and the knowledge that there was a full bar a few meters away tempted him even more. He had to snap himself out of the daze and bring his mind back to the job in hand. "Is there anything I can beat out of the scumbag out there that might help?"

"Honestly I don't know. The bomb is triggered by a mobile phone, which suggests that there is someone somewhere waiting to make a phone call."

When Whitburn awoke from his deep sleep, he found himself alone in the living room; he sat up feeling an incredible ache throughout his body as he did. On the pine coffee table in front of him was a small plastic cup filled to the top with water, he took a quick sip then stood up. It was a struggle to get up after such a deep sleep, but he shook the temptation to lie back down and go back to the dream he was actually quite enjoying.

He walked through the door at the back of the room which led straight to the kitchen, sitting at the centre breakfast unit; Connors was nursing a cup of coffee and a sandwich of some kind. He was watching the evening news, which to Whitburn's surprise, mentioned nothing about the bomb threat or the fact that he had been evacuated from the capital. His thoughts turned to his staff, who he realised must have been working solid to make sure the public were kept in the dark about the threat. He felt slightly cruel keeping his people in the dark, especially when a huge number of people would be killed if the bomb went off. He had great faith in his defence team though and knew full well that they would save the people of London.

The kitchen was relatively modern compared to the rest of the house. The pine coloured units seemed like they had been recently installed and the black worktops looked as if they had never seen any form of home cooking. Whitburn walked through he kitchen and over to the stainless steel kettle in the corner and flipped the switch down. He pulled a mug from the rack next to it and spooned some coffee in, and then he filled it up with the boiled water. He turned to Connors who had said nothing to him since he entered the room.

"Any word from York or Henshaw yet?" Henshaw asked after taking a sip of the coffee.

Connors sighed then said "I am afraid I received some bad news from ATS whilst you were asleep, it seems that Henshaw moved Jazir away from the building and shot him at point blank range. A witness said he did it in cold blood."

Whitburn couldn't believe what he was hearing. All the years he had known Henshaw, he would have never had him down as a cold blooded murderer. He was always the one who seemed to have a personal vendetta against any kind of criminal, even when they were just new recruits in the Air Force.

"Are they sure it was him?" Whitburn asked "I just can't imagine Henshaw being a killer."

Connors shook his head "I am sorry sir, I know you were very good friends."

Whitburn shook his head; questions began to roll around in his mind. What the hell had happened to his best friend? Why would he do such a thing? He took another sip from his coffee then left the room and headed straight back to the lounge.

Connors finished his sandwich then walked through to the front door and out to the gardens. Murphy was at the front gate briefing the guard. He walked round to the rear of the property where he saw the man he wanted.

They hadn't seen each other in a good few years and Reign was even bigger than Connors remembered. He had a full head of hair back then so looked slightly different now he was bald.

"I trust you have the perimeter secure?" Connors asked.

Reign threw a hard glance back at him "If you're gonna start slating my work, then I suggest you fuck off back to where you came from."

Connors looked slightly shocked at the remark but then stretched a smile across his face "You never change do you Danny?"

They shook hands the started to walk away from the house, keeping their voices as low as possible.

"What's your status so far?" Connors asked

"We have the entire perimeter covered; no one can get in or out."

"Good, everything is going perfectly. Just make sure that you do exactly as we planned and nothing should go wrong."

"Yes sir, I will."

Connors took his phone from his pocket and pressed the menu button. He opened the contacts page and highlighted the only number stored in the list and stared at it for a moment then he hit the send button.

34

York burst through the kitchen doors and stood staring at Ahmed. He had been sitting quietly in the same position where York had left him a few minutes earlier. He had been calm before, but now, after seeing the look on York's face he was nervous. He could see the killer instinct in the agent's eyes. .He began to feel beads of sweat start to run down his face and his whole body was beginning to shake, he knew what was coming next.

York walked over to Ahmed and sat down calmly on the chair in front of him once again "How do we disarm that bomb?" He asked in a cool, polite manner.

Ahmed looked at him for a second before answering; the expression on York's face was free of any emotion. This kind of interrogation, he knew, needed someone who could switch off sympathy and mercy and York seemed to be able to do both.

"I am sorry." Ahmed finally replied. "I was never told how to disarm it."

York looked his captive straight in the eye. He continued to show no form of emotion. Fear was what he was going for. Although he had been trained to go beyond the realms of Human Rights and ignore any such law that would prevent him from using any means necessary, he was well prepared to go all the way and inflict severe pain when it was needed. That was always the last resort though. If he could use any other method he would.

His thoughts turned to the Russian he had interrogated earlier in the day. He had given him no chances then, he went straight in to the hard questions. This was different though. Ahmed looked half the man that Sergei was. Ahmed was thin and looked seriously under nourished. He wasn't sure if it was intentional or not but any high level of torture would surely be way too much for him to cope with.

"I am going to ask you again." York informed him, this time in a slightly harder tone. "How do we disarm the bomb?"

Silence.

"Listen to me Ahmed." York said as he moved in close "My team have all the information there is about you. I know you have family back in Iraq. If you don't help us, I swear I will make it my personal goal to make their lives as difficult as possible. So I am going to ask you one more time, how do we disarm the bomb?"

Again, it was met with the same answer. York believed him too. He could see the fear in the Iraqi's eyes and knew if he had been told how to, he would have spilled by now, the threat to his family would have surely triggered something

"How does it feel Ahmed, huh?" York inquired, trying to take another approach as a last attempt. "How does it feel to know that you have failed your mission?"

Ahmed sniggered "I have not failed. My mission was to plant and set the device, not to get away from it. I am willing to die for our cause."

"No, I don't think so. I have looked in to the eyes of martyrs on many occasions and you are no martyr."

There was a brief silence; York knew he had read Ahmed correctly. Many of the terrorists he had dealt with in the past who had been willing to end their lives to complete their mission showed no fear of the thought of death. They had no emotional signs in their eyes, they were blank and merciless. Ahmed however was none of those things. Granted York had only known him for just over half an hour, but in that time he had learnt a lot about the man by the way he spoke and his mannerisms. His English was excellent which made York believe he had perhaps either grown up in the country or been educated here. Also, in the time it took for them to find out that the conference centre was the target to the point where they caught him, he should have been in and out and half way out of the city. This, York mused, meant one of two things, either he was incompetent and had trouble setting the device, or his conscience had stopped him from doing it straight away.

"Tell me Ahmed, what possessed you to take on a mission like this?" York asked. "I mean, you strike me as a man beyond this kind of petty terrorism."

Ahmed looked at him and screwed his face. For the first time, York was beginning to hit some nerves "How dare you judge me." Ahmed replied with hate in his voice "You know nothing about me or what kind of man I am. I do what I am paid to do because if I don't my family starve. If murder is what is on the list, then that's just what I will do. I don't care if I am killed in the process, as long as my family get paid."

This was the first York had known about Ahmed's family, he had lied earlier about being aware of Ahmed's family. Now he had learnt that Ahmed really did have a cause that most men would be willing to die for. With this in mind, there was no more need for questions, now he had to take action.

He walked over to the bar area to look for anything

that he could possible use as a tool. At first glance he found nothing. As he looked a little harder though, he fond a set of drawers, in the top drawer, he found a cork screw. He picked it up, walked back over and sat down. He placed the cork screw down on the table and sat in silence, giving Ahmed a chance to think over his options. There was no doubt in his mind that Ahmed knew exactly what the screw was for.

"So, Ahmed. What's it to be?"

The Iraqi looked down at the cork screw on the table. He had heard of the sorts of things that people like York do to get the information they required. Although he had never been in this kind of situation before, he could only imagine what the utensil was going to be used for and he mused it would not be to open a bottle.

"I am sorry Agent York, but as I said before, I was never told how to disarm it."

York picked up the Cork screw and stood up. He walked around so Ahmed's back was to him. He lifted the arms of the screw so the coil was fully exposed then pressed it down on Ahmed's shoulder.

"Last chance Ahmed." York warned.

There was no answer. York waited for a few seconds, reluctant to take the action he was threatening. Still, he had no reply. This was it, now he had to act. He applied pressure to the screw so the point would pierce the skin. As he was about to twist the screw further in to Ahmed's shoulder, Myers burst through the door.

"Alex." He shouted. "Stop."

York stopped immediately and pulled the screw out. He walked over to Myers after placing the utensil back in the same place on the table where it had been before, this time, the end was covered with blood.

"What is it?" York asked.

"It's done; I've disconnected the charge from the explosives."

York let out a long sigh of relief. For a moment, he doubted their chances of success, but as always his pal had come through.

"How the hell did you do it?"

Myers walked back in to the kitchen and York followed closely. They walked up to the device and Myers picked up a pair of tongs he had found in one of the drawers.

"I used these to grip the charges. All I had to do was get them down to the right temperature before I did it."

York looked at him and smiled. It was a simple solution, so simple he couldn't believe he hadn't thought of it earlier.

"You are a genius Andy Myers." York complimented with enthusiasm. "An absolute genius."

"I'm gonna finish dismantling it here. I'd like to get a better look at the design before it is ripped to shreds back at HQ. I think you had better get him plasters for that boo boo." Myers said jokingly pointing through the door to the dining room.

York smiled and walked back out to Ahmed. He grabbed him up off the chair and escorted him down the stairs and out of the centre. He guided him past the police cars and straight in to the back of an ambulance so they could patch him up. He sat on the back step contemplating the devastation the bomb would have caused had it gone off. All the innocent men, women and children who would have lost their lives for no reason just because some psycho had a beef with the PM, it was hard to come to terms with.

He was trained for everything the job involved. He could easily take the life of a terrorist if that was what was needed. He could inflict pain to get information. That was the easy part in his mind. The hard part was accepting the loss of innocents. His mind turned to the youngsters killed the previous morning and he suddenly felt sorry. Not only for the fact that they had died, but that the man responsible had been given the easy way out.

As he thought about it, he remembered what Kirk had told him. Henshaw had murdered Jazir. That wasn't his style at all. If anything, he would have loved to see him rot in prison with thugs who hate terrorists. It would have mad him the happiest man alive.

He began to think back over the last thirty six hours. Henshaw had been the first to arrive at the club bombing and he had arrived stupidly fast. His explanation regarding his connection to Reign was shady at best and he had been acting a lot different to what he normally did. He had been a lot tenser.

York was not sure what he was getting at, but he didn't like it. He turned his attention back to Ahmed.

"Tell me Ahmed, Who were you working for?" He asked, not expecting an answer.

Ahmed simply sat in silence. York smiled and turned back to his own thoughts until he was disturbed by the Iraqi.

"My boss was not Jazir," He said. "If that is what you are thinking."

"Really," York responded. "So who is?"

"This goes higher than you would believe. I am not sure who the brains behind it is, but I answered to the same man you do."

The allegation hit a nerve with York, even though he sort of believed him. He launched himself in to the ambulance and brought his fist down on to Ahmed's jaw. Ahmed fell flat on his back. York figured it might have made him feel a little better and it did.

Myers took care while tried to dismantle the explosive. It took his all if fifteen minutes to have the whole thing out on the floor. He looked at all the pieces with detail, taking in the design and build of the device. It was like a hobby of his, it gave him a great sense of achievement knowing he had stopped a disaster. The thrill he got from it he could never explain to anyone who had never experienced it first hand. As he looked at the pieces, he realised that there was something missing. He went back to the case and looked around it. There was a panel in the centre which separated two compartments. He lifted the panel out and as soon as he did he dropped it to the floor. His whole body froze as he was faced by his worst nightmare. Below the panel was an exact replica of what he had dismantled a few minutes ago. This time it was different though. There was no heat sensors on this one, it was simply a phone connected to two blocks of C4. As he stared in fright the phone lit up, he instinctively made a grab for the charges.

York was walking towards the doors when the blast happened. The glass doors and the windows surrounding shattered and rained down on him as he fell to the floor to take cover. As soon as the last shard of glass fell, he jumped to his feet and ran as fast as he could in to the building screaming Andy's name as he moved faster than he had ever before.

The visibility was almost zero under the heavy smoke and dust filling the corridor. As he ran further in, the ability to keep going under the strain for breath became too much to bear. He held back whilst the breeze flowing through struggled to clear the smoke.

He fell to the floor keeping his face below the smoke line and crawled slowly back towards the doors until he reached the outside. The lungful of fresh air was bliss after being inside.

He stood up, holding on to the railings for support. The sight was devastating, emergency service crew were running around, checking those who might have been hurt in the blast.

York looked in to the dark abyss that was once the huge corridor. Everything around him had now become non existent. Silence encircled him as he stood alone hoping that his life long friend would walk out of the abyss. He knew however, that there was no possibility of that happening. The one who had pulled him though most of the trials in his life was now gone. He felt a sudden fear come over him; he was alone for the first time in his life. Even when his parents had been killed, he had Andy to help him though, now there was no one.

When he finally came too from the trance, he found himself face to face with a female paramedic. Her face was black with dust from the blast. She was saying something to him; he struggled to understand what it was. When he did, he realised she was trying to calm him down as he was screaming Myers name.

35

York sat in the back of the ambulance staring out across the car park towards the building. Mental pictures of what Myers must have felt when the bomb went off kept flashing through his mind. He had dealt with death all through his working life. Pretty much since the day he left school and joined the armed forces he had to deal with seeing violent deaths. He had never once imagined what it was actually like for the victim though. He never once asked himself if they felt any pain. Then again how could he know?

A paramedic quickly dressed the cuts on his arms he sustained when the bomb went off then left to tend to another patient. As he left, the Chief Inspector stepped up to the rear of the ambulance.

"How you doin' son?" He asked sincerely.

York didn't bother replying, not to an obviously daft question. He looked at the CI for a moment, trying to take in what he must have been feeling. Although these sorts of things do happen on a regular basis, York assumed it didn't happen every day on his watch. He must have been shaken up. He then realised that the question wasn't really that stupid, it was genuine.

"I am fine considering." He finally answered. "I wish I could have done something you know."

The CI nodded "A few years ago I lost a good friend. We were out on a routine drugs raid." He paused for a second, seemingly still having trouble dealing with the tragedy. "We busted ten people in one house. They were all thrown in the back of the van and he went back in to check the contents. If only I had known that there was one more in there."

York looked at him; for once there was actually a person who really understood. York knew all to well that there were many people out there who try to offer support when you are going through hardship, but unless they have been through it themselves, there is only so much they can do.

"What happened to him?" York asked, not really k=understanding why.

"The last man left inside was armed with a pistol. My friend took a bullet in the head, clean shot. The thing is, it took me a long time to get over it, but I kept going because that's what he would have wanted." The CI didn't say anything else, he simply walked away.

York thought for a moment about what he said. He was right. There was two ways he could go from here. He could fall to pieces, which meant Myers death would have been for nothing. Or he could take down the man who killed him. There was no real choice; he knew what he had to do.

He stepped down from the ambulance and headed for his car. Once inside, he pulled his phone from his pocket and dialled the number. There was only one person now who he was sure was the only one who could lead him to the man responsible.

The line rang a few times then it was answered. The voice on the other end was low and soft, like he had been dreading the call.

"Hello Alex." Henshaw greeted.

"You know what I want Captain." York stated harshly.

"I guess you are feeling less than talkative. I have just heard about Andy, I am sorry Alex."

"I don't need your sympathy; all I need from you is an answer. Are you involved in this?"

There was a brief silence that followed a long sigh. York knew Henshaw was carefully choosing his words correctly.

"I never knew that this many people were going to die Alex, I swear. But fell victim to the temptation of money."

York could feel his blood begin to boil "How could you Captain. I used to look up to you, now you are nothing but a cold blooded killer."

"Alex, please. I am not the one who ordered the bombing. It was put in place by the man I work for in case you didn't do as you were instructed by Jazir."

York lowered the phone from his ear and took a few seconds to calm his nerves. He couldn't come to terms with the fact that the man who was once the leader of a team who protected the innocent public from terrorism was at the helm of an attack himself.

He placed the phone to his ear once more "Who do you work for?"

"Please understand, I had no idea that Myers was going to be killed, I'm sure they didn't either."

"I'll ask you again." York said, this time in a harder voice. "Who do you work for? If you don't tell me I will personally track you down and make you feel pain like you could never imagine."

After another sigh and short silence, Henshaw answered "Sheldon Murphy."

York couldn't believe it; the country was being attacked by not one but two anti-terror bosses. "Where is he?"

"He has escorted the Prime Minister to the safe house. Don't try anything stupid Alex, it is under heavy guard by Reign and his men, there is no way you can take them down on your own."

York didn't bother to answer; he hung up the phone, started the engine and drove off.

Sheldon Murphy finished briefing Reign and his men as soon as he received the notification from Henshaw that York was on his way. His plan was working perfectly. As soon as Jazir was captured, he had to come up with something a.s.a.p. It didn't take him long to think of it and put it in to action. He knew the destination of the explosives, simply because Ahmed had been working for him as well as Jazir..

He had found Ahmed a few months earlier in the streets of London. After being forced out of his country by the authorities for theft and assault, he had been forced to enter Britain illegally and live on the streets. Sheldon offered him a home and a job in return for his help with certain matters from time to time. When this mission came up, he could think of no one better.

All he had to do really was swap the device Jazir had given him with one exactly the same, except less powerful. It was simple, if York wasn't going to come to him when innocent lives were at stake, maybe he would come after him with revenge in mind. He knew that Myers was a bomb expert so he would resist the opportunity to be a national hero.

The bomb was designed with two separate devices, one under the other. As soon as the first was dismantled, the second was triggered, with a ten minute delay. The design had been Murphy's idea, one which he was proud of.

For the first time since the mission had begun, everything was going perfectly. He knew at the start that Jazir was going to be a dangerous man to deal with, and the consequence of using him was the death of all those innocent young people in the club. He hadn't planned for many of the public to die. But that was a risk he had to take, the mission had a purpose which was far bigger than anyone of those few.

He walked up to the front door of the house, as he opened the door, he was disturbed by a call on his radio, "Mr Murphy, this is the gate, I have a Tom Henshaw here to see you."

"Send him in." He replied.

He turned and waited for Henshaw's car to pull up outside the door. He walked down the steps and opened the car door. Henshaw stepped out and gave Murphy a nod as a sign of thanks.

"Good to see you again Tom." Murphy greeted. "I have to say this is an un-expected visit."

Henshaw shut the car door then held out his hand to shake Murphy's. "I thought you might be able to use my help."

Murphy smiled "I think I have enough fire power here. Reign and his men are more than enough to overcome one man."

Henshaw shook his head; he had known York for many years and knew his past, even the areas which were deleted from all files. "It seems to me that you are under estimating the talents that Alex possesses." Henshaw said as he followed Murphy up the stairs and in to the house. "He is smart and I know he won't come in without being fully equipped."

Murphy tuned and looked Henshaw in the eye "When he gets here, we will be ready, until then we have a bigger problem to deal with."

"What's that?" Henshaw asked.

"We need to take care of Connors. I wasn't prepared for him to still be here. We need to make sure he doesn't suspect our involvement."

Henshaw nodded in agreement, they had to make him believe that York was the one who was after the PM. The problem in Henshaw's mind; was that if York came in all guns blazing, it wouldn't take long for Connors to raise the alarm. Which ever way he tried to play it out in his mind, the end for Connors was the same, death.

36

York pulled up a few hundred yards down the road from the safe house. He had to get things clear in his mind before he even thought of going in. With the PM inside, only the best security staff would be on hand to protect him, at any cost. York was also aware that there would be high tech security equipment dotted all over the grounds, from motion sensors to CCTV cameras.

He typed a text in to his phone then scrolled through the contacts page until he found Kirk's number. He waited a few minutes for the reply. When it came, there was a link to a secure ATS site. When the link was opened, a live satellite feed of the house and the surrounding area filled the screen. He could see security guards positioned twenty metres apart around the perimeter fence. There were also three positioned around the house and one by the door, he guessed there would at least be another three inside. The odds were not in his favour. If he was going to succeed, he had to find some way of getting in unnoticed.

He got out of the car and walked round to the boot. He opened it up to and then pulled open the doors to the cabinet inside, which housed his assault equipment. He took off his jeans and threw on a pair of black combat trousers and a bullet proof vest over the top of this ATS T-shirt. Then he pulled out a Heckler & Koch MP5 SD and lifted the strap over his shoulder, he also strapped an MP5 K to the back of his belt. Two Desert eagle hand guns came next; he placed them in their holsters and then grabbed three extra magazines. Once he was fully equipped, he took another look at the satellite image, apart from a few of the guards pacing up and down, there had been no change in their position.

He took a map from the glove compartment and opened the page that showed the area. The ground covering the thousand yards between him and house looked rough. It consisted of mostly woodland with a small stream running along the edge of the garden He calculated it would take him approximately ten minutes to cover the distance providing there were no unseen obstacles.

Visibility was almost non existent under the cover of the night. If it wasn't for the faint light of the moon, York would never have been able to navigate using the small torch he grabbed from the car before setting off. All it really proved useful for was reading the map, which he had to do to gain his bearings every so often. He used certain landmarks to navigate through the overgrowth such as public trails and small openings in the trees.

He was used to these sorts of surroundings; many of his friends were unaware of what he got up to between the times of leaving the marines and joining ATS. He had been selected as a member of a small, government funded task force specialising in special surveillance operations. Although none of the members were trained to the level of the SAS, they all had their unique skills.

The team only lasted a year and within that time they had only completed three missions. All three missions were long and occasionally uncomfortable; they required the team to camp out for weeks at a time. Each member felt as though the missions were the SAS' cast offs, but in reality they brought excitement and a sense of purpose to their lives.

After around twenty minutes, he finally saw the lights from the safe house. He ducked down below the weeds and brambles in amongst the trees and looked around the perimeter as far as he could see. There were only two guards in view. They both looked tired and fed up, obviously both coming towards the end of a long shift. This would work perfectly in York's favour; Tiredness would slow down their reactions, giving him time to secure them before they raise the alarm.

He took the MP5 SD from his shoulder and checked the magazine was fully loaded, and then he placed the silencer on the barrel. He then made his way slowly towards the edge of the fence line. The satellite images Kirk had sent hadn't shown the six foot high chain link fence surrounding the grounds, but he had made sure he planned for every eventuality. He pulled the wire clippers from his belt and began slowly and quietly snipping away at the fence while keeping himself concealed under a shrub.

Once he had cut a hole big enough for him to squeeze through, he took one final look around, to ensure no one was watching then climbed through. He crept along the ground beside the fence, trying his best to keep out of the light shining from the house. The black combats kept him almost invisible in the darkness.

He came to a stop around five meters from the first guard, who was sitting on the grass, facing the house and smoking a cigarette. He raised himself on all fours then slowly and silently moved towards the guard, who barely had time to make a sound before York covered his mouth with his hand. He wrestled the guard to the ground then with one punch to the head, rendered him unconscious.

The guard to his left had witnessed the struggle and began to run to the aid of his colleague. York lifted his weapon and fired two shots in to the man's shoulder. The large guard crumbled to the floor. The hits by the bullets seemed just a minor set back to him though. He rose to his feet and continued heading in York's direction. York new he couldn't kill the guard, it wouldn't be right. He was just doing his job and doing it well.

The guard launched himself at York. The man who must have weighed at least seventeen stone of pure muscle slammed his shoulder in to York's abdomen. Both of them fell to the floor. York acted quickly and began to ram his fists in to the guard's kidneys repeatedly. He could feel his assailant begin to give up the fight, he swung his gun in the air and brought it crashing down on to the guards head.

He pushed the unconscious body off of him and sat up to catch his breath. So far, so good – He thought. He had managed to take down two of the security team without killing them. It was becoming harder though, these guys were tough.

He grabbed his rifle and stood to his feet. What happened next took him by surprise he was surrounded by at least five of the other guards. They had come from as if from no where. He knew the PM's security staff were good, but not this good, these guys were too swift, too silent in their movement. If he had to guess, he would have said they were Special Forces. There was only one group like that he knew had anything to do with the events over the past couple of days, Reign's group.

From any normal mans point of view, he was trapped.

York was not about to give up that easily though. He threw the rifle in the air, which momentarily caught the attention of the guards. He then pulled the two desert eagles out of their holsters and fired at the legs surrounding him. Two of the five guards managed to let off a round each, one of which hit York in the arm just above the elbow. He didn't scream, the shock of the impact sent a burning feeling though his body then he felt a sharp sting. Two of the guards still stood fast, they kept their weapons trained on him. He found it strange that they weren't firing though. By rights, he should have been plastered all over the lawn by now. They had been ordered to keep him alive and unharmed, he figured. This could work for him. He lifted his leg up and kicked the gun from the hands of one of the guards. As his leg came down, he grabbed the barrel of the other's and pulled it downwards. He slammed his fist in to their faces. Then again. They fell to the floor, both completely still. He knew for a fact that there would be more on their way, so he had to work double time. He threw the pistols across the lawn then began to run towards the house.

Inside Connors, Henshaw and Murphy were sitting around the coffee table in the main reception room when they heard the fist gunshots. Connors immediately jumped to his feet and headed for the window, an action that wouldn't have normally been recommended by the Director General of MI5. But he knew that if Connors was killed by a stray bullet from outside, the task would be lifted from him. His hopes didn't come true; Connors stepped back from the curtain to find himself face to face with Murphy.

"We need to call for backup immediately." Connors

ordered in a panicked manner.

Murphy simply looked at him. He had a calmness that sent a chill down Connors' spine. "I don't think that will be of any use to you sir." He stated coldly.

Before Connors could say another word, a pain like none he had ever felt in his life overcame his whole body. He began to shake slightly then he felt his legs begin to loose strength. He looked down towards his abdomen to see a knife had been fully thrust in, the hand of the man who he thought he knew and trusted was still clutching on to it. He looked Murphy dead in the eye, there were no words he could find to say and even if he did; his ability to speak had been taken.

Murphy pulled the knife out from Connors stomach. Blood gushed from the wound and began to drip on to the floor. He coughed which added to the pain and brought blood up in to his mouth. As he fell to his knees, everything began to blur. The room started to spin uncontrollably and then he fell to the floor, still and lifeless.

Whitburn ran in to the reception room when he heard the commotion. He looked down at Connors' body lying in a pool of blood, and then he looked at Murphy, who was covered in the Defence Secretary's blood.

"What the hell is going on?" He asked in a panic.

Henshaw immediately grabbed the PM and pushed him against the wall. Murphy grabbed a large candle holder that was sitting on the windowsill and slammed it down on Whitburn's head. Henshaw let his grip go and the PM fell to the floor.

Henshaw looked down at the PM then at Murphy and said "I hope this works Sheldon, if not; we are in a whole lot of trouble."

York managed to reach the front door before a barrage of gun fire headed in his direction. He launched himself through the door and fell to the floor instantly. There was a door directly in front of him which he noticed led in to the kitchen. This was the best place to gain some form of cover from the rain of bullets he was about to suffer. He jumped to his feet and ran as fast as his legs would carry him towards the door then crashed through it. After flipping the light switch to off, he took up position behind the centre units, this gave him cover from and gun fire from the window and gave him full view of the door. He couldn't quite understand why they were shooting at him now when they had neglected to do so earlier.

He holstered the side arms then readied the MP5K and aimed it towards the doorway. He waited patiently for the shadows of the guards to appear on the floor, it wasn't long before the first guard was at the door. He was still set on not killing the guards, but he had no choice but to go for the body shot and hope they were all wearing bullet proof vests. He took down he first guard and then another two after that. The next two held back behind the door frame, ensuring they didn't give him a clean shot. At the same time as they fired, another storm of bullets crashed through the glass of the patio doors and slammed in to the units.

For the second time he had become trapped. He peered in the direction of the rear doors only to be forced back by more gun fire. He was now out of options, it was either give himself up or die trying to get out. In truth, he didn't care for either one, but at least if he gave himself up, there was a slim chance of him succeeding. He cursed himself for taking such a forceful action in revenging his friend's death.

After a few moments of thought, he threw the MP5 across the floor then followed it with the handguns. The gun fire stopped as he raised his arms above the units. He didn't stand, if he did the guards could have possibly seen it as a reason to defend themselves and open fire, he simply waited for them to come to him. There was also no reason for him to try and tackle them hand to hand as he knew there would be at least one guard holding back with his weapon trained on him if he did.

Two of them grabbed his arms and dragged him to his feet, and then they pulled his hand behind his back and threw a pair of handcuffs around his wrists, tightening them as much as they could. York screwed his face as a pain shot up his arm.

They dragged him in to the reception room where he came face to face with Henshaw for the first time since leaving ATS headquarters earlier in the day. This time though, his feelings towards his captain were much different. This time he felt hate, disgust and slightly sorry towards the man who once called him self a patriot to the British Nation.

"Hello Alex." Henshaw said with a genuine look of concern on his face.

"Don't look at me as if you give a shit," York replied, showing the hate in his voice "You turned your back on me and the rest of the team at ATS the moment you agreed to sign up to this mess."

Henshaw took a step towards York "Don't misinterpret everything that has happened over the last couple of days. Things are not always as they seem."

"Don't tell him anything Tom." Murphy's voice came

from behind Henshaw.

As Henshaw turned, York could see Murphy sitting comfortably on the sofa, with Reign sitting next to him clutching his rifle.

York turned back to Henshaw and said "You know what, I should have known you were a traitor the moment I found out you were involved with that fat shit bag."

"Do you have to use that sort of language in the presence of the Prime Minister?" Henshaw asked nodding over York's shoulder

York looked over to see the PM unconscious and bound by the feet and hands. He looked back towards Murphy, who was sipping at a glass of scotch. "I guess you got what you wanted. So why the hell did you have to get me involved if it was that easy?"

Murphy put the glass down on the table and stood. He walked towards York and looked him up and down, turning up his nose as he did "Because," he replied "For some bloody reason, you are the conciliation prize."

37

"What the hell do you mean?" York asked. He couldn't understand what anyone would want with him. He had pissed off plenty of people in the past, but all of those were either dead or behind bars. There was no one he could think of who would want to go to all this trouble for his benefit.

"All will be revealed Alex." Henshaw answered. He turned to Reign "Put him in the car and wait for us. And let the PM ride in the boot, he will take up to much space in with us"

Reign grabbed York's arm and forced him out of the door. Henshaw turned to Murphy "I'm beginning to have doubts about this whole thing, the crimes we are committing here are completely observed. As I said before, if we get caught, we are in deep."

Murphy laughed. Henshaw had known him for many years; they had worked together on a vast number of occasions. There was something different about him now. In years past, he had been one of the most genuine people Henshaw had ever met. He worried about others a lot more than himself. Now though, his eyes told a different story. Henshaw saw nothing but hate, an evil glare that could send chills down the spines of the toughest.

"We have come too far to back away now," Murphy replied. "And besides I have put in place measures that ensure we are never blamed for this."

Henshaw didn't bother to ask what the measures were, it wasn't important now. He knew the Director General was right. They had worked way too hard to make this whole mission a success and they were now so close to the end that they could almost taste the victory. If he backed out now, he would more than likely get thrown in prison any way.

There was still something in Henshaw that made him want to call the whole thing off though. He knew exactly what it was too. Throughout all of the planning, of all of the people who had to sacrifice their lives in order for them to succeed, there was one he felt guilty about, Myers. He was fond of him and he wasn't afraid to acknowledge it. In fact, they had built up quite a relationship over the past few years. He knew too that Myers and York were like brothers, which didn't help with the guilt one bit.

He walked out of the house and jumped in to the limousine. York was sat at in front of the separation glass between the rear seating and the drivers cab. Reign was sat right next to him.

Henshaw sat next to Murphy at the rear of the car. Murphy opened the mini bar and pulled out a small bottle of scotch whiskey. He grabbed a glass from the rack above the fridge and poured the scotch in to it. He took a few sips then looked at York.

"The past couple of days have been quite eventful for you haven't they Alex." He said with a self-satisfied look painted on his face.

York stared at him, he too had known Murphy for a while and he had in fact begun to gain some respect for the man. His position at MI5 was probably one of the toughest in the UK's defence system. He was the man who had to answer for cock ups when they happened. Then again, he could take all the glory when things went to plan. Now, that respect had all gone and just like Henshaw, York could see a sadistic look in Murphy's eye.

"I've seen a lot of shit in my time." York said, "But I never thought I would see the day that a high ranking member of the British Government…"

"Let's cut the rubbish shall we." Murphy interrupted. "I don't have time for this waffle."

York took a deep breath, "OK, I am guessing you didn't want me here for my extreme charm and good looks. So why don't you tell me what the hell I have to do with any of this."

Murphy looked at Henshaw; he gave a single nod as approval for him to tell all.

"It's simple really," Henshaw Began "When we had Salim Jazir's father study the Dark Gold, and he made some astonishing discoveries. He found that when it is mixed with the correct substances and in the correct way, it can be used in many ways. We found that in war zones, we could destroy enemy camps with a simple grenade strike. We could also use it as a form of extracting information from prisoners. By simply mixing it with water and injecting it in to the blood, it induced minor heart attacks and nerve malfunctions. No one could withstand the pain of the torture."

"Who the hell would commission such lethal substance to be distributed for use?" York asked

"The PM, he was the man who began the investigation when he read about what happened to the three kids who found it back in the 1800's. He became obsessed. Just like the one of those three kids who survived the trip to find it. The other two were killed after ingesting small amounts of it neat.

He was killed a few years later when he tried to stop anyone else from getting to it."

York shook his head; he could hardly believe what he was hearing "So what happened? I have never heard of this before."

"You wouldn't have." Murphy interjected. "It was decommissioned almost as soon as it began. It turned out that some one had alerted high ranking officials within the military. They put a stop to it straight away. That's why Whitburn went in to politics, so he would have the power to implement the operation once more."

"It didn't quite go as he planned though." Henshaw came in. "He began the process again, as before. It was used to gain information from a known terrorist, to give it a trial run. He died in the interrogation. Whitburn came under attack immediately after and has done ever since."

York looked confused "So why the hell have you kidnapped him? What will that achieve?"

"There are people who have personal vendettas against him." Murphy explained. "We are being rewarded greatly for his abduction and execution."

"So the Defence Secretary and the Director General of MI5 have a price. I have to admit, I would have never suspected you for a second." He could hardly believe that his boss had turned his back on his country for money. It was completely out of character.

"Would you like to know who grassed Whitburn up originally Alex?" Henshaw asked.

York couldn't see the relevance of the question, but he was interested none the less "Who?"

"Your father"

Suddenly he understood why his parents had been killed. It wasn't the work of a simple terrorist, of that of a psychopath. They died at the hands of someone who now ran the country, for nothing but revenge.

"So, you're going to kill the Prime Minister, get paid a shit load for doing it, then what?"

"Simple," Murphy said firmly "For the past few years, we have been at war with the middle east. We all want that to stop, so I figured we can sell a load of the gold to the Iraqi's and the Afghans. Then we turn them against each other and they can destroy each other."

York took on a shocked expression "You have gone absolutely insane. You will be aiding in the deaths of millions of innocent people."

Murphy laughed and leaned towards York "Try and stop me."

York lunged towards Murphy. His head slammed in to the DG's stomach, forcing him in to the back of his seat. Reign immediately grabbed York and threw him back to the seat. Then he grabbed his pistol, took it by the barrel and brought it crashing down on to York's head. Instantly, York's body flopped in to the seat.

38

The driver pulled the Limo up at their destination. Henshaw had never seen the Royal Britannia up close before. In fact, the only time he had ever seen it was on TV or in the papers. He was awe struck by the sheer magnitude of the super liner. The lights were fully illuminated now which, he felt, made it even more spectacular. The glimmer of the lights seemed to reflect off of the hull like a mirror. There was not a scratch on her as she floated gracefully on the dock. Having not been out to see since she had been unveiled, she hadn't had the chance to accept the imperfections the saes would cause.

Murphy and Henshaw stepped out of the car. Two of Reign's men dragged York and Whitburn out of the car and up the boarding platform. Murphy stood next to Henshaw and stared up at the ship.

"Fantastic piece of craftsmanship isn't she." Murphy declared. Feeling as awe struck as his companion even though he had seen the ship many times. All aspects of maritime engineering and sailing had been an interest of his since he was a young boy. The interest had stemmed from his father being a fisherman. He had wanted to follow in his dad's footsteps and become a fisherman himself; that was until his dad went to work one evening and never returned. The boat had run in to a harsh storm just off the coast of Ireland. The trawler couldn't withstand the thrashing from the wind, waves and heavy rain. From that day on, Murphy had vowed never to step on to a boat, until today.

"That she is." Henshaw returned. "I have seen a few

ships in my time, but none as amazing as this."

They pulled their attention away from the ship and made their way up the boarding platform. They walked on to the deck and through the door to the inside. The carpet through the corridor was a soft, thick pile. The walls were decorated in a deep red paint that brought a warm feeling to the inside.

They walked along the corridor to the end. Murphy pressed the button to call the lift. They waited in silence for it to arrive. When it did, they stepped in and pressed the button for the fifth floor.

"There is something I have been meaning to say to you Sheldon." Henshaw said, breaking the silence. "I am slightly apprehensive about the plans you have made to attack enemy countries using the Gold. You have seen the power it possesses. We would be putting a lot of innocent people to death."

"Actually." Murphy came back. "The plan was Connors' idea. I just had the balls and the resources to make it happen."

"Why the hell would he plan something like that?"

"I know you have known Whitburn for a long time Tom. You have to admit, since he has become a politician, he has become weak. He knew that someday, an attack like the one Jazir was responsible for would happen. He came up with this because he felt retaliation would be necessary. Of course, when he put it forward to the PM, it was written off."

Henshaw thought about it for a moment. He agreed that retaliation would always be necessary. But he couldn't help but feel that Whitburn had been right to write the plan off. Ok, he was about to put the plan in to action himself, but for the PM to allow it to happen would have been a political nightmare. For it to be put in to action without proper authority would have far less repercussions.

They stepped out of the lift and walked along the corridor in the direction of the crew's resting room. They walked in to the room and headed for the coffee machine. After fixing a drink, Murphy turned to the other twenty people in the room who had been waiting for them, all Reign's men.

"Ok gentlemen." He said firmly. "It is time to show me what you are made of. Each and every one of you is being paid well for this, so don't let me down."

With that they all left the room and headed for their stations. Murphy sipped his coffee happy in the knowledge that the hardest part of his mission was finally over. They were now leaving the country and would never need to return.

When York eventually awoke, the surroundings had changed. He was no longer in the car. The air was damp around him and it had a distinct taste to it, a salty taste. There was a continuous roaring sound in the distance too. It was a combination of those two things and the fact that the room seemed to be ever so slightly rocking that confirmed he had to be on a boat.

The room he was in was big, at least a hundred square meters and surprisingly empty. Judging by the temperature in the room, it was used as cold storage for perhaps food or drink. There were bundles of rope and straps that were used to secure crates placed ten metres apart along one side of the compartment. The one thing he did notice was that every thing looked new and amazingly clean. No time had been taken to decorate the room either, the walls were simply left in there original steel form. The floor was also made from steel to help keep the temperature regulated.

There was no doubt in his mind what boat he was on either. Henshaw would not have gone to the trouble of killing Jazir if he wasn't going to get anything out of it. He had always insisted that every action taken should always have a worth while outcome.

As he fully pulled himself back to a conscious state, he took notice of the pounding feeling in his head. The last thing he remembered was leaping towards Murphy, then nothing. He looked up to see his hands were still in the cuffs, only now they were attached to some piping. He couldn't believe he had been so foolish. His temper had gotten the better of him again. When Myers was killed, the only thing his mind was set on was revenge. He didn't even bother to way out the odds, which were always one hundred percent against him.

York's thoughts were disturbed by the door opening. Reign and two of his men walked in to the room. They all wore tough, emotionless expressions as they mad their way towards him. As Reign stopped in front of him, he looked deep in to the thugs eyes. He couldn't tell if they were here to hurt him of just keep an eye on him. He figured the fact that he was safely chained to an eight inch thick steel pipe suggested they had no need for the latter.

"You boys here to join the party?" York said with a huge smile on his face. He had been in situations like this before. The one thing he had come to learn was that if he let the mental strain consume him, he was a dead man.

Reign couldn't help but smile. The strength of his captive impressed him greatly. He had heard of some of the missions York had successfully completed and often wondered if he could have been persuaded to join the team. There was one thing that stopped him from confronting York though, the baggage he carried. One of his men had been given the task of spying on him for a few days, watching every move he made. When Reign found out about the drinking, he immediately aborted the thoughts of recruiting him.

"You will be needed on the bridge in a while." Reign stated. "Until then, there is a small matter we need to rectify."

"Which is?" York asked, having an idea already.

"Sergei."

York smiled. He never knew that what he did to the Russian would come back and bite him on the back side. Even if he did, he still would have gone the same way.

Reign signalled to his men who turned their rifles around and slammed the butts in to York's abdomen. He grimaced as the wind was stolen from him. A pain shot through his stomach and up his back. After a few seconds, the pain died and he stood tall once again. They looked at him, and then looked at their boss. Reign nodded, and then they repeated the action. York knew with the punishment he had given Sergei, this was going to go on for a while.

39

Murphy stood on the bridge of the Royal Britannia staring out of the window over the pitch black sea. The whole day had been a complete success so far. The one thing he regretted was killing Connors. They had worked together on many occasions and he had grown fairly fond of the man. But he was working for himself now. Anyone who got in the way of him completing his mission had to be eliminated but that didn't stop him from thinking he could have found another way. Perhaps he could have been hidden away until it was over, he thought. It was done now, he couldn't go back and change what he did, and he just had to live with it.

Being the captain of such a magnificent ship made him feel almost indestructible. He had built a passion for the seas when he was a young boy. He had his dad would often go on long fishing trips or sailing holidays. The passion had been in the family for many generations and he hoped to have one day been able to pass the same knowledge down to a son of his own, but that day had not yet come and he was starting to wonder of it would.

The bridge itself stretched the entire width of the superstructure. The windows surrounded the front and sided leaving only the rear out of view. Along the frond window, twenty or so chairs were bolted to the floor. In front of them were touch screen computers each loaded with the latest technology in navigation, engineering and other software. In the centre of the room was the captain's station. The computer there had access to everything in the ship. If there was a problem anywhere, he could manage it from his chair. The state of the art technology meant that the ship could run with minimal crew.

Murphy turned from the window and peered in to the eyes of Whitburn, who had just woken from his deep sleep. He seemed dazed still but aware enough to notice he was chained to the captain's seat.

"What the hell is going on here?" Whitburn demanded. "Where am I?"

"Nice of you to finally join us James." Murphy replied. "I thought perhaps you were never going to wake."

Whitburn looked at Murphy and then at Henshaw who was sitting on one of the seats in front of the window. He could hardly believe his eyes, he was being held captive by two men he trusted and one whom he called his best friend. There were three other men in the room too; all of them were armed with rifles. Suddenly he felt a wave of fear overcome him.

"What do you want with me?" He asked, a little calmer this time around.

"It's not us who want you James. You have pissed off half of the world for nearly twenty five years by commissioning the use of the Dark Gold. Now they are hitting back at you."

"That's absurd; the use of the gold is strictly for interrogation purposes. I never meant for innocents to get harmed."

"Don't treat us like fools James." Henshaw cut in. "I know that you have used it on more than a few occasions to wipe out towns and villages across the globe."

Whitburn shook his head in disbelief. "What can I say, you have been miss informed. I have never agreed for it to be used as an accelerant for explosives. I know how powerful it is.

I never even wanted the world to find out about it."

Henshaw looked at Murphy with confusion written all over him. Murphy walked closer to Whitburn.

"How can you sit there and deny it. You are responsible for a great many deaths James. People want you to be punished like the criminal you are. I am just the judge who is giving you your sentence."

"Sheldon, you have to believe me." He looked at Henshaw "Please Tom, you are my best friend. You know me better than anyone. You know in would never willingly commit murder."

Henshaw looked at Whitburn; he wasn't sure if the plea was one of a desperate man who knew what his fate was or if it was the honest truth. His friend had been right about one thing, he knew that Whitburn was the sort of man who would never let innocents perish. Maybe he was telling the truth, Henshaw thought.

"If you didn't sign it off; then who did James?" Henshaw inquired. "You were the man in charge of the unit that deployed the arsenal. You were the only one who could make that call."

"I am sorry James." Murphy offered "But this is how it has to be. I have to trust my instincts here and I am afraid they are telling me not to trust you."

Whitburn slumped in his chair. He no longer felt afraid, he felt sorry more than anything than anything else. He felt sorry for himself. This was obviously his time to die; either that or he was to be handed over to people who would do him some serious harm before allowing him to die. He hoped for the first option.

Murphy walked over to the communication radio sitting on the docking station. He held it up to his mouth and radioed for York to be brought in.

"Sheldon, are you absolutely sure we're barking up the right tree here?" Henshaw asked quietly.

Murphy could hardly believe what he was hearing, after all of the hard work that had gone on to making the mission a success. He looked at Henshaw with a shocked look on his face.

Henshaw could see the hate for Whitburn in Murphy's eyes. It seemed raw and unchangeable. Henshaw was beginning to have doubts about everything. About whom the real criminal was. From the start all those twenty odd years ago, Sheldon had been at Whitburn's side, all decisions had been joint.

When the original team they created were separated. They seemed to separate with them. Murphy joined MI5 and Whitburn went in to politics. They had only begun to work closely again since Whitburn became Prime Minister.

The one thing Henshaw had noticed about the relationship between Murphy and Whitburn was the competitive rivalry. When ever they did something, it always had to be bigger and better than the others. Henshaw had always found it amusing. When he thought about it deeper however, he remembered that they once both said they had a dream of one day becoming Prime Minister. He also remembered that when the Dark Gold operation was shut down, a few months afterwards he and Whitburn had discussed it and both agreed that the substance was too dangerous to be used.

His mind began running at hyper speed. Maybe Whitburn was innocent, he thought. Was this just rivalry gone out of control? He couldn't let anything happen unless he was sure. But there was no way he was going to be able to stop it. If he tried to be a hero, the three soldiers, all armed to their teeth would intervene.

His thoughts were interrupted by the door opening. Reign and his men dragged York in and sat him in one of the chairs. He looked as if he had been in the ring with Mike Tyson. His face was covered in blood and bruises. His shirt had been ripped off to reveal even more bruising on his torso.

Murphy looked him up and down the looked at Reign. "At what point did I say you could beat him to within an inch of his life?"

"You didn't." Reign replied "Let's get one thing straight Sheldon. I work for one man, me. If you have a problem with that then perhaps you and I should step outside."

Murphy paused momentarily then laughed "As long as he can still do what I need him to." He turned to Henshaw. "Is the link ready?"

Henshaw reluctantly tapped a few commands in to one of the computers. The screen was now filled with the CCTV image of the bridge.

Murphy dialled the number he wanted on the phone. "It's ready." He said when the line was answered.

He walked up to York and grabbed him round the arm then lifted him up out of the chair. He took a Beretta 9mm pistol from Reign and handed it York.

"It's time to make yourself useful to us Mr York."

York looked down at the gun "What exactly am I going to do with that?"

"I thought you would have figured that out yourself." Murphy answered "You're the one who is going to execute Whitburn."

40

York stared at the gun in his hands. After years of waiting, he was now in the perfect position to get the revenge he had been yearning for. But he couldn't help but think that this was the second time in a day that he had been here. Before, he had been made to believe that Salim Jazir was the man he wanted. Now he was being told it was Whitburn. The thought that he was being played for a fool was growing ever more present.

He looked at the PM, who seemed terrified to his bones. That life changing moment flashed before his eyes again, the moment he was orphaned. He couldn't imagine though, that Whitburn was the man who planned it. He was no murderer. York had known the man for while and he had been able to gain a pretty good insight to the type of man he was. He always put everyone else first. He never set out to intentionally hurt anyone, especially his friends. That was the real clincher, Whitburn and York's dad had been good friends.

"Well, we're waiting." Murphy said, interrupting York's thoughts.

York looked at him, then at Henshaw. There was something in his captains eyes, he had seen it before on one occasion but recognised it instantly. It was nervousness. Henshaw was a tough character. He never showed any sign of fear over anything. The only other time York had seen it in him was when he had made a big mistake and York could tell that was what he was feeling now.

"It's your call captain." He said.

Henshaw nodded.

York walked up so he was behind Whitburn. He checked out the three soldiers in the room and the ones with Reign. If he was going to launch an attack, the odds were dead against him and not for the first time in the day either. He began going over scenarios in his mind of what might happen if he just started shooting. The outcome was not good for him or the PM. He had to wait for the right moment and this was definitely not it.

He held the gun out and rested the barrel against the back of Whitburn's head. He could feel the PM shaking. A rush of adrenaline began to pump through his body. He had killed many people in his life, but none like this. Killing in self defence was easy to live with, but if he pulled the trigger now, he wondered if he would ever recover from it.

"Mr Prime Minister." York said, "I need to know for sure. Is everything they have said true? Are you the man who slaughtered all those innocent people? And most importantly, did you kill my parents?"

Why he was asking the question, he wasn't sure. In this type of situation, Whitburn would say anything to spare his life. But York had a respect for him. He had based his entire life on honesty and truth. He never made promises he couldn't keep and he always ensured if he said or started something he would see it through to the end.

Whitburn took a few moments to answer. The intense fear running through is veins were beginning to cause a panic attack. He managed to control it enough to speak "Alex I loved your dad." He muttered "He was like a brother to me. I would have never brought any harm to him, your mum or any other innocent lives. You know that."

"Just pull the trigger Alex." Murphy ordered.

One of Reign's men held up his rifle and aimed it at York. He had a choice to make now, Him or Whitburn. But he remembered what Murphy had said to him before, he was the consolation prize. He had to run with the thought that they needed him alive.

"I have a question for you Henshaw. Why did you get involved in this crap?"

"Alex I have been working hard all of my life to get to where I am now. But that isn't where I should be. I should be high in the government ranks by now. I needed a way out, a way to retire. So when Murphy came to me, I accepted. It was mostly because I was in agreement that the use of the gold was in-humane." He paused for a moment and looked at Murphy. "Something has changed since then though. I now realise that it wasn't Whitburn who was in control of it." With that he pulled out his gun and aimed it at Murphy's head.

York pulled his gun away from Whitburn and aimed it at Reign. The soldiers all aimed at him and Henshaw.

"Well, well." Murphy said with a grin on his face. "It seems that we have a slight predicament here." He turned to Henshaw "Do you know what Tom. In all the years we have known each other, I never thought you were that smart. But I guess I was wrong."

"So your saying I am right then" Henshaw asked.

"Maybe. Our government are cowards Tom. We tip toe around the rest of the world trying our best not to tread on any toes. It's been the same for many years now. There are places and people in the world who need to be taught a lesson. Seeing as no one else was willing to do it, I decided to take it on myself. And now I am being compensated for my actions."

Henshaw tightened his grip on the gun "You son of a bitch. You launched the attacks on that wiped out communities. You're a monster. How could you do something like this?"

Murphy pulled his gun out and aimed it at Whitburn's chest. "I'm human Tom. I fall under the same temptations as everyone else My reasons are simple really, take this bastard here, he thought as he was the leader of a country he was invincible. I proved every one wrong. He is a fake, a coward like the rest. I just did what he and the rest of them should have done along time ago. People will realise I had the country's best interests in mind. We will be looked upon as one of the toughest countries in the world I will make us invincible."

"Your fucking crazy" York interjected in a hateful manner. "What about my parents and all of the other people on that plane?"

"Your dad found out that I had gone in to business for myself. He was going spill the beans. I had to put a stop to that. The rest of them were just collateral damage."

York knew trusting his instincts were the right way to go. They had never failed him before and today was no different. He knew Whitburn was no the man he wanted. Now he just had to get out of the current situation and get the man he did want.

He looked around to see if there was any sure way of saving everyone. With three rifles aimed at him and ready to fire, it would be more than difficult to find one. He looked behind him to see the door a few feet away and the light switch on the wall. With the moon being behind them, there would be almost no light if the lights were killed. If it was going to work he needed help.

Henshaw couldn't believe he had been conned. Murphy had hooked him in to believing the PM was the one responsible for all of the deaths over the past few years and now he was learning Whitburn had nothing to do with it. He had to wonder how Murphy had gotten away with it. He remembered that every time one of the attacks on the villages happened, terrorist groups all over the world came forward to claim responsibility. Each attack had been so horrific, that they all wanted it to make them feared throughout the globe. Murphy had it easy when it came to covering it up really. He could have gotten away with anything.

"So you really thought you were going to get away with it?"

Murphy smiled "I already have Tom. I already have."

The prefect moment had now presented itself. Reign and his men had their attention on Henshaw and Murphy as they looked as though Henshaw was about to pounce. He took one last look at the light switch then took a deep breath. York leapt towards the switch and flipped it to the off position. Both he and Henshaw fired one round of the weapon; Henshaw's was aimed at Murphy. The soldiers automatically began to fire in retaliation. York dropped to the floor for cover and waited for the gun fire to stop.

There was a cold silence in the room when the carnage finally came to a close. York kept low for a few moments. There was no way he was about to switch the lights back on if the soldiers were ready to fire the moment he did. He listened carefully; you could have heard a pin drop.

He ran his arm up the wall towards the switch and flipped it on. The room instantly illuminated. Now though, the view was much different. Most of the area around him was now blood stained. Bodies of Reign's men were lying still on the floor. There was something missing now though; three things actually; Murphy, Reign and Whitburn.

York couldn't believe that they had been able to get away without being hit by a stray bullet him seeing them. He stood up to see the rest of the room had blood spayed over it. It was like a scene from one of those gory horror movies. As he was about to leave the room in pursuit of the others, he caught eye of Henshaw lying on the floor behind the captains chair. He ran over and knelt beside him, he was still breathing but there were two bullet wounds in his chest and stomach.

"Captain." He said softly.

Henshaw looked up at him. His eyes looked tired and blood stained. "Alex." He muttered. "The bow of the ship, they're heading for the bow of the ship."

"What's there?" York asked, he wanted so desperately for Henshaw to stay alive, but he knew that was not a possibility. All he could do was try to get as much out of him as possible.

"A helicopter. Murphy........Murphy has probably rigged the explosive to go off soon. He will want all evidence destroyed."

"What explosive?"

The question was not answered. Henshaw took his last breath then his body fell limp.

York was more than angry now, to many people he

cared about had died because of some power hungry, money grabbing psychopath. It was time to show him what happens to traitors.

He grabbed two of the H&K MP5's from the soldier's bodies and ran out of the door. The crucial moment in his life had now come. There was no doubting the truth now. The man he had been hunting all his life was just a short distance away and he was going to stop at nothing to get him.

41

York was under no illusion there would be many of Reign's men waiting for him. The giant soldier seemed to have an entire army on his side. He counted at least twenty throughout the ship when he was dragged up to the bridge. He needed a plan to get through them. Every single one was no doubt a trained killer, and a good one at that.

He headed down a corridor towards the stairs to make his decent down to the deck. As he got to within ten feet, he had to fall to the floor to dodge the first wall of bullets that headed his was. There was a door to his left, he opened it and dived in. It was a service cupboard. Inside there were all kinds of cleaning materials from detergents to mop and buckets. He crouched down by the door the pointed the gun round the frame and fired. The action was met by another wall of attacking fire.

He searched around the cupboard to try and find anything that he could use as an explosive of some kind. He rifled through the bottles of bleach and packets of cloths and dusters. Then he hit the jackpot. There were six cans of air freshener in total and they were wrapped up as a multi-pack. He grabbed the pack and moved back over to the door. He quickly peered round the corner to see where his targets were. They had now regrouped and were closer to him.

There was a cross junction in the corridor about fifteen feet away from him. He hoped that they were positioned on each side, if they weren't, his plan would fail. He got to his knees then grabbed the pack of cans and threw them down the corridor. As they landed he fired at them. The cans exploded in a fireball that engulfed the corridor. Any one who was in the direct path of the blast would have been killed instantly.

York waited for a few moments before peering around the corner. There was no movement. He stood and moved slowly out of the cupboard, keeping his weapon at the ready. He walked up to the cross junction. Sure enough, as he thought, there were three bodies, two on one side and one on the other. He searched their bodies and took some full magazines for his rifle and a couple of grenades. He made his way to the staircase and down the stairs to the deck level.

At the bottom of the stairs, he was met by another soldier who opened fire on him as he came down. A bullet ricocheted off the hand rail and grazed York's leg. He fell to the floor momentarily before gaining his composure again and filling the soldier's body with a barrage of lead.

York walked through the door and on to the deck. The cool, crisp air struck him and he couldn't help but take a second to enjoy the breath of fresh air. The smell of blood and death had filled the air inside the bridge and the corridors for pretty much the entire time he was in there.

He walked along the railings towards the bow of the ship. The route looked clear. Ahead of him was s set of stairs, the sign above them read 'Pool'. He walked up them slowly and aimed his rifle dead ahead of him as he reached the top. Just as sure as the sun was going to rise, his arrival was met by yet another attack. He fell to the floor and used the stairs as cover. Taking down this one was going to be a lot more difficult as he had no idea where he was. He looked all around him, but could see no one.

He opened fire and covered the entire area he could

see. Another rain of fire came his way. This time he could see where it was from. The soldier had used the same method as him. Across the pool area, on the opposite side, he had crouched down below the level of the stairs. York took one of the grenades he had taken from the men in the corridor and pulled out the pin. He threw it as hard as he could in the direction of his target and crouched back down to the deck.

As before, he waited a few seconds before rising to his feet, just in case had hadn't hit his target. He stood and walked out on to the pool platform. As he passed the pool, he was stunned by what happened. Reign seemed to have flown out of the pool and into the path of York. The huge man hit him with the force of a ten tone wrecking ball. York immediately fell to the floor; his rifle flew out of his hand and fell over the side.

Reign stood to his feet and looked down at York. "It's about time you and I had our moment together." He said as he took off his bomber jacket to reveal the huge muscle he had worked hard for years to build. "I've been looking forward to finding out what you are really made of."

York looked up at him. He was good at hand to hand combat, but he had never had to take on someone the size of Reign. The thought scared him a little, yet he wasn't the type of person to decline a challenge. He got to his feet and clenched fists.

"Let's get it on big boy." York said as he took his fighting position.

Reign didn't bother taking a fighting position. He just stood and waited for York to attack. York ran at Reign and jumped in the air in a kick position. Reign almost effortlessly grabbed his leg and threw him in to the railings to the side.

York let out a wail as he hit the steel bars with an enormous crash. He quickly got to his feet again but not before Reign had walked up to him and grabbed his leg again.

"Oh shit!" York screamed as Reign threw him across the pool to the other side.

York knew Reign was strong, but he had seriously underestimated him. He seemed to posses the strength of ten men. He was now beginning to wonder if he could win this fight. For the first time in his life, he felt like giving up.

Reign followed him over and picked him up off the floor, after slamming his gigantic fists in to York's abdomen he lifted him above his head and threw him to the floor.

York was now feeling like his body was giving up on him. The fight was almost over and so was his life. If he was going to survive, he needed for find some way of weakening the huge warrior. As Reign approached for another attack, York lifted his leg and smashed it in to Reign's groin. The lug screamed out in pain. This was his chance. He stood as fast as he could and began to hit Reign repeatedly in the face and stomach.

After a few seconds, he could finally feel his opponent begin to weaken, until he grabbed York's fist and twisted his arm backwards. York grimaced then readied himself for the next blow.

Reign slammed his fist in to York's abdomen then gave him a full blow to the face. York crumbled to the floor again, only to be thrown towards the railing. As he hit the railing, he felt a sharp pain shoot through his shoulder and down his left arm. He knew instantly that his shoulder had been dislocated. As he laid waiting for the next beating, he noticed the MP5 hanging by the strap over the edge. It had become caught on a bolt as it fell over the edge. He reached down and grabbed it by the barrel.

Reign walked up and dragged York away from the edge by his feet. As he did, York swung the gun around and caught Reign on the side of the face. The impact caused him to fall back slightly, giving York time to ready the weapon for fire.

Reign looked down at the gun aimed at him as he regained his balance. "You cheating fuck."

"You lose slap head." The he pulled the trigger.

Murphy dragged Whitburn towards the Helicopter. The pilot he had hired fired up the engine and got everything ready to take off. Whitburn stepped up and sat in the seat, closely followed by Murphy.

"Do you really think you will get away with this?" Whitburn shouted. "I have people looking for me as we speak."

Murphy laughed "You seem to forget that those people work for me. Besides, no one will look for you if they think you are already dead."

Whitburn looked at him, the confusion written like a book all over his face.

"Let's just say the house we were at got a little hot after we left." With that he pulled a hand held computer from his pocket and showed the display to Whitburn. On the screen was a clock. This was not telling the time, this clock was counting down.

Whitburn new what he meant. Actually, he was quite impressed with the lengths that he had gone to make it happen.

Murphy nodded for the pilot to take off. As the helicopter lifted off the deck, the windscreen shattered and the pilot slumped back in his seat. Murphy leaned forward and saw the bullet hole in his helmet. He looked out over the ship and saw York standing at the top of the steps which lead to the helipad. He pulled out his pistol and emptied the entire magazine towards him. None of them hit.

York ran up to the copter, grabbed Murphy and dragged him out. He stared him dead in the eye before punching him as hard as he could in the face. He fell to the floor, blood erupted from his nose.

"You stupid shit." Murphy said as he shook off the pain and rose to his feet. "I have rigged this place with the bomb that was meant for the Excel Centre. In about tem minutes, we are all toast"

York smiled "Not all of us." Then he slammed his fist in to Murphy's stomach and brought his knee up in to his face.

Once Murphy was on the floor, York jumped in to the Copter and dragged the pilot out. He sat in the pilot's seat and grabbed the yoke.

"Have you ever flown one of these before?" Whitburn asked, now feeling more nervous than he had for the whole of the night.

"Of course I have." York replied. "When I was fifteen."

He lifted the aircraft off the pad slowly. It juddered as they rose in to the air. He gained control of the yoke and sent them flying in a forward direction.

"You might want to refrain from looking at the ship in about five minute's time." York told Whitburn.

There was no reply. He had been there when the bomb was set and he knew what was about to happen.

York kept his eye on the clock, as the last few seconds counted down he tightened his grip on the yoke. When the time was up, the entire sky was lit up by the blast. Once the light had dimmed, he looked back and saw the huge mushroom cloud behind them.

They were out of range of the blast radius, that wasn't what York was worried about. The blast had caused a tidal wave. Although he was flying to high for it to be a problem for him, he could see a coast line in the distance. He wasn't to sure what coast it was, but he had to alert them.

He put on the helmet with the comm. Radio inside and began to check the wave lengths. At first he had nothing back but after a few seconds, a voice responded.

"This is Portleven Coast Guard, How may we help?"

"This is ATS Agent Alex York, there is a huge mother of a wave heading your way, evacuate now."

The wave was travelling at an unimaginable rate, although it wasn't as big as the ones he had seen in movies, it would definitely do some damage. He just hoped he had done enough in time.

He watched as the street lights in the distance disappeared. Although he was to far away, he thought he could actually hear the scared cries from the residents of the towns along the Cornish coast. He couldn't really imagine what must have gone though their minds when they saw the wave heading their way. He just hoped that most of them would have been able to get to a safe height before it hit.

They flew over Portleven town five minutes later. The

damage wasn't as bad as he had imagined, he figured the wave must have lost momentum as it reached land. Cars had been over turned and anyone who had been close to the shoreline would have surely perished. However the wave hadn't travelled in land too far. It had only covered half of the town.

A large portion of the water had subsided. There was still a lot left behind in certain places. He couldn't tell from air what damage properties had sustained or how many casualties had been suffered. But he was sure of one thing; it could have been a lot worse.

Epilogue

Four weeks later

The day was becoming the hottest of the year so far. The beach was packed with people topping up their summer tans. Kids were playing in the water enjoying the short time they had with the sun. The British weather was world renown for being hot for a few weeks in the summer then turning wet for the rest of the year.

York stood on his balcony looking out over the horizon. The bruises from the beating he took were now beginning to disappear. The memory of what had happened would live on for the rest of his life. But that day was a crucial one for him. It was the day that he was able to put the pain of his parent's death to rest once and for all.

He walked inside and put on his jacket. He grabbed his keys off of the side and walked out of the door. When he reached the garage, he couldn't help but smile. The choice he had to make every time he opened the garage door was upon him again and he could remember Myers constantly asking to take the Audi. He got in to the R8 and sat for a moment, remembering his best friend. After a slight tear began to form, he brushed the thought aside and started the engine.

Half an hour later, he arrived at the cemetery. He parked the car and walked slowly though the graveyard looking at the head stones as he walked. When he arrived at the stones he was there to see, he sat on the grass, as he had done every time he visited since he was nine years old.

"Hey mum, Dad." He said quietly, hoping no one would hear him and think he was crazy. "Well its twenty years ago today I lost you and as always I am here giving you an update. I have finally done what I set out to do. Justice has been served. I miss you guy's everyday. I know you are in a good place though."

He sat in silence for a while, just staring at the head stones. The thing that was different about this visit was the new one. He had made a point of burying Myers in the same place as his parents, so he could spend time with all of them at once. He loved each of them dearly and wanted to make sure they were all together on the same plot.

As he was about to leave, he noticed a man walking towards him. He was a tall man who seemed as though he had a slight weight problem. He wasn't fat, but judging by the double chin, he enjoyed his food. His eyes seemed almost two toned; they were dark brown round the edge and faded to a lighter shade in the middle.

"Hi." He said in a soft, friendly tone.

York smiled "Hey."

"You visiting anyone in particular?" The man asked.

"My parents and my best friend."

The man looked down at the stones "I see he died recently. What happened?"

York wasn't the sort of person to just talk to anyone, but this man was different. He had a quality about him that York just could put his finger on. He seemed so calm and collected so at peace with life.

"He was killed in an accident at work." York replied not wanting to give anything away about what he did.

The man nodded "I am very sorry to hear that. It was nice to meet you Alex."

"You too?"

"Sam." Then he began to walk away. Just before he tuned the corner and walked out of sight he turned back to York "Don't worry about Andy, he is in a good place now." The he disappeared.

York stood for a few minutes more before walking back to the car. He stopped midway as a thought hit him. He hadn't told the man his name.

He shook off the thought and headed for the car again, as he was about to get in, a Limo pulled up alongside him. The window rolled down and Whitburn revealed himself. York leaned in.

"Hello Alex, How are you?" Whitburn asked.

"I'm fine, thank you. And you?"

"I very well thanks to you."

York laughed "What can I do for you sir?"

Whitburn motioned for him to get in. he opened the door and sat down next to the PM.

"There is something that I owe you. Call it a gesture of good will for saving my life." He pulled out a file from his briefcase and handed it to York. "What I am about to tell you is going to hit you hard, so please, be calm."

York looked at him. He had a seriousness about him that only ever came with bad news.

"Your father didn't die in the bombing."

The revelation hit York like a meteor to the head. He felt a slight sick feeling begin to rise in his stomach. "What?"

"I only found out last week. Apparently, the C.I.A found out about the attack and sent an agent in to rescue him. They have been using him ever since. He wasn't allowed contact with his past family or friends."

York looked through the file. There were pictures dated within the last two years of him. He couldn't believe what he was reading.

"The thing is Alex, he went dark a year ago, and no one has found him since. The Agency believes he is responsible for what happened to us. That's why you were needed in the whole operation."

York shook his head "No way, that can't be. Why would he want you dead?"

"When he was going to grass up Murphy, he thought I was involved to. He was never informed otherwise."

"So he figured you were responsible for my mother's death. Now he wants revenge."

Whitburn nodded "I fear for my life Alex. That's why I need you to find him."

York was struggling to come to terms with everything he had just heard. Taking it in was going the hardest thing he had ever had to do. He took a deep breath as he closed the file.

"Where do I start?" He asked.

"I'll forward you the information." Whitburn replied. "I am sorry to have to burden you with this and then take off but I have many things I need to do. I will be in touch."

York stepped out of the car and shut the door behind him. He leaned in the window before the car pulled off "Sir. Thank you for telling me this. I'm sure you have broken a few rules to get this."

Whitburn nodded and then the car pulled away. As York was about to turn and get in to his own car, the Limo exploded in a ball of fire. York was thrown at least ten feet in the air. He slammed down on to the floor with a thud. His vision was blurred and he began to feel very faint. He looked up to see the burnt out shell of the Limousine. In the distance he could see something else. An image he hadn't seen in years. It was a face; a face that he never thought would come back to haunt him.